Elementary Studies in Plant Life

This edition published 2025
by Living Book Press

ISBN: 978-1-76153-906-0 (hardcover)
978-1-76153-900-8 (softcover)

First published in 1915.

NATIONAL LIBRARY OF AUSTRALIA

A catalogue record for this book is available from the National Library of Australia

Elementary Studies in Plant Life

by

F. E. Fritch & E. J. Salisbury

LIVING BOOK PRESS

Contents

1. THE LIFE-STORY OF A COMMON FLOWERING PLANT 1
2. HOW PLANTS GET WATER 7
3. HOW PLANTS GET FOOD FROM THE AIR 10
4. THE PARTS OF A FLOWER 13
5. THE FORMS OF PLANTS 17
6. LEAVES 24
7. THE ROOT 29
8. TREES AND SHRUBS IN WINTER 34
9. HERBS IN WINTER 39
10. HERBS IN WINTER (*continued*) 45
11. THE GERMINATION OF SEEDS 49
12. THE GERMINATION OF SEEDS (*continued*) 55
13. HERBS IN SPRING 60
14. TREES AND SHRUBS IN SPRING 66
15. PLANTS IN AUTUMN 70
16. THE PLANT AND THE SOIL 76
17. HOW PLANTS FEED 82
18. SPECIAL WAYS OF OBTAINING FOOD 86
19. HOW PLANTS GROW 91
20. PLANTS THAT GROW IN DRY PLACES 96
21. PLANTS THAT GROW IN WET PLACES 101
22. THE FLOWERING PARTS OF PLANTS 106
23. MORE ABOUT FLOWERS 111
24. FRUITS AND SEEDS 118
25. HOW FRUITS AND SEEDS ARE SCATTERED 124
26. MONOCOTYLEDONS: THE LILY-FAMILY 128
27. OTHER MONOCOTYLEDONS 133
28. DICOTYLEDONS: THE BUTTERCUP-FAMILY 137
29. THE WALLFLOWER- AND CHICKWEED-FAMILIES 141
30. THE ROSE-FAMILY 146
31. THE PEA- AND CARROT-FAMILIES 150
32. THE PRIMROSE-AND FORGET–ME–NOT–FAMILIES 156
33. THE DEAD-NETTLE- AND FOXGLOVE-FAMILIES 160
34. THE DAISY-FAMILY 165
35. A WALK IN SPRING 169
36. A WALK IN SUMMER 174

PREFACE

IN writing the present volume, we have hoped to provide a more complete account of the elementary aspects of plant life than is usually given in textbooks for beginners. To this end, we have included brief sections on the soil and different kinds of vegetation, a description of the commoner types of pollination mechanisms, and a considerable number of simple physiological experiments. A glance at the index will show that a large number of common wild or cultivated plants are included as examples. These have also furnished material for the illustrations, which are all original.

The subject matter, for which we are jointly responsible, has been treated, as far as possible, in relation to the seasons of the year. It is hoped that this will facilitate provision by the teacher of material for each lesson and for the practical work.

The first nineteen chapters are suitable for the period between autumn and spring, and many of these could be taken at any time of the year. The remaining chapters are intended for study in the late spring or summer.

Summaries and instructions for practical work are added at the end of each chapter. The practical work is intended to **supplement** the work done in connection with each lesson. A list of material required for the illustration of the lessons themselves is, for the convenience of the teacher, given after the list of contents.

The scope of the book is sufficient to cover all requirements for the Preliminary and Junior Local Examinations of Oxford and Cambridge. It also provides for the greater part of the syllabus of the Northern Universities' Joint Matriculation Board. Questions are included throughout, some of which are taken from the Local Examinations of Oxford and Cambridge. For permission to utilize these, we are indebted to the Oxford Local Examinations Delegates and the Cambridge Local Examinations Syndicate.

F. E. F. & E. J. S.
East London College,
June 1915

LIST OF MATERIAL REQUIRED FOR CLASS PURPOSES IN CONNECTION WITH THE DIFFERENT CHAPTERS

(N.B. - The material necessary for the practical work suggested at the end of each chapter is not included here, since what is required can be seen at a glance.)

CHAPTER I. - Young and old plants of the Shepherd's Purse, with roots, flowers, and ripe fruits.

CHAPTER II. - Plants of the Shepherd's Purse, flowers of the Jonquil; salt; two tumblers; oil; stamp paper; red ink; pot with soil; silver paper; pair of scales; white blotting paper; cobalt chloride; small sheets of glass.

CHAPTER III. - Plants of the Shepherd's Purse; pots with soil; methylated spirit; tincture of iodine; starch; lime water; taper; corked jar; glass rod; candle; saucer; glass jam jar.

CHAPTER IV. - Flowers and fruits of the Wallflower; muslin.

CHAPTER V. - Mosses; toadstools; branches of the Scotch Fir and Laurel; plants of Shepherd's Purse and Goosegrass or Stitchwort; branches of Bramble or Dog-rose; stems of Convolvulus or Hop; Ivy; tendrils of White Bryony or Sweet Pea; branches of Old Man's Beard; plants of Creeping Jenny or Ground Ivy (in flower); rhizomes of Dog's Mercury or Iris; first- and second-year plants of Mullein or Turnip; tincture of iodine.

CHAPTER VI. - Leaves of Violet, Lesser Celandine, Pansy, Garden Nasturtium, Shepherd's Purse or St. John's Wort, Grass, Privet, Chickweed, Garden Spurge, Ground Ivy, Convolvulus, Sorrel, Mallow or Garden Geranium, Enchanter's Nightshade, Ivy, False Acacia or Rose, Horse Chestnut, Primrose.

CHAPTER VII. - Cress seedlings (about 5 days old); pea seedlings (about 5 days old); bean seedlings (about 10 days old); pea seeds; roots of Shepherd's Purse or Jack-by-the-Hedge, Carrot, Grass, or Chickweed; cardboard or wooden box; blotting paper; pins; dry soil; flower pot; corks; jam jar.

CHAPTER VIII. - Branches of Horse Chestnut, Ash, Elm, Oak, Beech; Brussels Sprouts or Cabbages.

CHAPTER IX. - Leaves of Mullein; root stocks of Primrose or Violet; rhizomes of Solomon's Seal or Iris; corms and flowering plants of Crocus; bulbs and flowering plants of Tulip or Hyacinth; iodine.

CHAPTER X. - Rhizome of Dog's Mercury; plants of Yarrow, Perennial Sunflower, Jerusalem Artichoke; potato tubers; roots of Carrot, Lesser Celandine, or Dahlia; Beetroot; corm of Crocus; buds of Horse Chestnut; Strawberry or Cinquefoil with runners; iodine.

CHAPTER XI. - Pea and bean seeds; seedlings of Runner and French Beans of various ages; five pots; boiled water; cotton wool; two jam jars; iodine; two large (3 in.) soaked corks; pair of scales; pins and nails; soil; bowl of water. (Remaining chapters would follow in the same format for corrections.)

CHAPTER XII. - Grains of Maize; seeds and seedlings of various ages of Buckwheat and Castor Oil; rhizomes of Solomon's Seal and Dog's Mercury (winter condition); iodine; seedlings of Beech, Holly, etc.

CHAPTER XIII. - Young leaves of Primrose and Barren Strawberry; shoots of Beaked Parsley or Hogweed, Grass, Dock; plants of Daisy or Plantain; shoots of Dead-nettle or Horse Chestnut, Dog-rose; Pea-seeds: fresh and withered shoots of some herb; four pots with soil; plants of Ground Ivy.

CHAPTER XIV. - Opening buds of Flowering Currant, Ash, or Rose, Lilac or Privet, Beech or Elm, Horse Chestnut, Plane Tree; twigs of Apple and Scotch Fir, Horse Chestnut, Lilac.

CHAPTER XV. - Toadstools, Michaelmas Daisy; branches of Horse Chestnut, Ash, and Syringa or Plane Tree, Beech, Elm, or Lime, Lilac; stems of Vegetable Marrow, Buttercup, Maize; thick woody branches of some tree.

CHAPTER XVI. - Maize-seedlings (about 10 days old); Fuchsia plant in pot; soils of different kinds, humus, large bottles, firewood, vessel with water, distilled or rain water, large jam-jars, cardboard, glass tubing, rubber tubing, copper wire, a long stick.

CHAPTER XVII. - Seedlings or herbaceous plants, Canadian Pond-weed plants, some plant in a pot; leaves of Variegated Privet; saucer, pair of scales, glass cylinder or jam-jar, glass (4 in.) funnel, copper wire, test-tube, splinters of wood, warm and boiled water, ice, soda water, cardboard, methylated spirit, iodine.

CHAPTER XVIII. - Specimens of Dodder and Broomrape, with hosts; Mistletoe; plants of Yellow Rattle or Red Eye-bright with suckers; Bird's Nest Orchid, Toadstools, Puffballs, Sundew, Butterwort; jam-jar.

CHAPTER XIX. - Bulbs and tubers, some plant in a pot, Bean-seedlings with plumules and radicles (some in pots); Pea-seedlings grown in light and darkness; plants of Violet grown in light and darkness; shoots of White Bryony with tendrils; plants of Convolvulus, Tulip, or Crocus in flower; leaves of Wood Sorrel; growth-lever (this can be simply made from ordinary materials), rulers, Indian ink, jam-jar, garden sticks.

CHAPTER XX. - Plants from a wood or meadow; shoots of Arbor Vitae or Cypress; leaves of Cherry and Cherry Laurel or Holly; shoots of Gorse, Scotch Fir, Horsetail, Butcher's Broom; leaves of Sheep's Fescue or Marram Grass, and Heather; plants of Houseleek, Stonecrop, Mouse-ear Chickweed or Cudweed; twigs of Hawthorn or Sloe, Barberry, Rose, or Bramble; white blotting-paper, cobalt chloride, glass plates (old negatives).

CHAPTER XXI. - Plants of Milkmaid, Rushes, Pondweed, Brooklime, Ragged Robin, Water Plantain, Water Buttercup, Water Milfoil, Canadian Pondweed, Water Lily, Hornwort, Bulrush; land- and water-forms of Water Buttercup or Starwort; Duckweed.

CHAPTER XXII. - Inflorescences of Shepherd's Purse, Currant, or Lupine; Candytuft, Cowslip, or Cherry; Hogweed or Carrot; Plantain or Pondweed; Sunflower or Daisy; Buttercup or Herb Bennett; Campion or Chickweed.

CHAPTER XXIII. - Flowers of Wallflower, Marsh Marigold, or Winter Aconite or Hellebore; Tulip or Hyacinth; Geranium or Stitchwort; Primrose or Convolvulus; Willow-herb, Buttercup, Violet, Mallow, or Hollyhock; Pea or Bean; Campion or Pink; Canterbury Bell, Narcissus, or Apple; Dead-nettle, Honeysuckle, Figwort; pair of compasses.

CHAPTER XXIV. - Fruits of Hazel, Marsh Marigold, or Monkshood; Pea or Vetch; Wallflower or Jack-by-the-Hedge; Snapdragon, Campion, Poppy, Garden Nasturtium, Beaked Parsley or Hogweed; Mallow or Hollyhock; Buttercup, Acorn, Gooseberry or Bittersweet, Plum or Cherry, Blackberry, Strawberry, Mulberry, Fig; seeds of various plants; fruits of Maize and Sunflower.

CHAPTER XXV. - Fruits of Foxglove, Ash, or Elm; Maple or Sycamore; Honesty, Field Spurrey, Dandelion, Thistle, Old Man's Beard, Poplar, Willow-herb, Herb Bennett, Goosegrass or Enchanter's Nightshade, Gorse, or Touch-me-not.

CHAPTER XXVI. - Plants of Lily, Hyacinth, or Orchid; flowers of Tulip or Lily of the Valley; Herb Paris, Onion, Star of Bethlehem; fruits.

CHAPTER XXVII. - Flowers of Daffodil or Narcissus, Snowdrop, Iris, Crocus, Gladiolus, Grasses; plants of Grasses and Sedges.

CHAPTER XXVIII. - Flowers of Buttercup, Wood Anemone, or Winter Aconite; Monkshood, Larkspur, Columbine (the specimens should show the inflorescences and some fruits should also be shown).

CHAPTER XXIX. - Flowers, inflorescences, and fruits of Wallflower, Shepherd's Purse, Honesty, Radish, Charlock, Pink or Campion, Stitchwort or Chickweed, Ragged Robin.

CHAPTER XXX. - Flowers, inflorescences, and fruits of Strawberry, Cinquefoil, Rose, Apple, or Pear; Agrimony, Blackberry, or Raspberry; Cherry or Plum.

CHAPTER XXXI. - Flowers and inflorescences of Gorse or Broom, Sweet Pea or Clover; fruits; flowers and inflorescences of Carrot and Hogweed; also fruits.

CHAPTER XXXII. - Flowers, inflorescences, and fruits of Primrose, Pimpernel, Yellow Loosestrife, Forget-me-not, Viper's Bugloss.

CHAPTER XXXIII. - Flowers, inflorescences, and fruits of Deadnettle, Bugle, Foxglove, Snapdragon, Mullein, Figwort, or Penstemon; Speedwell.

CHAPTER XXXIV. - Flowers and inflorescences of Sunflower, Cornflower, Dandelion or Sow-thistle, Coltsfoot, or Thistle; fruits of Dandelion, Burr Marigold, Thistle.

CHAPTER XXXV. - The flowers, etc., mentioned in this chapter are best studied in the field.

CHAPTER XXXVI. - The whole subject matter in this chapter should be studied in a number of afternoons in the field.

CHAPTER I

THE LIFE-STORY OF A COMMON FLOWERING PLANT

IN the early spring, we sow seeds in our gardens so that we may have flowers in the summer. Plants that bear flowers usually grow from a seed. This, as you will learn later on, always contains a baby plant. Most weeds produce seeds in large numbers, which is one reason why we find them springing up on every waste piece of ground. One of the commonest of our weeds is the Shepherd's Purse (Fig. I), the story of whose life we shall now briefly follow. We may begin by sowing some seeds of this plant on damp sawdust.

The plant and its enemies.—The seed at first gives rise to a small plant that is quite simple in form. This is called the **seedling** (Fig. I, B). Like many other seedlings, it will be found to possess a short white root (Fig. I, B, r.r.) buried in the earth. Above ground is a little curved or upright **stem** (Fig. I, B, h.) bearing two green **leaves** (Fig. I, B, c.). At the tip of the stem and situated between these two leaves is a tiny bud. As the plant grows up or becomes mature, this bud gradually lengthens into the main stem, bearing leaves, branches, and finally flowers. Meanwhile, the root has also been growing and branching so that it fixes the Shepherd's Purse firmly in the soil.

During this gradual development, the plant is exposed to many dangers. Birds may pick up the seeds before they can sprout, and the leaves of the growing plant may be eaten by snails and caterpillars. Seedlings, like children, are often the victims of diseases. You can easily recognize one of the commonest diseases of the Shepherd's Purse, since the parts attacked look swollen and as though they had been whitewashed. At any time, too, a spell of dry weather may make it difficult for the plant to obtain the large amount of water it must continually suck up from the soil.

The mature plant.—When you pull up a full-grown Shepherd's Purse, you can clearly distinguish the buried part, or root, from the overground part, or shoot (Fig. I). The root is white and bears many branches that are all alike (Fig. 2).

FIG. 1. — Complete plant of Shepherd's Purse (slightly reduced). The surface of the soil is shown by the dotted line on the left.
a.i., main stem of the inflorescence; a.r.b., axillary bud; c.h., upper leaf; A., flowers; fr., fruit; in., internode; n., node; r.l., leaf of rosette; Rt., root; Sh., shoot; A and B, two stages in the sprouting of the seed (somewhat enlarged); C., cotyledon; h., hypocotyl (p. 57); r., radicle; S., seed-coat.

The **shoot** is green and bears leaves and flowers in addition to branches (Fig. I). You will also notice that the branches of the shoot always join onto the stem just above a leaf.

The angle between a leaf and the stem upon which it is borne is called the **axil** of the leaf (Fig. 3, E). Since all the branches arise in these angles, they are said to be **axillary**.

If a number of specimens of the Shepherd's Purse are examined,

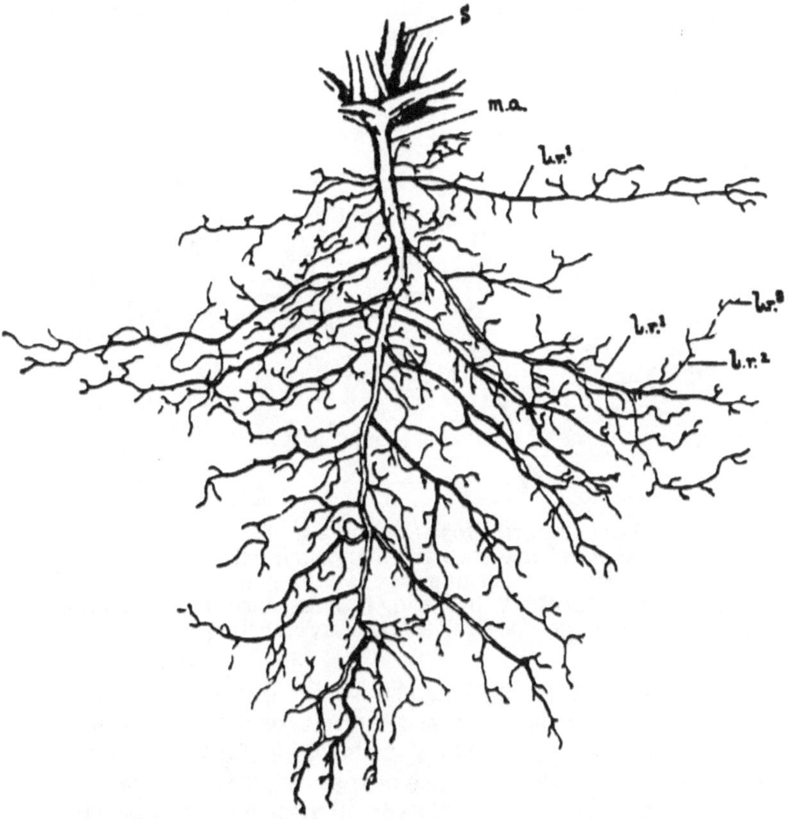

FIG. 2. — Root-system of the Shepherd's Purse (about natural size). s., lower end of the stem; m.a., main axis of root; Lr.1, Lr.2, Lr.3, successive branches of the root.

you will find that the lower leaves generally form a **rosette**, close to the surface of the ground (Fig. I). The others are far less crowded and situated at intervals up the stem. The part of the stem to which each leaf is attached is called a **node** (Fig. I, n.), whilst the bare length of stem between one leaf and the next is termed an **internode** (Fig. I, in.). Between the leaves at the base of the stem, the internodes are very short,

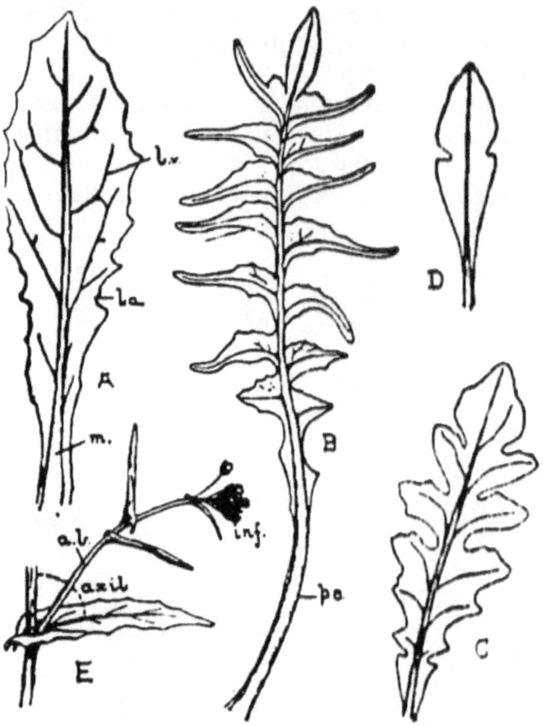

FIG. 3. A.D. — Leaves from the rosette at the base of the stem of the Shepherd's Purse (about half the natural size). m., midrib; l.a., blade; l.v., vein; pe., petiole; E., node with leaf and axillary branch bearing inflorescence (inf.) (about half the natural size); a.b., axillary branch.

so that the leaves are closely crowded.

The leaves. — The lower leaves are flat green structures with a varying outline. Each is borne at the end of a short green stalk, the **leaf-stalk** or **petiole** (Fig. 3, B, pe.). This is continued into the flat part of the leaf or **leaf-blade** as a thick **midrib** (Fig. 3, A, m.), which runs right up to the tip.

If you hold the leaf-blade up to the light, thinner ribs, the **veins**, are seen branching off on either side of the midrib (Fig. 3, A, l.v.). The midrib and veins together form a framework, between which the thin green substance or **tissue** of the leaf-blade is spread out. You will soon learn, however, that they also serve as channels for the passage of water.

The upper leaves of the Shepherd's Purse (Fig. I), unlike the lower ones, have no petioles. The base of their blade is enlarged in such a way as to clasp the stem (Fig. 3, E). In all the leaves, the blade is placed so that one surface is directed towards the ground, whilst the other turns away from it. You can therefore speak of an **upper** and a **lower surface**. The former is of a deeper green than the latter.

If you look carefully at the stem or at one of the leaves, you will notice numerous white branched **hairs** (Fig. 119, C, p. 151) scattered over the surface.

Cells. — Such a plant as the Shepherd's Purse is composed of innumerable tiny units, or **cells**, which are of many different kinds. They are so small that you cannot see them without using a microscope. Near the tips of all the branches of the stem and root, there are special groups of cells. These form the **growing points**, which carry on the growth of the particular branch.

The flowers. — In the mature plant, the main stem and some of its larger branches end in groups of small white **flowers** (Fig. I). At the very top, they appear as tiny green buds, which gradually open out and expose the white **petals.** Still further from the tip, you will find that the petals have fallen off and that the flower-stalk ends in a little flat green triangle — the young **fruit** (Fig. I, fr.). At the same time, the internodes between the flower-stalks lengthen out, so that the enlarging fruits become widely separated (Fig. I). The whole of this part of the plant which bears the flowers and fruits is called the **inflorescence.**

The fruits and seeds. — At the bottom of the inflorescence, the triangular fruits have reached their full size. In an old plant, some of them will have **split into two halves**, leaving a small white membrane at the end of the flower-stalk. If you squeeze a slightly younger fruit, before it has opened in this way, a number of little oval bodies will be pressed out. These, which are green or yellowish in color according to their age, are the **seeds.** They are usually shed when the fruit splits open.

The seeds fall onto the surface of the ground and gradually get washed by the rain into the soil. There they sprout or **germinate** to form new plants. Since each Shepherd's Purse forms numerous seeds, one plant may produce many seedlings. Soon after the seeds are shed, the parent itself dies away.

Summary.—The ordinary plant consists, then, of a green overground part or shoot and a white underground part or root. Both are branched. The shoot bears leaves at its nodes and axillary branches. Some of the branches bear groups of flowers or inflorescences at their ends. The flowers form fruits within which are the seeds.

PRACTICAL WORK

1. Examine a number of seedlings, such as the Sunflower, the Cress, the Marrow, the Beech, the Nettle, the Buckwheat, etc. Make drawings of several and name the different parts.

2. Examine full-grown plants of the Shepherd's Purse, Groundsel, Chickweed, and Red Dead-nettle. Notice root and shoot and how the leaves and branches are attached in the different cases.

3. Look at any plants that have been flowering for some time. Notice that as the flowers wither, their places are taken by fruits. Examine the latter and see that they contain seeds.

QUESTIONS

1. Describe and name the different parts of some common plant.
2. Enumerate the differences between the shoot and root of a Flowering Plant.

CHAPTER II

HOW PLANTS GET WATER

The taking up of water (absorption). — You have already been told that the plant is continually sucking up the moisture present in the soil. You know also that unless a plant grown in a pot is watered, it soon droops and dies. The water is taken up by the root and is passed through the stem into the leaves.

If a substance like salt is placed in water, it rapidly becomes dissolved. In the same way, the water in the soil dissolves some of the salts present, so that the root really **takes up** a weak **solution of substances in the earth.** In this manner, the plant obtains an important part of its food.

The large amount of moisture which is sucked up is shown by a simple experiment (Fig. 4). Place a plant of the Shepherd's Purse with its roots in a tumbler of water. Pour oil (Fig. 4, o.) on the surface so as to form a thin film, and mark its level on the outside with a strip of stamp-paper (Fig. 4, p.). Fill another tumbler with about the same quantity of water, covering it with a layer of oil as before, and again mark the level of the liquid. Each day the level of the water in the tumbler containing the plant will be found to have dropped slightly (Fig. 4, p'.), whilst there is no change in the other tumbler. This is because the oil prevents evaporation, and so the water lost in the first tumbler must have been taken up by the plant.

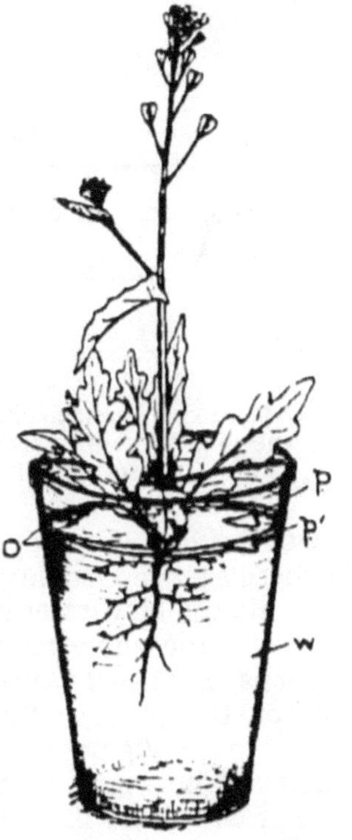

FIG. 4 - Experiment to show the absorption of water by the roots of a plant. o., oil; P., p successive levels of the liquid in the tumbler; w., water

The course of the water. — You can easily follow the course of the water through the plant by placing a Shepherd's Purse with its roots (whose tips must be cut off) in red ink diluted with water. After a few days, the midribs of the leaves will appear red when held up to the light. The red solution must therefore have travelled **through the root and stem** into the leaves. You will get a more striking result by putting the cut stalk of a white flower, such as a Jonquil, in the colored liquid. In a few hours, the petals appear streaked with red. You will sometimes see flowers which have been treated in this way in a florist's window.

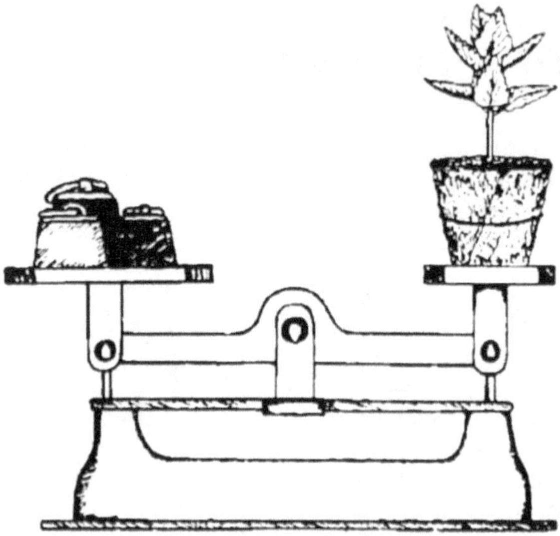

FIG. 5. - Experiment to show loss of weight due to the giving off of water-vapour by a plant. Description in the text.

What happens to the water. — What becomes of all the water which the plant takes up? A few simple experiments will answer this question for you. Plant a few healthy specimens of the Shepherd's Purse in some garden soil in a pot and give them plenty of water. Allow all the water which the soil will not hold to drain away. Then cover the whole pot and the bare soil between the plants with "silver paper." You thus prevent any moisture being lost by evaporation from the surface of the soil or pot.

Now place the pot on one pan of a pair of scales and put sufficient weights in the other pan to counterbalance it (Fig. 5). After a day or two, you will find that the pan bearing the pot has risen; it has become lighter. This can only be due to **loss of weight by the plant**. The next experiment shows that this is a result of the escape of water-vapor.

Dip some white blotting paper in the pink solution of a substance called cobalt chloride, and then dry it in front of a fire. The color of the paper gradually changes to bright blue. If you breathe on the paper, it will become damp and again turn pink. Now place small pieces of the blue paper on either surface of a leaf of the Shepherd's Purse, with a small sheet of glass on both sides to keep off the moisture of the air.

After a few minutes, you will find that the blue color is disappearing, and that the paper against the lower surface of the leaf fades more rapidly than that against the upper. This shows that the leaves are **giving off water-vapor**, a process known as **transpiration**. The loss of weight noticed in the previous experiment was due to this cause. The water-vapor passes out through innumerable minute holes or **pores** in the surface skin. Since these are mostly situated on the lower side of the leaf, transpiration is most active from this surface.

The substances in the soil-water. — When a solution of salt is exposed to the air, the water gradually evaporates, and the salt is left behind as white crystals. In the same way, the substances dissolved in the water absorbed from the soil remain in the plant and accumulate as the water evaporates. The soil-water is a very weak solution of these substances, so that, unless large quantities of water pass through the plant, it does not obtain enough of them. You will learn later that a constant supply of these salts is necessary for the growth of the plant.

Summary. — We have thus seen that there is a constant stream of water through the plant, bringing with it mineral substances obtained from the soil. Only a small amount of this water is kept in the plant, whilst most of it evaporates from the foliage (transpiration). In fact, the larger part merely serves to carry food substances from the soil to the leaves.

PRACTICAL WORK

1. Perform the experiment described on p. 7 with a number of different plants, and compare the rates at which they take up water.
2. Take leaves of these same plants and compare the rates of transpiration from their under surfaces by means of the cobalt method described on p. 9.

QUESTIONS

1. What experiments would you perform to prove that roots absorb water from the soil?
2. Describe carefully two experiments to show that water is given off from the leaves of a plant.
3. Plants use a large amount of water. Why is such a large quantity taken up?

CHAPTER III

HOW PLANTS GET FOOD FROM THE AIR

YOU have learnt that the roots take nourishment for the plant from the soil. But this is not the only source of the plant's food supply, since an important part is obtained from the air. Air consists mainly of a mixture of the gases oxygen and nitrogen, with a small quantity of carbonic acid gas.

The necessity of light. — If you grow some plants in the light and others in the dark for a few weeks, you will find that those in the light remain quite healthy, whilst those in the dark become sickly, yellowish, and eventually die. Evidently, then, **light is necessary** for the well-being of the plant.

In order to find out why this is so, we may see whether the plant grown in the light contains any substance which is not present in that grown in the dark. As a matter of fact, **starch**, which is an important plant food, is only found in the leaves of plants which have been exposed to the light. You can prove this for yourself as follows.

Light and starch-formation. — Take some leaves from the plant grown in the light and some from the plant grown in the dark, and put them separately into boiling water. When they have become limp, pour off the water and add a little methylated spirit. After a short time, the green color passes into the spirit, and the leaves become colorless.

Now paint a leaf from each set with tincture of iodine. The one from the plant exposed to light becomes darkly colored, whilst that from the plant grown in the dark remains unchanged. Next, add some of the iodine to a piece of starch, such as you get from the grocer's, and you will find that it also turns a dark color. This is a certain means of recognizing starch, i.e., it is a test for that substance.

The above experiment has therefore shown you that **starch is only formed when the plant is exposed to light.** You will learn later that the green substance in the leaves is also necessary for its production. The starch is manufactured from **carbonic acid gas** taken in from the air and **water** sucked up from the soil. The processes leading to starch-formation are spoken of as assimilation.

The breathing of plants (respiration). — Like all animals, you breathe so long as you live. At every breath, you **take in oxygen** from the air and **give out carbonic acid gas**. This you can easily recognize by blowing down a tube whose end dips into lime-water and noticing how the latter turns milky. This is because the carbonic acid gas from your lungs unites with the lime to form a white insoluble powder (carbonate of lime). All **plants breathe** in just the same way as animals, and they too die if deprived of oxygen for any length of time. The breathing process, both of animals and plants, is termed **respiration**.

The taking in of oxygen. — Place a number of plants of the Shepherd's Purse in a securely corked jar and a similar number of dead ones in a second jar. Keep both in the dark for about two days. Then quickly place the end of a lighted taper in each jar. You will find that it immediately goes out in that containing the living plants, whilst in the other, it continues to burn. Since burning can only take place in the presence of oxygen, the living plants must have used up all of this gas. In the jar containing the dead ones, on the other hand, there is nearly as much oxygen as at the beginning of the experiment.

The giving out of carbonic acid gas. — Next, instead of the taper, hold a glass rod that has been dipped in lime-water in each jar. In that containing the living plants, the lime-water rapidly becomes milky, whilst in the other, there is scarcely any change. You must, of course, be careful not to breathe on the rod whilst performing this experiment. You have thus learnt that the living plants have not only **used up the oxygen** but have given out and so **increased the amount of carbonic acid gas** in the jar.

FIG. 6. - Experiment to show that living plants give off oxygen during assimilation. Description in the text.

If both jars are left in the light, you will obtain no such result. This is because, in the daytime, the plant uses up the carbonic acid gas produced in breathing to form starch from it in the way described above. There would consequently be no increase in the amount of carbonic acid gas in the jar. During the formation of starch, moreover, plants give out a large quantity of oxygen. Part of this is used for breathing, whilst the remainder escapes into the air. In the light, therefore, enough of this gas will be formed to enable the taper to go on burning.

The giving off of oxygen. — You can show that oxygen escapes during starch-formation in the following way. Heap up some living plants around a short length of burning candle placed in the middle of a saucer containing a little water (Fig. 6). Cover the whole with a glass jam-jar placed mouth downwards. Soon the candle goes out, having used up all the oxygen. Keep your experiment in bright sunlight for a few hours, and then, rapidly lifting up the jar, push into it a lighted taper. You will find that the latter goes on burning, so that the plants in the jar must have **given off a new supply of oxygen.**

Summary. — You have now learnt that plants obtain oxygen and carbonic acid gas from the air by way of their leaves, water and various dissolved substances from the soil by means of their roots. Also, that the important plant-food starch is only formed by the green parts and in the presence of light. When plants breathe, oxygen is taken in and carbonic acid gas is given out (**respiration**). When starch is formed, on the other hand, carbonic acid gas is taken in and oxygen is given out (**assimilation**). Since the amount of gas taken in and given out during assimilation is much greater than in breathing, the latter process is hidden unless the plant is in darkness.

Plants thus use much more carbonic acid gas than oxygen, whilst animals inhale large quantities of oxygen and give out a constant supply of carbonic acid gas. The latter does not, however, accumulate, as it is used by plants in assimilation and replaced by the oxygen which they give out.

PRACTICAL WORK

1. Perform the different experiments described above.

2. Collect leaves of a number of different plants in the afternoon. Decolourise them as described on p. 11, and test for starch.

QUESTIONS

1. Give a short account of the different kinds of work done for the plant by a leaf. Describe an experiment which shows the existence of *one* of the activities you mention.

2. If you want a plant to live, why must you let it have (a) light, (b) fresh air, (c) water?

3. Describe, as far as you can, how plants and animals resemble and differ from one another in the way in which they live.

4. How will the plants in a closed greenhouse alter the composition of the air (a) in the daytime, and (b) at night?

CHAPTER IV

THE PARTS OF A FLOWER

SOONER or later, plants, like the Shepherd's Purse, always form flowers, and we will now study them a little more fully than we did in the first chapter. The flowers of the Shepherd's Purse are so small, however, that we will substitute for them the similar, but larger, flowers of the Wallflower.

The floral leaves. — All the different parts of such a flower arise from the top of the **flower-stalk** or **peduncle** (Fig. 7, p.). Outside, you will find four small pale green leaves (the **sepals**), which come off at almost the same level, and together form what is called the **calyx** (Fig. 7, i.s.). Two of the sepals are enlarged into small pouches at their base.

Within the calyx are four coloured **petals** situated opposite the gaps between the sepals (Fig. 8, A, p.), in other words, the two kinds of floral leaves **alternate** with one another. The petals together form the **corolla**. Pull off a petal and notice that it consists of two parts: the broad blade and a narrow tapering portion, the claw. The four upright sepals and the claws of the petals form a tube, at the top of which the blades of the petals spread out (Fig. 116, p. 149).

The stamens. — If you remove all the sepals and petals, there remains a green central body surrounded by six green stalks, each ending in a little oval swelling (Fig. 8, A). Each of these six structures is called a **stamen**, the stalk being known as the **filament** (Fig. 8, C, f.) and the yellow swelling as the **anther** (Fig. 8, C, a.). By squeezing one of the anthers, you will press out a yellow powder, the **pollen**. In some flowers, the anthers will have split open of themselves (Fig. 8, C), thus shedding their pollen, a little of which still remains clinging to them.

The ovary. — The green body or **ovary** (Fig. 8, O.) in the centre of the flower is oblong in form and ends in two little sticky swellings, the **stigmas** (Fig. 8, B, st.). If you examine the latter carefully, you will probably find some of the yellow pollen adhering to them. Now cut open the ovary and notice the small greenish bodies which it contains. These are the unripe seeds or **ovules** (Fig. 7, O.; Fig. 8, D, Ov.).

When you have pulled off all the parts of the flower, you will see that the end of the peduncle to which they were attached is slightly

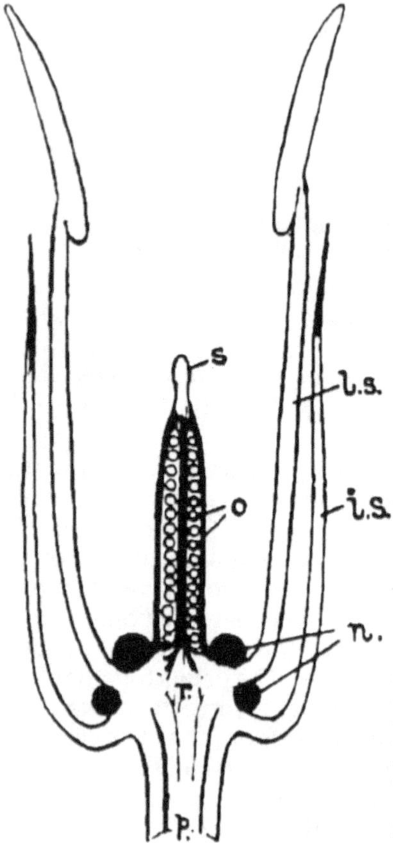

FIG. 7. — Section cut up the middle of a Wallflower (enlarged about four times). i.s., inner sepals; I.S., side-stamens; n., nectary; O., ovules; P., peduncle; T., receptacle; S., stigma.

swollen. This swelling is termed the **receptacle** of the flower (Fig. 7, r.).

The fruit. — The inflorescence of the Wallflower, like that of the Shepherd's Purse (p. 5), lengthens out as the flowers fade. When the sepals, petals, and stamens have fallen off, the ovary will be seen to be much enlarged. It is now developing into the ripe **fruit**, which is long and pod-like and still bears the stigmas at the top (Fig. 9, A). Here, as in the Shepherd's Purse, you may find ripe fruits at the base of the inflorescence. These have split into two halves and shed their **seeds** (Fig. 9, B).

What makes the ovary and ovules develop into fruit and seeds? Remove all the stamens from the flowers of an inflorescence before they have shed their pollen. Then cover the whole with a fine muslin bag to prevent any pollen being brought from outside. Under these circumstances, no ripe fruits are produced. The conclusion is that **pollen is necessary for the formation of seeds and fruits.** The same result is obtained in whatever way you prevent pollen from reaching the stigma.

Pollination. — We may now enquire how the pollen, which you have already seen on the stigma, comes to be there. Watch some Wallflowers on a bright sunny day, and you will notice that they are frequently visited by bees. These insects settle on the spreading corolla and stay for some little time on each flower. Meanwhile, they are sucking up the **honey** which is present in the flower. No doubt the bee finds its way more readily to the flower because of its scent and colour.

If you pull off the two pouched sepals (Fig. 7, i.s.), you will notice a little liquid honey in each pouch. Now examine the two stamens

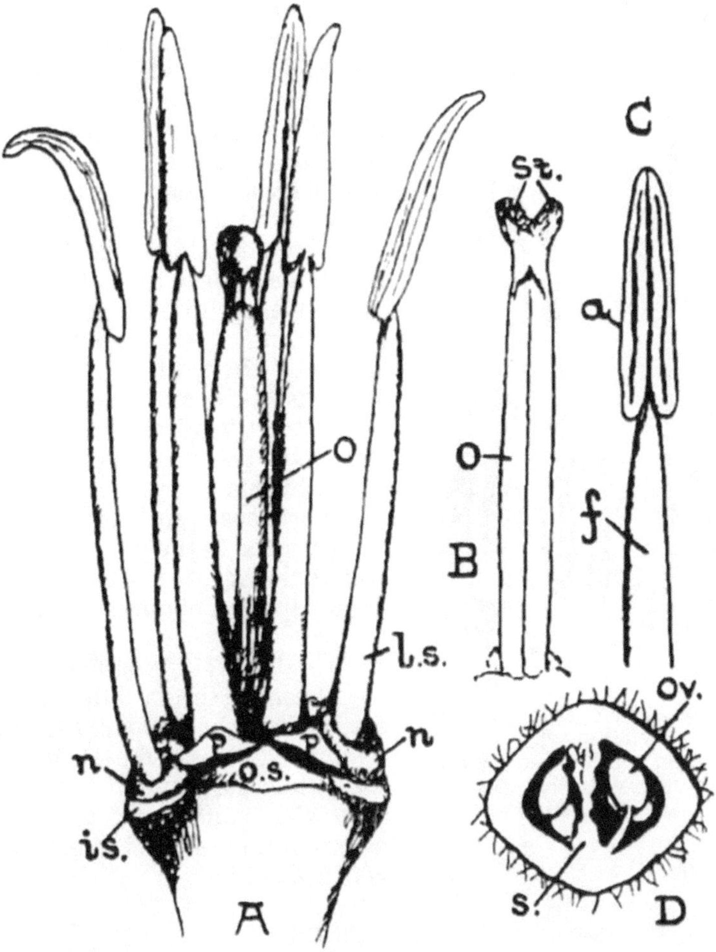

FIG. 8.
A. Flower of Wallflower, with sepals and petals removed (the scars of the latter are indicated): B, ovary: C, single stamen: the long black lines on each side of the anther mark where it has split open; D, ovary cut across (all figures enlarged): a., anther: f., filament; i.s., inner sepal scar: I.S., side-stamen: n., nectary: O., ovary; O.S., scar of outer sepal; Ov. ovule: P., scar of petal: S., partition in ovary: st., stigmas.

exposed by pulling off these sepals. You will find that each has a little green swelling or **nectary** (Fig. 7, n.; Fig. 8, A, n.) at the base of its filament. These nectaries produce the honey which gradually collects in the pouches.

While the bee is sucking honey, its tongue touches the anthers

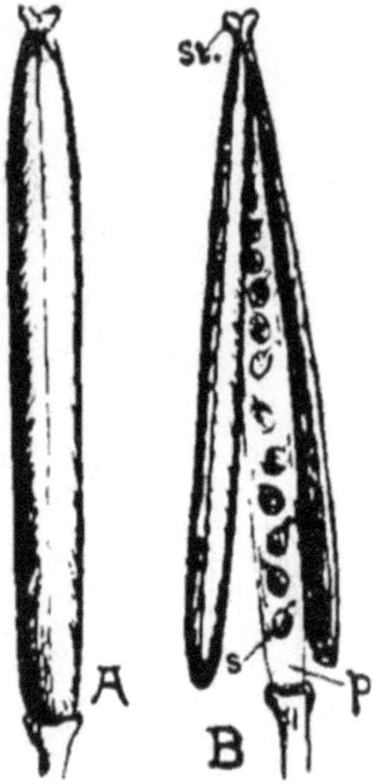

FIG. 9. - Two fruits of the Wallflower.
A, before, and B, after opening (about natural size); P., partition S., seed st., stigma.

which nearly fill up the opening of the flower. The pollen, which is picked up in this way, is **carried to the stigma** (generally of another flower of the same kind) as the bee continues its search for honey. This is what is called the **pollination** of the flower. After the pollen has reached the stigma, certain changes take place which lead to the formation of the young plant within the seed.

Summary. — A typical flower consists, then, of calyx, corolla, stamens, and ovary. The flowers are really structures for producing fruits and seeds. This depends on pollination, which in many cases is brought about by insects, such as bees. These are attracted to the flowers by their colour and scent, and especially by the prospect of obtaining honey.

PRACTICAL WORK

1. Examine several different flowers, such as the Poppy, Stitchwort, Geranium, Jack-by-the-Hedge. Note the various parts and their number.

2. Watch different flowers in full bloom and notice the different insects which visit them.

QUESTIONS

1. What are the different parts of a flower and what are they used for?

2. How would you show that pollen is necessary for the formation of fruits and seeds?

3. What benefit does (a) the plant, and (b) the insect receive in visiting a flower?

CHAPTER V

THE FORMS OF PLANTS

IN this book, we shall only study plants that bear flowers. But there are, of course, a large number which have no flowers, such as Sea-weeds, Mosses, Toadstools, and Ferns. The Flowering Plants are very numerous and differ very much in their manner of growth; in other words, they show many differences of **habit**.

Trees and shrubs. — It is easy to distinguish between **trees** and **shrubs**, whose woody branches live from year to year, and herbs, in which all the overground parts generally die back at the end of each season. Trees differ from shrubs in having a thick main trunk (Fig. 10) from which the smaller branches arise. Shrubs have several equally large stems emerging from the surface of the ground. In both trees and shrubs, the leaves are usually shed on the approach of winter; that is to say, they are **deciduous**; sometimes the branches also die back a little way. **Evergreen** trees and shrubs, such as the Scotch Fir and the Laurel, keep their leaves throughout the year.

Herbs. — Herbs show a much more varied habit. Thus, the main stem usually grows **erect** (Fig. 1), but in some plants it **creeps** above or below the surface of the ground. Herbs having upright stems, such as the Shepherd's Purse and the Sunflower, easily expose their leaves to the light, and their flowers are readily seen by insects. You will notice that such plants keep their shoots erect without any outside help.

Climbing plants. — Some herbs, however, use other plants as a support, since their thin stems are too weak to keep erect of themselves. The Goosegrass (Figs. 11, A, and 12, g.) and the Stitchwort of our hedgerows grow upright when very young. As they get taller, however, they lean over against surrounding plants and gradually sprawl over them, clinging through the roughness of their stems (Fig. 11, A). If you pass your finger in both directions along the stem of the Goosegrass, you will notice that it feels much rougher when stroked upwards. The Bramble and the Dog-rose are woody plants which **scramble** in the same way. Here you can see plainly that the stem is covered with bent prickles that hook the plant on to its support (Fig. 11, B).

FIG. 10. - Photograph of an Elm tree in winter, showing the bare twigs. The trunk is clothed with Ivy. (Photo, E. J. S.)

Another way in which weak-stemmed plants use stronger ones to help them grow towards the light is by **twining** their stems around them. Here again, you will find good examples growing in hedges, as, for instance, the Convolvulus, the Hop (Fig. 13), and the Black Bryony. The Honeysuckle twines its woody stems round those of trees and shrubs. Another woody climber is the Ivy, which becomes attached to walls and tree-trunks by numerous little roots on its stems (Fig. 10).

Tendrils. - The White Bryony (Fig. 12, b) and Sweet Pea climb in

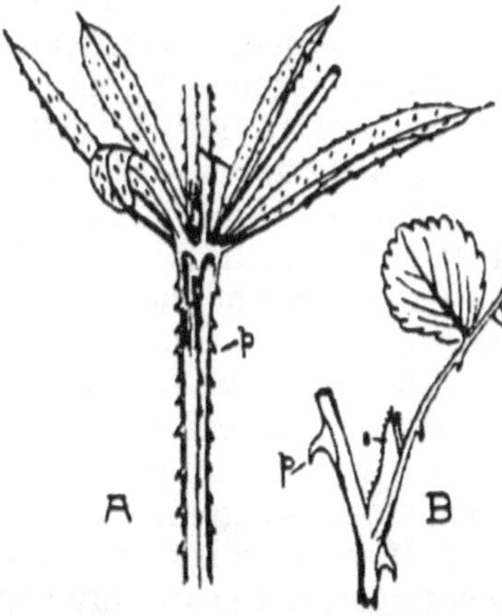

FIG. 11.

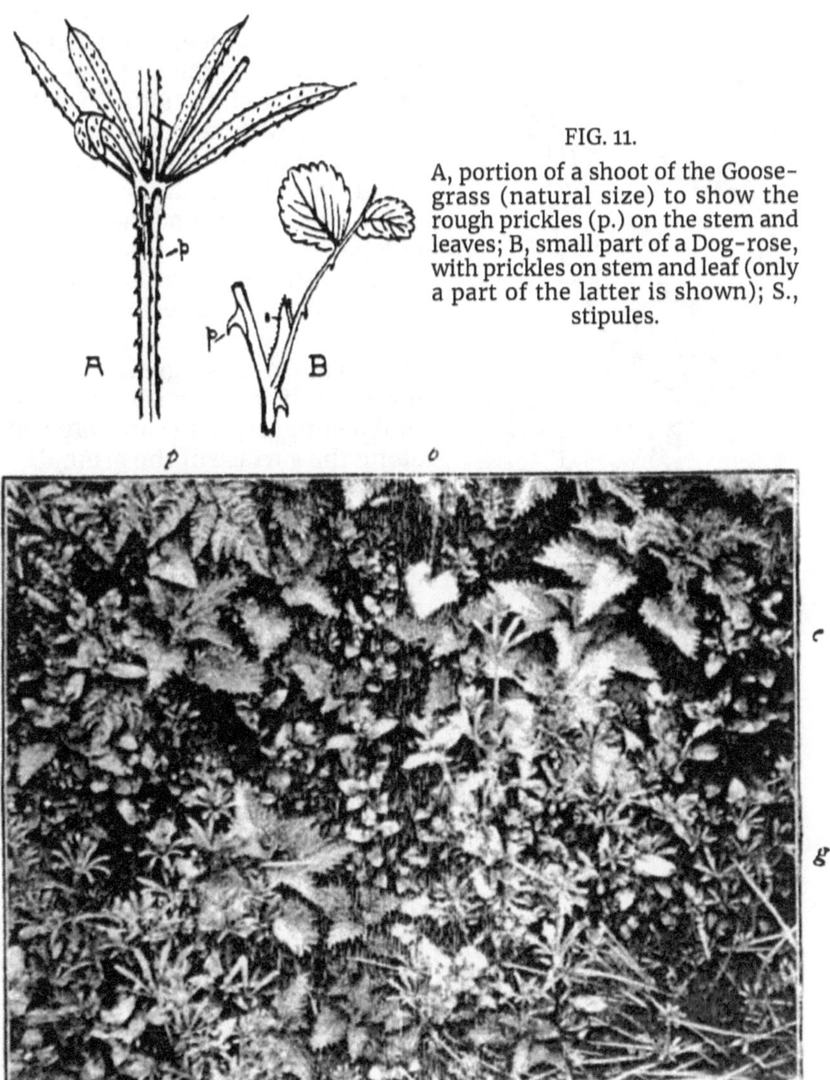

A, portion of a shoot of the Goose-grass (natural size) to show the rough prickles (p.) on the stem and leaves; B, small part of a Dog-rose, with prickles on stem and leaf (only a part of the latter is shown); S., stipules.

FIG. 12. – Photograph of the foot of hedgerow. (Photo, F. J. S.)
b., White Bryony: e., Chickweed; g., Goosegrass; p., Beaked Parsley; s., Stinging Nettle.

quite a different way. These plants are attached to their supports by means of spring-like threads or **tendrils** (Fig. 14). The latter are at first almost straight (Fig. 14, A), but when they touch any slender object they coil round it (Fig. 14, B). Afterwards, the lower part of the tendril also coils up, so that as the plant gets older it is attached by numerous spiral springs, each formed from a tendril. It can thus sway about without being torn away from its support. In the Wild Clematis or Old Man's Beard, the long **petioles** of the leaves **coil round** the branches of other plants and thus support it.

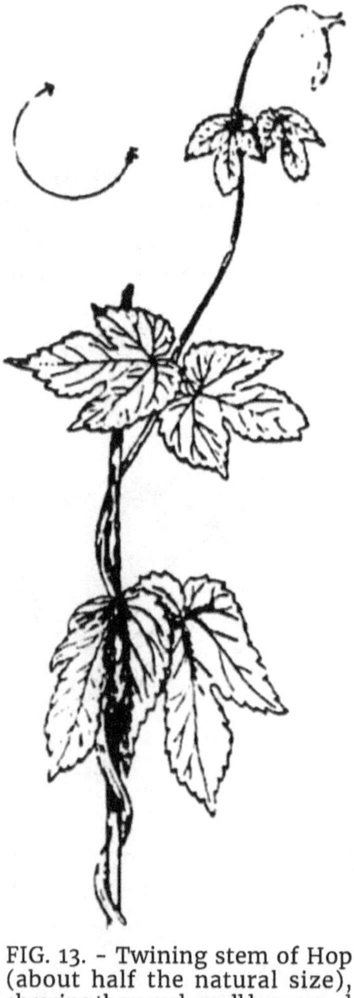

FIG. 13. - Twining stem of Hop (about half the natural size), showing the usual small leaves and long internodes of the twining tip. The arrow shows the direction in which twining takes place.

The different kinds of climbing plants are able to expose their leaves and flowers without forming a thick stem. This means a great saving of material. If, however, they fail to find a support, they can only trail along the surface of the ground.

Creeping plants. - Plants which creep on the top or below the surface of the soil rapidly spread over ground left bare by others. By completely covering the soil, they are often able to keep out taller growing plants, but if they fail to do this, they become shaded and suffer in consequence.

When the stem creeps along the surface, as in the Ground Ivy (Fig. 15) and Creeping Jenny, it bears leaves rising up into the air, and bunches of roots at intervals on the underside. The flowers of the Ground Ivy are borne on short upright shoots (Fig. 15, f.s.) coming off from the creeping stem, a common feature of such plants.

Underground stems. - The stems of the Dog's Mercury, Solomon's Seal (Fig. 29), and Iris creep just **under the surface** of the earth, such a stem being called a **rhizome**. In the Iris, the long flat leaves arise in a group from the tip, whilst in the Dog's Mercury,

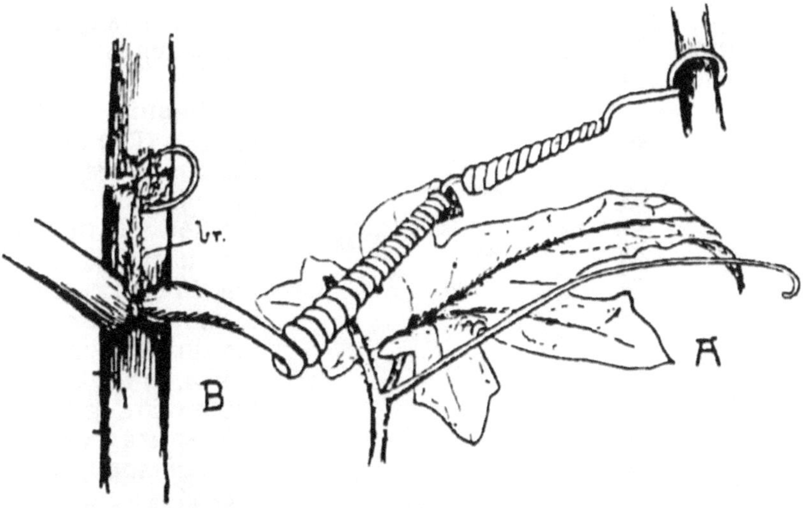

FIG. 14. - Tendrils of the White Bryony (natural size). A, before; B, after clasping the support; br., branch.

leafy shoots branch off from the rhizome at intervals and grow up into the air.

The rhizome of the Iris is thick and fleshy. This is usual in such underground stems, and is due to their being filled with **stores of food**. If you cut off a piece of the Iris stem and paint it with iodine, it at once turns almost black owing to the presence of starch.

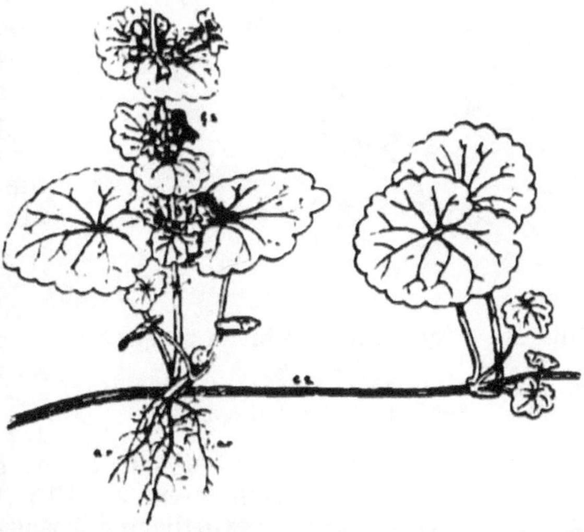

FIG. 15. - Creeping stem (c.s.) of the Ground Ivy, showing adventitious roots (a.r.) and an shoot (S.S.) (about half the natural size). The full length of the flowering shoot is not shown.

Annuals. - Plants, like the Shepherd's Purse and the Poppy, grow rapidly after germination, flowers and fruits are soon formed, and death takes place towards the end of the season. Such plants are called **annuals**, and use up all their strength in the formation of flowers and fruits. The reappearance of the plant in the next year depends on the sprouting of its seeds.

FIG. 16. - The Mullein, a biennial (greatly reduced).
B, in the rosette-stage (first year) A, in the stage found in the second year.

Biennials. - The Mullein (Fig. 16) and the Turnip are examples of plants that do not flower in the first year of their life. All this time is occupied in making and storing up food in the fleshy root, which, in the case of the Turnip (Fig. 24, D), is eaten as a vegetable. Until the spring of the second season arrives, the stem remains quite short, and the leaves appear as a **rosette** on the surface of the ground (Fig. 16, B). Then, with the help of the food that was stored up in the root, a tall erect stem, bearing flowers, is produced (Fig. 16, A), seeds are formed, and after that, the plant dies. Such plants, which take two years to complete their life, are called **biennials**.

Perennials. - Shrubs and trees last for many years and are known as **woody perennials**. But there are also herbs which live for many seasons, and are hence called **herbaceous perennials**. All such perennials, when grown from seed, seldom flower in the first season and sometimes not for several years, but afterwards, flowers usually appear annually. Each autumn, a portion of the plant dies back. The remainder (the woody roots and stems in the case of trees and shrubs, the underground parts in the case of herbs) lives on and contains **stores of food** for next spring's growth.

Summary. - According to the way in which they grow, you can distinguish erect, climbing, twining, and creeping plants. Whilst according to their length of life, they are either annuals, biennials, or perennials. The latter are either herbaceous, or woody trees and shrubs.

PRACTICAL WORK

1. Look at the trunks of various trees and make a list of their differences.

2. Examine the plants of a hedgerow and group them, according to their habit, into erect, scrambling, climbing, and creeping forms. In the case of the climbers, state the method of attachment adopted by each plant.

3. Examine first-year plants of the Foxglove, Thistle, Teazle, and Mullein.

4. Look at the underground parts of a number of herbaceous perennials, such as the Nettle, Cuckoo Pint, and Dog's Mercury.

QUESTIONS

1. What are the advantages and disadvantages of the different habits of plants?

2. Describe and draw one plant which climbs in each of the following ways: (a) by tendrils, (b) by rootlets, (c) by twining stem. Describe, and make plain by your figure, the relation of each of these climbers to its support, and the way in which it holds its leaves to get light.

3. Name one biennial plant and one perennial plant, and describe briefly the life-history of each.

CHAPTER VI

LEAVES

The work of leaves. - You have learnt that leaves play a very important part in the life of plants. From their broad thin blades most of the water-vapour escapes in transpiration. Their **flat shape** suits them well to catch the light which is so necessary for assimilation. The numerous pores on their under surface are the main passages by means of which, apart from the water-vapour, carbonic acid gas and oxygen pass into and out of the plant.

The parts of a leaf. - Such a leaf as that of the Violet, which can be obtained at nearly all times of the year, shows three distinct parts. First, there is the heart-shaped **blade** (Fig. 17, b.). This is pointed at its tip, and has two rounded lobes on either side of the notch, in which the petiole (Fig. 17, p.) is attached. Blades of this same shape, which is described as **cordate**, are also seen in the Lesser Celandine and Hedge Woundwort (Fig. 18, A).

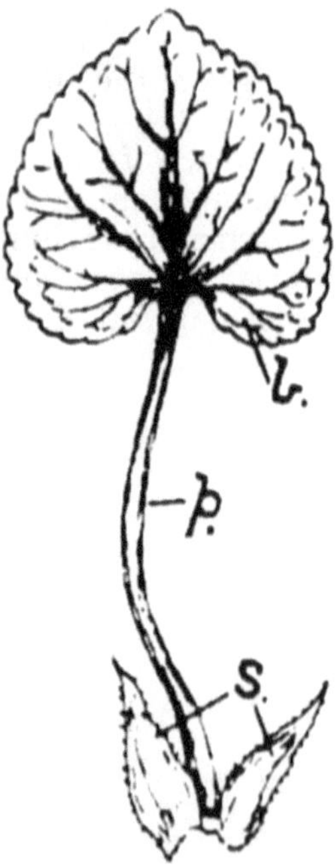

FIG. 17. - Leaf of the Sweet Violet (about three-quarters the natural size).
b., blade: p., petiole; S., stipules.

The second part of the Violet leaf is the long slender **petiole**. This, where it is attached to the short underground stem, broadens out to form the third part of the leaf, the **leaf-base**. In the Lesser Celandine and Garden Geranium (Fig. 19, l.b.), the latter is easily recognised, since it forms a large sheathing structure, partly surrounding the lower end of the internode above.

On either side of the leaf-base of the Violet, there is a narrow membranous outgrowth called a **stipule** (Fig. 17, s.). When such structures are present, the leaf is said to be **stipulate**.

Stipules are not met with in all leaves; for instance, there are none in the Chickweed (Fig. B) and Lesser Celandine, which are hence termed **exstipulate**. Sometimes, as in the Pansy (Fig. 43, B, p. 65), the stipules are large green structures, which serve to increase the assimilating surface.

The petiole. - In many plants, for instance in those just mentioned, the upper surface of the petiole is flat or grooved (Fig. 19, p.). But this is not the case when the leaf-stalk is attached to the middle of the blade, as in the Garden Nasturtium (Fig. 60, B, p. 85) or Pennywort. Such mushroom-like leaves are said to be **peltate**.

The second part of the leaf or leaf-stalk is not uncommonly absent, so that the blade arises directly from the stem. Such leaves are sessile, and are found on the stems of the Shepherd's Purse (Fig. 1, c.l.) and in the St. John's Worts.

Shapes of leaves. - If the two edges of the leaf are almost parallel, as in Grasses (Fig. 18, G), the blade is said to be **linear**. When it tapers at both ends, as in the Privet (Fig. 18, I) and Dog's Mercury, it is **lanceolate**. In the Chickweed (Fig. 18, B), the tip of the blade is pointed, whilst its base is rounded, so that it is egg-shaped or **ovate**. This differs from the **cordate** leaf of the Violet (Fig. 17) in not having the deep notch at the base. Sometimes, the blade, though egg-shaped, has its pointed end attached to the petiole; this is the case in the common Garden Spurge (Fig. 18, F), and such a blade is said to be **obovate**.

The outline of the blade in the Ground Ivy (Fig. 18, E) is like that of a kidney, for which reason it is termed **reniform**. In the Field Convolvulus (Fig. 18, J) and the Sorrels, the blades are somewhat like those of a cordate leaf, but the lobes at the base are sharply pointed; this shape is described as **hastate**. The leaves of the Common Mallow and the Garden Geranium have rounded blades with a very deep notch at the point of attachment to the petiole. In such **orbicular** leaves (Fig. 19), the petiole appears fixed almost at the centre of the blade.

The edge and tip of the blade. - In some of these leaves, the edge is almost smooth or **entire** (e.g., Privet, Fig. 18, I; Chickweed, Fig. 18, I B), but in most of them it is more or less cut. Thus, in the Woundwort (Fig. 18, A), the margin resembles the edge of a small saw, having pointed teeth all directed towards the tip, i.e., it is **serrate**. When all the teeth point outwards, as in the Enchanter's Nightshade (Fig. 18, K), the margin is described as **dentate**. In the Ground Ivy (Fig. 18, E), all the teeth are rounded, and the margin is said to be **crenate**.

The tip of the blade is either blunt (i.e., **obtuse**, as in the Spurge, Fig. 18, F) or sharply pointed (i.e., **acute**, as in the Chickweed, Fig. 18, B), whilst the surface may be smooth or **hairy** (Fig. 18, A).

Simple and compound leaves. - All the leaves with which you have as yet become acquainted are **simple** leaves, since their blade

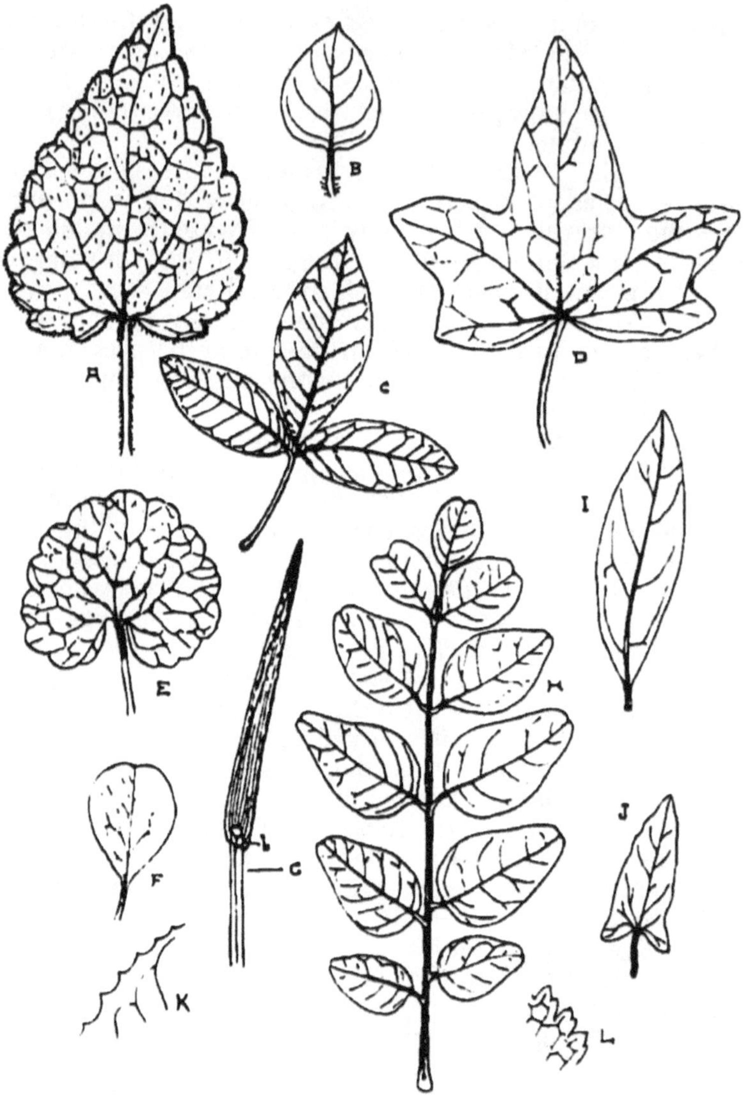

Fig. 18. - Different kinds of foliage-leaves (all about one-half natural size). A, Hedge Woundwort (cordate, acute): B, Chickweed (ovate, acute): C, Laburnum (compound, with three leafleis): D, Ivy (palmately lobed); E, Ground Ivy (reniform, crenate); F', Garden Spurge (obovate, obtuse); G, Grass (linear): 1., small ridge at top of leaf sheath: H, False Acacia (pinnate): I, Privet (lanceolate, entire); J, Field Convolvulus (hastate); K, Enchanter's Nightshade (showing dentate margin only): L, White Dead-nettle (showing margin with teeth of two sizes).

consists of one continuous piece. Very often, however, simple leaves are deeply lobed, as in the Shepherd's Purse (Fig. 3, B, C) and the Ivy (Fig. 18, D). When the divisions between the lobes reach the midrib, the leaf is said to be **compound** (Fig. 18, H), and the separate parts of the blade are called **leaflets**. The latter may be stalked or sessile, and vary in shape, margin, etc., in the same way as the blades of simple leaves.

In the False Acacia (Fig. 18, H) and the Vetch, the leaflets are arranged on either side of a central stalk. Such a compound leaf is said to be **pinnate**. When all the leaflets arise near together from the top of the petiole, as in the Horse Chestnut, the leaf is described as **palmate**. The leaflets of compound leaves are distinguished from simple leaves by the fact that there are no buds in their axils. On the other hand, a bud is found in the usual position between the main stem and the stalk of the compound leaf.

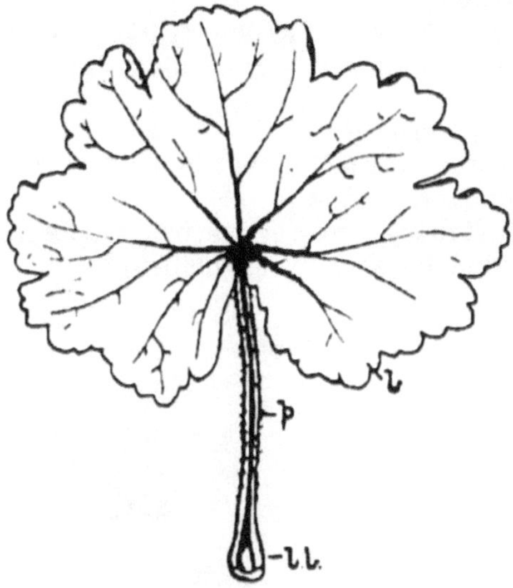

FIG. 19. - Orbicular leaf of the Garden Geranium (about half the natural size). b., blade; 1.6., leaf base P., petiole.

The veins. - In the blade of the Shepherd's Purse, you recognized a prominent central **mid-rib**, from which **lateral veins** branched off on either side (Fig. 3, A). The same arrangement of the veins is found in many other leaves. If you look at a leaf of the Primrose or Woundwort (Fig. 18, A), you will see that the side veins branch into smaller and smaller ones. The whole system forms a network which is plainly visible on the underside of the blade of the Primrose.

Such **reticulate** vein-ing is found in the leaves of most **Dicotyledons**, which form one of the two great groups of Flowering Plants. In some cases, however, there is not a single midrib, but several main ribs spread out from the top of the leaf-stalk. Between these, the finer veins form a network as before. A good example is furnished by the Ivy (Fig. 18, D).

In the other group of the Flowering Plants, the **Monocotyledons** (to which Grasses, Lilies, Hyacinths, etc., belong), there is seldom a prominent midrib. If you hold a Grass-leaf up to the light, you will see a number of larger veins which run parallel to one another (Fig.

18, G). These are joined by numerous parallel, but often indistinct, cross-branches. This kind of veining is described as **parallel**.

Summary. - The foliage leaf consists of three parts, namely, the blade, the petiole, and the leaf base. The latter frequently bears stipules. The blade varies in shape and margin, and may be simple or compound. Compound leaves are either palmate or pinnate. The veining of the leaf is either reticulate (Dicotyledons) or parallel (Monocotyledons).

PRACTICAL WORK

1. Examine as many simple leaves as you can find, and describe their shape and margin and the form of the tip.
2. Look at a number of compound leaves and group them according to the arrangement of the leaflets.
3. Place various thin leaves with their stalks dipping into a solution of red ink, and after a day or two, examine the arrangement of the veins.

QUESTIONS

1. What are the different parts of a leaf? How would you distinguish between a simple and a compound leaf?
2. What is meant by the following terms: entire, peltate, pinnate, acute, obovate, hastate, exstipulate, serrate, and palmate?

CHAPTER VII

THE ROOT

The root-system. - You have already learned that the root serves two purposes or **functions**, namely, to fix the plant in the soil and to absorb water. If you dig up any plant, you will, in most cases, find that the roots are richly branched. The mass of soil threaded by the roots is generally proportional to the size of the shoot. In woody plants, the growth of the whole mass of roots (the **root system**) keeps pace with the enlargement of the overground shoots. Sometimes, the washing away of the soil leads to the exposure of the horizontal branches of the roots of trees. You can then see that they extend a long way out from the main trunk.

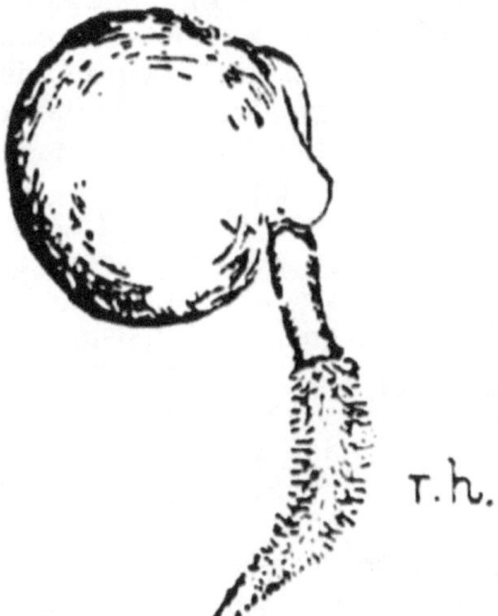

FIG. 20. - Young Pea-seedling with root showing root hairs (r.h.) and root-cap (r.c.), after being kept in water (about twice the natural size).

The root-hairs. - To see what the young root is like, place some Cress seeds on blotting paper, which is kept damp, and examine them after a few days. The roots, which have grown out from the seeds, bear, a little way behind their tips, a mass of hairs (r.h.) and root-cap (r.c.) after being kept in white water (about twice the natural size). These are the **root hairs**. They are present in the same position on the roots of almost all plants and also occur on every branch-root.

By means of the root hairs, the plant absorbs the moisture which surrounds the small particles of the soil. When you pull up a plant, you will notice that the earth remains clinging to the tips of the roots. This is because the root hairs are in such close contact with the particles of the soil that these cling to the parts where the root hairs are found.

The root-cap. - At the tips of the roots of the Cress, in fact, on almost every root, you will see a little brown covering, the **root cap** (Fig. 20, r.c.). This serves to protect the tender growing tip (p. 5) as it pushes its way down through the earth. Notice that the root hairs do not arise immediately behind the root cap, but that there is a short space of bare root between them and the tip (Fig. 20). Near the seed, you will find that the older root hairs have withered away.

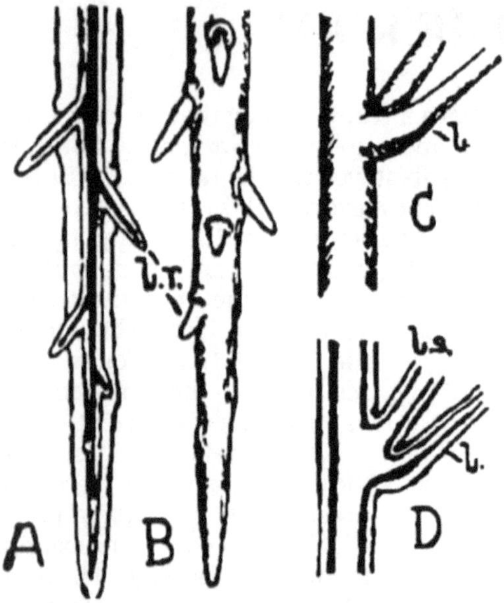

FIG. 21. - Diagram to show the way in which lateral roots and shoots are produced.
A, the root cut lengthwise; B, the same root, shown entire; C, drawing of the node of a stem; D, the same cut in half lengthwise. I., leaf; Lr., lateral roots; I.s., lateral shoots.

The branch-roots. - Now take a well-grown Bean-seedling, and split the branched main root up the middle. You will see that there is a **central woody core** which appears rather darker than the rest (Fig. 21, A; Fig. 54, B). This is the skeleton of the root. It gives the necessary strength to resist the frequent pulls to which the root is subjected, as the stem and leaves sway to and fro in the wind.

Arising from this central core are the branches. These begin growth **right inside** the main root and gradually push their way to the outside (Fig. 21, A). If you now look at the surface of an entire root, you will see that the side or **lateral roots** come out of small slits (Fig. 21, B). The branches emerge from the surface of the main root only **above** the region bearing root-hairs.

The root and gravity. - The main roots in all cases grow vertically downwards. We may now endeavour to find out the cause. Plant some soaked Peas in damp sawdust and wait until the roots have grown about an inch long. Then take a small wooden or cardboard box and line the whole of the inside with damp blotting-paper (Fig. 22, b.). To one side, fix a few of the Peas (by pins passing through the seeds), so that the roots are horizontal (Fig. 22, p.); then put on the lid. Next day you will find that the tips of the roots have **curved downwards**, so that they again point towards the earth (Fig. 22, p.').

You know that there is a force, called the force of gravity, that makes bodies which are unsupported fall to the ground. The roots of the Peas in the box were surrounded on all sides by damp air and were in darkness. If other Pea seedlings were placed in the box with their roots pointing *vertically* downwards, they would continue to grow **without curving**. The only difference, therefore, lies in the **position which the roots occupy** in relation to the earth. Probably then, the force of gravity has some effect on the direction of growth of a root.

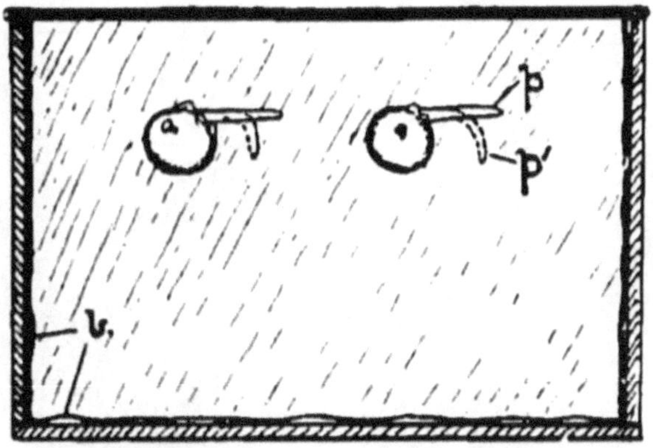

FIG. 22. - Experiment to show the influence of gravity on the root. Description in the text. b., blotting paper lining the box; p. original position, and p.' final position of the roots.

Next, grow a Bean-seedling for some little time in a damp jam-jar, with its main root vertically downwards. Wait until the side-roots have reached some length. You will notice that, although they are more slender than the main root, they spread out almost at right angles. Evidently then, it was **not the weight** of the main root which caused its tip to curve downwards when placed horizontally. It is also clear that the side-roots are influenced by gravity in a different way from the main root.

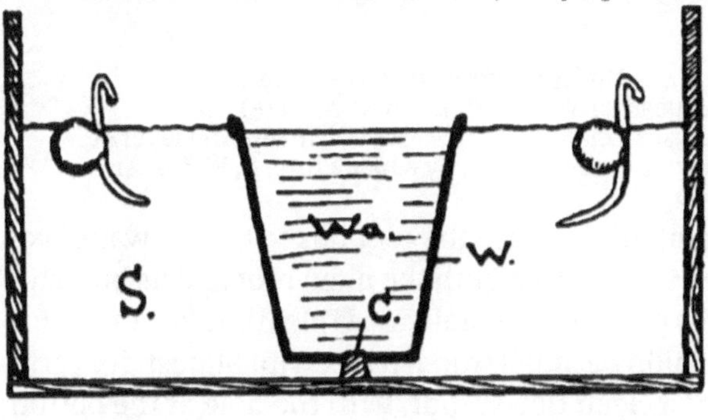

FIG. 23. - Experiment to show the influence of moisture on the root. Description in the text, p. 32. C., cork S., soil; W. side of pot: Wa., water.

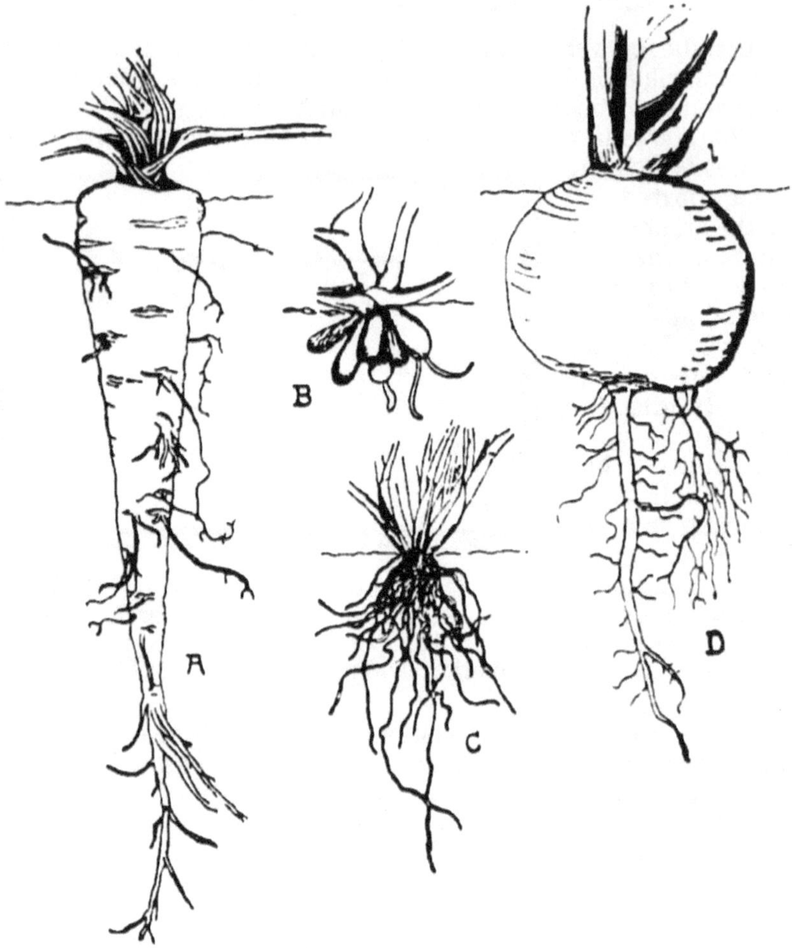

FIG. 24. - Different kinds of root-systems
(reduced to about half the natural size).
A, Carrot; B, Lesser Celandine; C, Grass; D, Turnip; the level of the ground is in all cases shown by a black line; l., leaf-scar.

The root and moisture. - Since the root has to absorb water, you will not be surprised to learn that both the main root and its branches tend to **curve towards** places where **moisture** is plentiful. You can follow this for yourself by filling a small wooden box with almost dry earth. In the middle, plant a clean flower-pot, with the hole at the bottom tightly corked, so that only the rim is above the surface (Fig. 23). Now sow about a dozen soaked Peas in the top layer of the soil, at some little distance from the pot. Keep the latter full of water, but do not water the soil, which thus only receives the moisture coming through the sides of the pot.

After about two or three weeks, carefully dig up a few of the Peas with a pocket-knife. You will find that in every case, the root-system has all its branches bending towards the pot (Fig. 23), i.e., the direction **from which the moisture came**. In nature, it is mainly the finer rootlets that are affected in this way, and these are uninfluenced by gravity.

Different kinds of root-systems. - If you pull up a number of plants, you will find that the root-systems are of two kinds. In the Shepherd's Purse (Figs. 1, 2), Jack-by-the-Hedge, and Carrot (Fig. 24, A), there is a large main **tap-root** growing downwards. This has a number of smaller spreading branches which themselves bear smaller and smaller rootlets. Compare such root-systems with those of plants like the Grasses (Fig. 24, C), the Chickweed, and the Hyacinth. These have no main root, but a number of similar **fibrous** roots forming a group at the base of the stem.

Summary. - On all the branches of the root-system you can recognise: (a) at the tip, a root-cap, protecting the growing point; (b) a short bare strip of root; (c) the region in which the root-hairs arise; (d) the region in which the branch-roots appear. The last develop from the interior of the parent-root and first appear at the edge of the central core or skeleton. The direction of growth of roots is influenced by gravity and moisture, though these affect the main and side-roots differently.

PRACTICAL WORK

1. Examine the roots of a number of germinated seedlings, and in each case note the different parts. (If the roots are grown in water, root-hairs and root-caps are more easily seen.)

2. Perform the experiment described on p. 31 on a number of other plants, e.g. Bean, Sunflower, Marrow, etc.

3. Pull up a number of plants and draw the different types of root-systems.

4. Cut off the tip from the root of a Bean-seedling and place it in water coloured with red ink. After some hours, slit up the root lengthwise and notice that the central core is alone coloured red. What do you conclude from this result?

QUESTIONS

1. Describe the form and structure of a young root, and show how it is suited to its life and work in the soil.

2. How would you show by an experiment that the direction of growth of roots is affected by gravity or moisture?

3. Describe, with diagrams, the way in which roots branch.

CHAPTER VIII

TREES AND SHRUBS IN WINTER

The markings on a twig. - Most trees and shrubs are bare in winter. You can nevertheless learn a great many things about them by examining their branches carefully. Thus, on a twig of the Horse Chestnut (Fig. 25), you will see a large bud (the **terminal bud)** at the end, and a number of smaller buds (the **lateral buds**) along the sides. Beneath each lateral bud, there is a somewhat triangular scar. This bears, near its lower edge, several dots (Fig. 25, vs.) arranged like the nails of a horseshoe. The whole structure is a **leaf-scar** (Fig. 25), formed at the node when the leaf dropped off. The dots are where the bundles of water-carrying pipes, passing from leaf to stem, have been broken across. You will notice that there is **no** leaf-scar below the terminal bud, so that it is **not axillary** like the lateral buds.

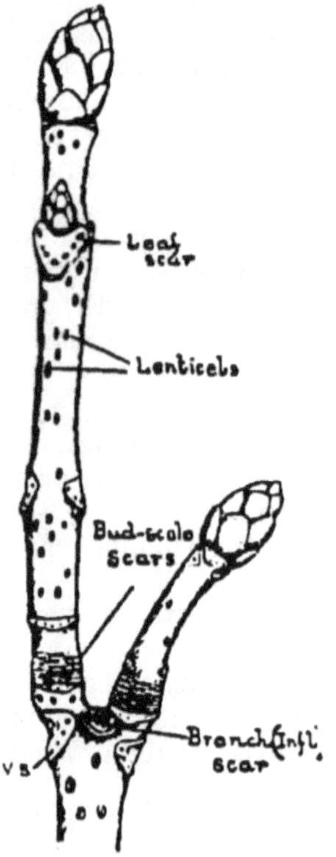

FIG. 25. - Portion of twig of the Horse Chestnut showing buds, leaf-scars, and lenticels (about two-thirds the natural size). vs., the broken ends of the water-carrying pipes.

On some of the twigs, you will find here and there a saucer-shaped scar (Fig. 25, branch-scar). This was left by one of the big inflorescences of the Horse Chestnut when it dropped off. All over the surface of the twig, between the scars, are pimple-like markings, the **lenticels** (Fig. 25). These are small openings through which breathing takes place, especially during the winter.

Twigs of different plants. - Now examine the twigs of other plants, such as the Ash, Elm, Oak, etc. (Fig. 26). Each of these bears buds, leaf-scars, and lenticels. They differ chiefly from

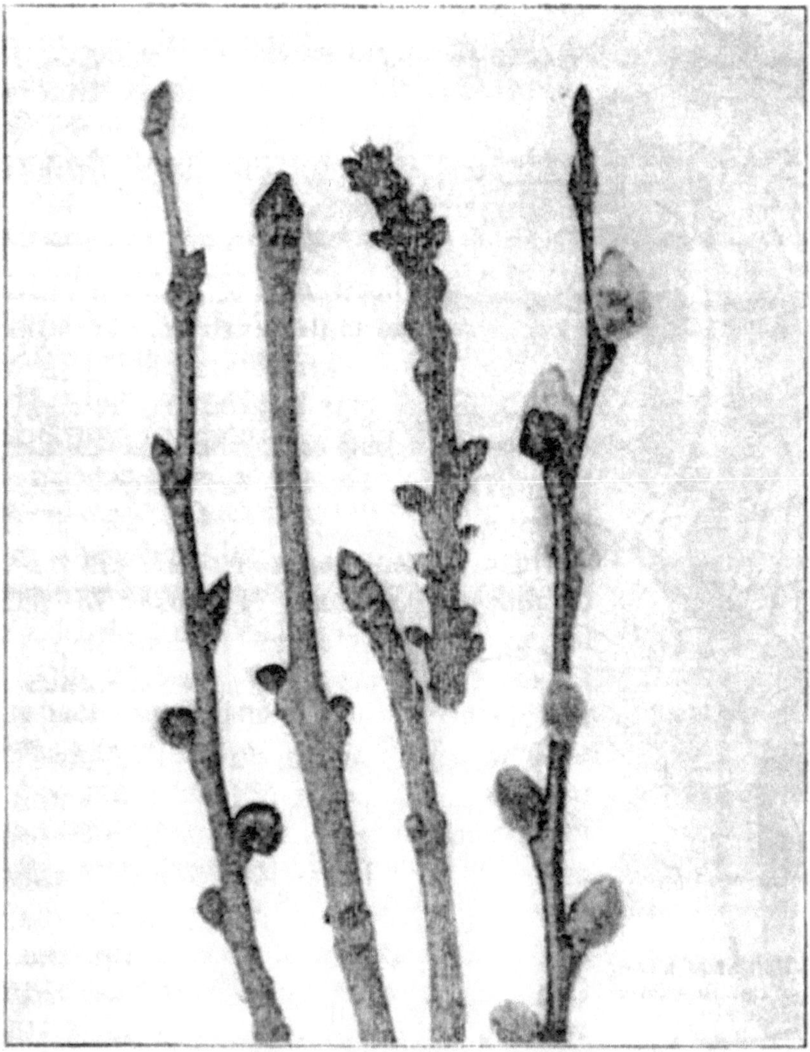

FIG. 26. - Photographs of the twigs of different trees.
From left to right: Elm, Ash, Sycamore, Oak, Goat-Willow. The large buds in the Elm and Willow are flower-buds.

one another in the shape, colour, and position of these structures. The surface of the branch may be smooth, as in the Ash (Fig. 26), or hairy, as in the Elm (Fig. 51, B, p. 76).

In the Beech, the buds are slender and pointed (Fig. 27); those of the Oak are short and form dense groups (Fig. 26), whilst those of the Ash are squat and black (Fig. 26). The leaf-scars of the Horse Chestnut are placed in pairs, one on either side of the stem (Fig. 25); in other words, they are **opposite**. Since, as you have learnt, branches always arise in the axils of leaves, the buds of this plant are of course also opposite. In the Beech (Fig. 27), however, the leaf-scars and buds stand singly at the nodes, i.e., they are **alternate**. You will notice that some of the buds on the twigs have grown out into branches, whilst others have remained undeveloped.

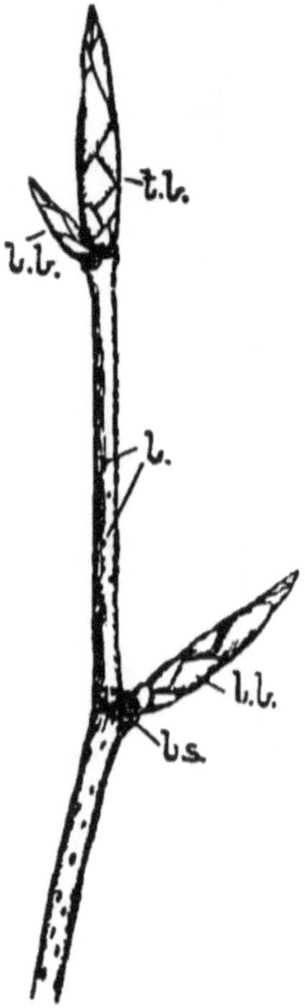

FIG. 27. - Portion of a twig of the Beech in winter time (about natural size). L., lenticels: l.b., lateral buds: 1.5., leaf-scar; t.b., terminal bud.

Structure of buds. - On the large buds of the Horse Chestnut (Fig. 25), the hard sticky **bud-scales** are plainly visible, overlapping one another. These scales are placed in opposite pairs. Each pair is arranged at right angles to the next, just as in the case of the leaves. If you take off all the bud-scales, which become thinner in the inner part of the bud, a white woolly mass remains. On pulling this to pieces, it is seen to consist of pale-green leaves densely clothed by long hairs. Sometimes there are tiny flower-buds in the middle.

The Brussels Sprout. - The inner part of the Horse Chestnut bud is too small to see its structure clearly. It is easier to make this out in the Brussels Sprout, Cabbage, or Lettuce, which are really huge buds. On splitting a Brussels Sprout up the middle (Fig. 28), so as to cut it into two halves, you will see a short stem tapering to a point at its upper end. This bears leaves which are large at the base, but become smaller towards the top (Fig. 28, P', P''). Where these leaves have been cut through their middle (i.e., through the midrib), little buds are found **in the axils** (Fig. 28, ax.b.). These, too, get smaller towards the tip.

The upper leaves of the bud are densely packed (Fig. 28), because the internodes between them are very short. When a Brussels Sprout is cut across, near its tip, the young leaves are seen folded like crinkled paper.

If, beginning at the outside of a Brussels Sprout, all the leaves are removed in succession, they will be found to get smaller and their parts less distinct. At the extreme tip, they appear as minute green pimples on the pointed end of the stem. It is here that the so-called **growing point** (Fig. 28, g.pt.) is situated. This not only adds to the length of the stem, but also forms new leaves and axillary buds. Since there is little room within the compact bud, the leaf-blades, as they enlarge, become folded. The structure with which you have just become familiar in the Brussels Sprout is that of a **summer-bud**, but this only differs from a **winter-bud** in the absence of bud-scales.

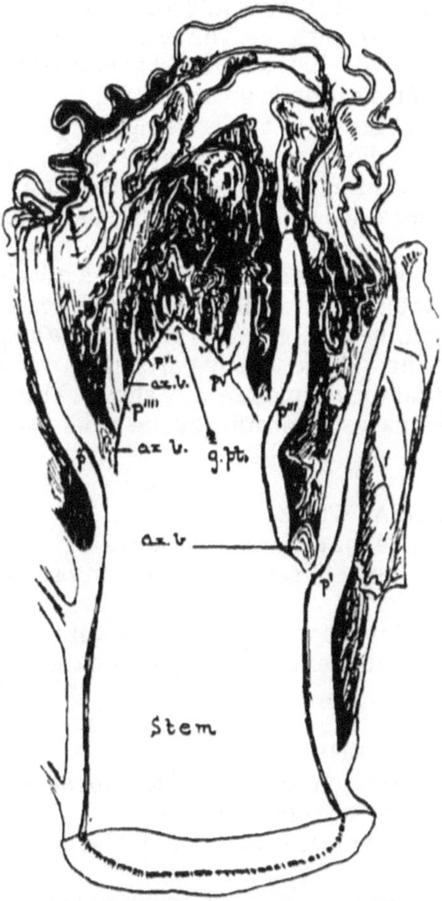

FIG. 28. A Brussels Sprout split in half lengthwise (considerably enlarged). a.x.b., axillary buds; g.pt., growing point of main stem; P.P. etc., leaves of successive ages, Note the folding of the densely packed leaves near the tip.

The bark. - The dark-coloured **bark**, which covers the surface of all the woody branches of trees and shrubs, consists chiefly of **cork**. In the Cork Oak, this becomes so thick that bottle-corks are manufactured from it. Cork has the property of preventing the escape of liquid and, as in the case of a soda-water bottle, that of gas also. In the winter, when the woody branches alone remain, the cork forms an envelope to the whole plant, the only passages through it being the lenticels (Fig. 25). Even the leaf-scars are covered in this way.

Transpiration in Winter. – Since the buds are also completely enveloped by thick leathery scales, it is clear that little transpiration can take place from the surface of a woody plant in winter. The leaves, which, as you know, are the parts from which water-vapour is mainly given off, are generally shed in the autumn. The only woody plants that keep their leaves during the winter are **evergreens**, where they are thick and leathery.

Why do plants thus strive to reduce the amount of transpiration in wintertime? The explanation is that most of them are only able to take up moisture from the cold soil **very slowly**. If, therefore, they could transpire as freely as in summer, they would lose more water than was taken up and would consequently die. The evergreen is able to keep its leaves in winter because the thick leathery skin with which they are covered only allows transpiration to go on slowly.

The cold of winter, then, is not generally a direct danger to plants. Evergreens, however, sometimes die from lack of water on a warm sunny day when the soil is frozen. This is because evaporation is much more rapid in the sun, whilst the frozen soil almost stops absorption by the roots.

Summary. – The twigs of woody plants show leaf-scars, lenticels, lateral, and terminal buds. In the buds, we can distinguish bud-scales, young foliage-leaves, and sometimes flowers. Only some of the buds grow out into branches in spring. All the woody parts are covered in winter by a corky bark, so that they transpire very slowly. This is necessary because the cold soil makes absorption by the roots a very slow process.

PRACTICAL WORK

1. Draw several twigs and name the different markings.

2. Pull to pieces the winter-buds of several plants, and notice their structure.

3. Seal up the ends of several twigs with melted wax, and place them in warm water. Notice that bubbles of air escape from the lenticels. Explain this.

QUESTIONS

1. Describe, with drawings, the structure of a bud. How do the buds of our common trees chiefly differ from one another?

2. What is cork? On what parts of plants is it found, and of what importance is it to them?

3. Give an account of the arrangements by which a supply of oxygen is ensured to all parts of a tree. Why is oxygen necessary to the tree?

4. Why are some plants able to keep their leaves during the winter, whilst others always lose them?

CHAPTER IX

HERBS IN WINTER

Annuals and Biennials. – In the winter, nothing of the annual is to be found except its seeds buried in the soil, awaiting the return of spring. You have learned, however, that biennials pass through their first winter with a rosette of leaves pressed against the surface of the ground (Fig. 16, B). The leaves are thus **sheltered** from the wind by surrounding vegetation. This is important since wind greatly encourages evaporation, as is shown by the fact that a wet road dries much more rapidly on a windy than on a quiet day. Also, in the rosettes, the lower sides of the leaves, which give off most water-vapour, face **downwards**.

In addition, the leaves of some biennials, such as the Mullein, are densely covered with **hairs**. These still further hinder the escape of moisture. Owing to all these **means of protection**, the biennial is able to keep its leaves during winter, in spite of the little water that can be absorbed.

Perennials. – In most perennial herbs, the bulk of the overground parts **die back completely** in the autumn. The parts that live on are of many different kinds. They are buried beneath the surface and are thus protected. In the Primrose or Violet, the perennial part is a short erect underground stem, from the upper end of which the leaves arise in the spring. This is what is called a **root-stock**. More commonly, the underground stem grows parallel to the surface, as in the Solomon's Seal (Fig. 29). Such a stem you have already learned to speak of as a **rhizome**.

Rhizomes. – The rhizome of the Solomon's Seal is a white fleshy structure (Fig. 29), which, like the twig of a tree, bears buds and scars. The most striking difference from a twig is that it bears **numerous roots**, chiefly on the lower surface.

Each branch of the rhizome ends in a pointed bud (Fig. 29, a.s.) that turns slightly upwards and is enveloped in white bud-scales. These buds grow out in the next spring into leafy overground shoots. The latter die back, after bearing flowers and fruits, and leave round sunken **scars** (Fig. 29, sc.), the so-called "seals," on the upper side of the rhizome. These bear numerous dots which again mark the broken

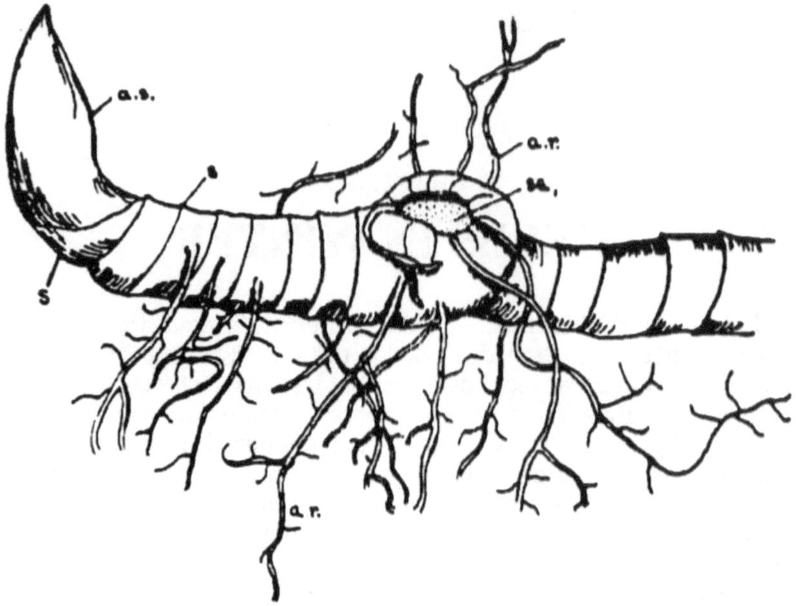

FIG. 29. - Rhizome of the Solomon's Seal in winter (about three-quarters the natural size). a. adventitious roots; a.s., bud of next year's overground shoot; S., scale-leaves on rhizome; sc., scar of overground shoot of past season. The portion of the rhizome to the right of this scar was formed a year earlier than the part to the left of it.

ends of water-carrying tubes. Encircling the rhizome at intervals are raised lines (Fig. 29, s.), the scars of bud-scales that have died away.

Such a rhizome is distinguished from a root by the fact that it **bears buds and scales**. These show that it is a stem. The roots which arise from it are called **adventitious**, because they are not borne as branches of another root.

The Corm of the Crocus – In the Crocus, the well-known **corm** (sometimes wrongly called a bulb) is all that remains of the plant in the winter. The corm, which is situated underground, is really a short swollen root-stock of a special kind. On the outside, there are several brown papery scales (Fig. 30, D, t), whilst one or more pointed buds peep out at the top (Fig. 30, B, b.).

As you remove the scales, you find each attached all the way round to the central stem. The latter forms the greater part of the corm and shows a dark-coloured scar at its base. When cut in half from top to bottom (Fig. 30, C), the corm is seen to be **quite solid**. If you happen to halve one of the larger buds, you will find within, the young foliage-leaves and a tiny pale-coloured flower (Fig. 30, C.f. 1914).

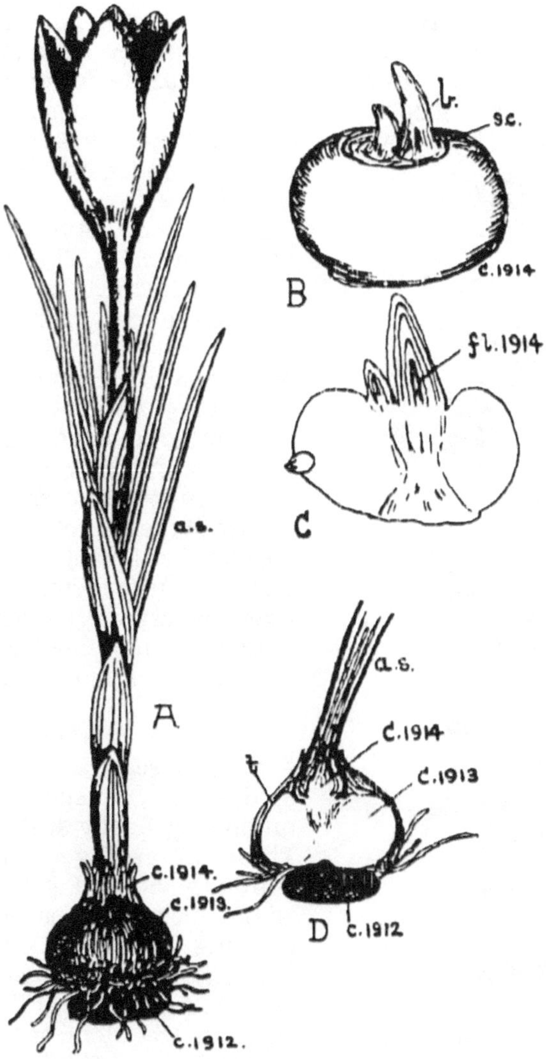

FIG. 30. – Development and structure of the Crocus-corm. A, spring condition, with overground flowering shoot; B, winter-condition of the corn, showing two buds which will produce two flowering shoots in the next season; one of the scales has been removed near the top of the corm, leaving a ring-shaped scar (s.c.): C, the corm cut lengthwise at the stage shown in B: all the scales have been removed: P, a similar section of the base of the corn and of the flowering shoot at the stage shown in A. (All figures about natural size.) a.s., overground flowering shoot: b., buds for next season's flowering shoots; A. 1914, flower which will unfold in 1914; t, envelope of scales.

During the winter, Crocus plants in flower are usually on sale at the florists, and you may now examine one of these (Fig. 30, A). A number of long slender **roots** have sprouted out from the edge of the scar on the underside of the corm, whilst the buds have grown out into the **flowering shoots**.

If you carefully halve a flowering shoot at its lower end (Fig. 30, D), you will see a small round swelling (c. 1914) surrounded by the lower parts of the leaves. This swelling is joined to the top of the corm below and passes into the flower-stalk above. It is the **new corm** for the next winter, which is thus formed from the **base of the flowering stem**. If Crocus plants are dug up later in the year, the swellings will be found to get bigger and bigger. At the same time, the upper parts of the leaves gradually wither, whilst the lower parts around the new corm form the brown scales. The old corm slowly shrivels away, leaving the **scar** you have already noticed at the base of the new one (Fig. 30, A and D, C. 1912).

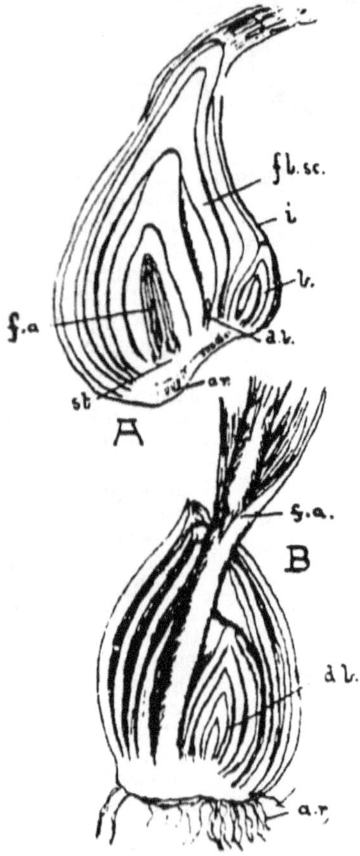

FIG. 31. - Structure of the Tulip-bulb (natural size).
A, bulb in the winter-condition, cut in half lengthwise: B, the same in the spring. condition, only the lower end of the flowering shoot being shown: a.r. adventitious roots: b., incompletely developed daughter-bulb; d.b., bud which will give rise to a herbaceous daughter-bulb: f.a., flowering shoot: fl.sc fleshy scales of the bulb: l. papery covering on from year to year, are therefore of dry scales: st., flattened stem.

Since one corm may bear several flowering shoots and a new corm is formed at the base of each, the number of plants generally becomes increased. After several years, a single Crocus plant may thus have developed into quite a large clump.

Bulbs. – True bulbs, such as those of the Tulip or Hyacinth, consist of a number of **fleshy scales**. These are arranged one within the other (Fig. 31), and are enclosed in a papery covering (i). When a Tulip bulb is halved up the middle (Fig. 31, A), an almost flat structure (the stem, st.) is seen at the base. This bears the fleshy scales (f.sc.), as well as a central flower-bud surrounded by a few young yellowish-green leaves (f.a.). In the lower portion of the **flat stem** are a number of narrow streaks, the future roots (a.r.). When the bulb is cut across, the fleshy scales appear as complete rings encircling one another.

Next, cut lengthwise through the bulb of a Tulip which is in flower (Fig. 31, B). The roots have now grown down into the soil, whilst the flower-bud and young leaves have developed above the surface. The fleshy scales, especially the outer ones, have **shriveled**. One or more large **buds** will be found developing between them, i.e., **in their axils** (Fig. 31, B, d.b.). These are next year's bulbs. You can find them already as tiny buds (Fig. 31, A, d.b.) in bulbs which have not yet sprouted, by pulling off the scales one by one.

These **daughter-bulbs** increase in size until at last they are just like the parent bulb. The thin brown papery covering, noticed above, is formed from the shriveled scales of the parent bulb. Here again, as with the corm, the bulb of one year is generally replaced by **several** in the next.

Bulbs and Buds – The structure of such a bulb is very similar to that of a bud. Each contains young green leaves and flowers. The chief difference is that the scales in the bud are **dark and leathery**, whilst those of the bulb are **white and fleshy**. The fleshy nature of these scales is due to the fact that the **food** necessary for early growth **is stored up** within them. That this food is starch in the case of a Tulip bulb can be easily seen by placing a drop of iodine on the cut surface.

Summary. – The parts of herbaceous perennials, which live from year to year, are therefore very varied in form. Thus, you have got to know the short erect root-stock, the creeping rhizome, the swollen corm, and the bulb. In all but the last, the food for the next season's growth is stored up in the underground stem, but in the bulb, the food is found in the scale-leaves. These are consequently large, while the stem itself is small.

PRACTICAL WORK

1. Examine the rhizomes of the Solomon's Seal, Enchanter's Nightshade, Dog's Mercury, and Wood Anemone. Distinguish the scale-leaves and adventitious roots in each case. Note also the buds for next season's growth.

2. Treat cut surfaces of each of the above rhizomes with iodine and see whether starch is present.

3. Examine the winter condition of the Hyacinth, Cuckoo Pint, Snowdrop, Daffodil, and Crocus. Find out whether the structure is a corm or a bulb.

QUESTIONS

1. Describe, with examples, how annuals, biennials, and herbaceous perennials pass through the winter.

2. Write the story of the life of a crocus (or some bulbous plant) from the time of planting till the fruit is ripe.

3. What is a bulb? Give an account of the structure of the bulb of any plant you may have examined. Of what use is a bulb to a plant?

4. How would you distinguish between a root-stock, a rhizome, and a corm? Describe and draw an example of each.

CHAPTER X

HERBS IN WINTER (continued)

Vegetative reproduction – When new bulbs or corms are formed, you have noticed that there is generally an **increase** in the number of plants. Rhizomes, like those of the Solomon's Seal or Dog's Mercury, also multiply, but in a slightly different way. Here, the older part of the main rhizome gradually decays, so that the branches become separated off as new plants. These kinds of multiplication are known as **vegetative reproduction**, and generally take place by means of those parts of perennial herbs that last during the winter. We will now study some further examples.

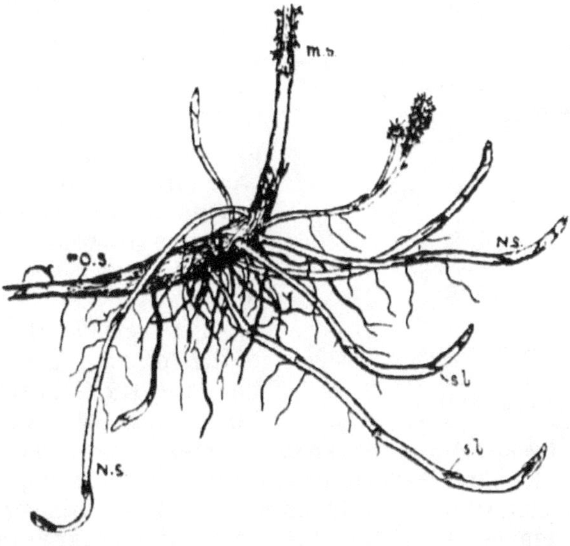

FIG. 32. - Lower end of a plant of the Yarrow or Milfoil, showing the remains of an old sucker (n.s.), whose upturned tip produced the main stem (m.s.): also numerous new suckers (n.s.) (about two-thirds the natural size); s.l., scale-leaves.

Suckers – First, dig up some plants of the Yarrow or Milfoil (Fig. 32). Arising from the base of the erect stem of last year (m.s.), you will see a number of whitish horizontal branches or **suckers** (Fig. 32, n.s.), the tips of which turn upwards. These suckers are formed at all times of the year, but it is only in winter that their tips do not grow straight up to the surface.

In spring, the terminal buds lengthen into the overground leafy shoots. The latter remain connected with the parent-stem for two or

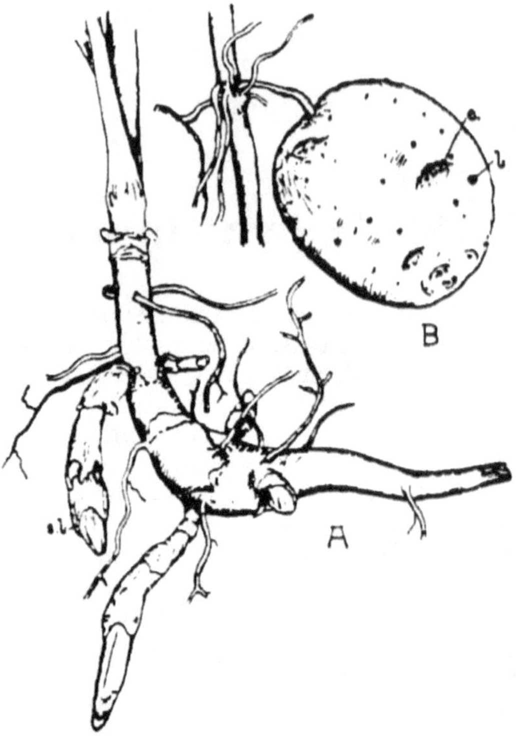

FIG. 33 - Storage of food in tuberous stems
A, Perennial Sunflower; B, Potato:
l., lenticels; s.l., scale-leaves.

more years. Ultimately, the **horizontal parts** of the suckers **die away**, thus leaving a number of separate plants. Similar suckers are formed by the Poplar and many fruit trees (e.g., Damson, Plum).

The Perennial Sunflower (Fig. 33, A) forms underground shoots during the summer in the same way. In this plant, however, the parent-stem always dies towards the end of the year. The underground branches likewise only live for one season, during which their tips grow out into the erect flower-bearing shoots.

A sucker, like that of the Yarrow, is slender, and there is **no large store of food**. This is unnecessary, because the sucker grows at the expense of nourishment taken from the parent-stem, to which, as you have seen, it remains attached for some time. In the Perennial Sunflower, however, where the parent-stem dies at the end of the year, the underground branches are dependent on **food stored up** in their slightly enlarged tips (Fig. 33, A). In another kind of Perennial Sunflower, the Jerusalem Artichoke, the tips are hugely swollen and eaten as a vegetable.

All such suckers are seen to be **stems** and **not roots**, because they bear small scaly leaves of a white or brown color. In the Yarrow (Fig. 32, s.l.), these scales occur singly (i.e., are alternate), whilst in the Sunflower (Fig. 33, A, s.l.) and Jerusalem Artichoke, they are opposite. Little knobs, visible especially at the tips, are the future adventitious roots. Some of these may already be growing out.

The Potato-tuber. – Potato (Fig. 33, B) is a similar structure, covered with a thick brown peel which consists of **cork**. Like the bark of trees, this is pierced by a number of little apertures or lenticels

(Fig. 33, B, 1.). Here and there, especially near one end, you will see dents, the so-called "eyes" (Fig. 33, B, e.). These are **small buds**. Each arises in the axil of a scale-leaf, which appears as a minute ridge on one side of the dent.

The Potato is an example of a structure called a **tuber**. It is formed, in the same way as the Jerusalem Artichoke, at the end of an underground branch (Fig. 33, B). The farmer cuts up the Potato into several pieces, each including an eye, and when these are planted, they give rise to new plants.

Root-tubers – All the underground structures described in this and the last chapter are **special kinds of shoots**. They store up food and carry on vegetative reproduction in various ways. Moreover, they differ from ordinary green shoots in bearing **scales** in place of foliage leaves, and adventitious roots.

In some plants, however, the chief part to last through the winter is the root-system, which becomes **swollen with food**. As examples, you may look at the Carrot (Fig. 24, A), Horse Radish, Dahlia, and Lesser Celandine (Fig. 24, B). In the first two, it is the main root that becomes tuberous, whilst in the Dahlia and Lesser Celandine, a number of roots swell up to form **tubers**. These structures are evidently roots, since they bear **no scale-leaves**. In such cases, the bud, which gives rise to the new plant, is quite an insignificant structure at the tip of the swollen root.

The storage of food. – All the different parts of perennial herbs that live underground through the winter thus tend to be swollen with **reserves of food**. In many cases, the food consists mainly of starch. You can prove this by cutting open a corm of the Crocus or of the Cuckoo Pint, a Potato, or a rhizome of the Iris, and painting the surface with iodine. In the Solomon's Seal, the Beetroot, and the Wild Hyacinth, however, the food present is **sugar**. To this, the sweet taste of the Beetroot is due.

All these food reserves are **used to make new growth** in the springtime. Similar food reserves are stored up **beneath the buds** of woody perennials, as is easily seen by applying

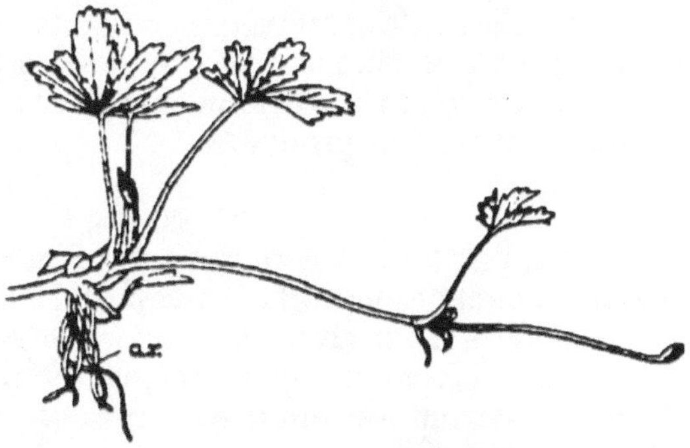

FIG. 34 Runner of the Cinquefoil (about half the natural size). One plant produced from a runner is seen on the left, a younger one on the right. a.r., adventitious roots.

iodine to a halved bud of the Horse Chestnut. You will learn later that seeds also contain food for the growth of the young plant.

Vegetative reproduction by overground shoots – Vegetative reproduction may also take place during the summer in the overground parts. Thus, creeping plants increase by the **rotting away** of the stem between the rooted portions (p. 22, and Fig. 15).

The Strawberry and the Cinquefoil (Fig. 34) produce creeping branches, called **runners**, which root at intervals and thus serve to multiply the plant. These runners are bare slender stems, with only one or two scale-leaves. A small bud develops at their upturned tip, and eventually becomes a new plant attached to the soil by its own adventitious roots. This plant may immediately produce a new runner. Sooner or later, however, the daughter plants **become independent** by decay of the runners.

Plants spread rapidly by vegetative reproduction. All the new individuals are, however, near one another, and may therefore interfere with each other's requirements.

Summary. – The parts of perennial herbs which live from year to year are usually situated beneath the surface. Here they receive protection during the winter months. By branching, and subsequent decay of the parent structure, an increase in the number of plants commonly takes place. In nearly all cases, the new season's growth, whether it be that of the parent or its offspring, is provided for by stores of starch, sugar, etc. Owing to such storage, the perennial roots or stems are often swollen.

PRACTICAL WORK

1. Examine the underground parts of the following plants: Yarrow, Rose-bay Willow-herb, Perennial Sunflower, Lesser Celandine, Dahlia. Treat a cut surface in each case with iodine.

2. Note the mode of origin of new plants in the Bugle, Wild Strawberry, Silverweed, Cinquefoil, Ground Ivy, and Houseleek.

3. Cut up a Potato into a number of pieces, each containing an eye, and plant them in the ground.

QUESTIONS

1. Many plants usually reproduce themselves by means of seeds. Give an account of some other ways by means of which certain plants may reproduce themselves. (Cambridge Preliminary.)

2. In what different organs may plants store up supplies of food? When and in what way are these stores used up afterwards? (Cambridge Preliminary.)

3. Compare the structure and functions of a bud and a bulb.

CHAPTER XI

THE GERMINATION OF SEEDS

IN spring, as soon as the weather becomes warmer, countless young shoots begin to appear above the surface of the ground. A large number of these arise from seeds that have lain dormant in the soil, whilst others grow from underground rhizomes, tubers, etc. We will now find out why seeds sprout or germinate, and how they do so.

The conditions of germination. - Plant ten Peas in each of three pots filled with soil. Leave one pot unwatered; each day give a very little water to the next, and plenty of water to the third. Keep all three in a fairly warm place. After about a week, the Peas which have been thoroughly watered will have germinated. Those which have received little water take longer to appear, whilst those left dry do not germinate at all (Fig. 35). **Water**, then, is evidently **necessary for germination**.

Now supply two pots of soil, each containing ten Peas, with equal amounts of water, but keep them at different temperatures by placing one outside in the cold and the other in a warm room. The Peas in the warm soil will germinate much more rapidly. In nature, there is always plenty of moisture in the ground during the winter, and it is the **rise in temperature** that causes germination to take place in spring.

Next, boil some water, which drives off all the dissolved oxygen, and allow it to cool. Place ten soaked Peas in this water, ten others in a vessel containing unboiled water, and a third set of ten on cotton-wool kept damp. After some days, the Peas on the cotton-wool will begin to germinate. Those in the unboiled water will take slightly longer, whilst those in the boiled water, which have no oxygen for breathing, will not germinate at all. Three things, therefore, are necessary for germination: a sufficient supply of **warmth, water, and oxygen**.

The seed of the Bean. - The dry seed of the Runner Bean (Fig. 36, A) is somewhat kidney-shaped and is covered with a tough skin, the **seed-coat** or **testa**. Along one edge, which is slightly hollowed, there is a narrow white scar, the **hilum** (Fig. 36, A, h.). This marks the former point of attachment to the pod. At one end of the hilum,

FIG. 35. - Photograph to show the effect of different amounts of water on the germination of the Sunflower. For details see the text.

there is a tiny hole termed the **micropyle**, more easily seen in a soaked seed (Fig. 36, A, m.).

When soaked, the seed is about double the size of a dry one, owing to the large quantity of water which it absorbs.

The seed-contents. - When you have peeled off the testa, you see a cream-colored mass. This is the **young plant** or **embryo**. It consists mainly of two thick fleshy leaves, the **cotyledons** (Fig. 36, B, c.). Between the latter, as you will find by separating them (Fig. 36, B), is a small bud with tiny folded leaves. This is the future shoot or **plumule** (p.). Projecting from between the cotyledons, and lying against their edges, is the white tapering root or **radicle** (r.). Break across one of the cotyledons and paint the exposed surface with iodine; the result shows that the cotyledons contain **reserves of food** for germination.

The absorption of water. - When such a seed germinates, it first takes up a large amount of moisture. Most of this passes **through the micropyle**, as is shown by the following experiment. A number of slots are cut into the edges of two large corks (Fig. 37), which have been well soaked in water. Dry Beans are wedged into the slots (Fig. 37, s.), so that those in the one cork have their micropyles facing upwards (Fig. 37, m.), whilst those in the other have the micropyles downwards. Now place one cork on each scale-pan of a balance, and into the lighter stick pins, or small nails, until the pans are level. Then

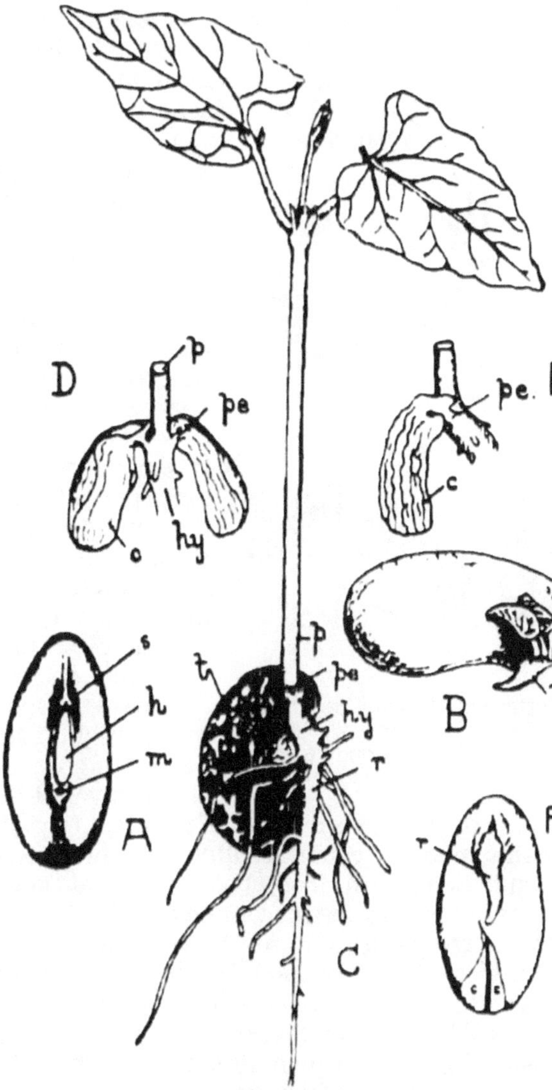

FIG. 36. - Structure and germination of the Runner Bean (all figures natural size).

A. soaked seed, seen from its edge, to show the hilum (h.), the micropyle (m.). and small swellings (s.) at the opposite end of the hilum: B. seed. with testa and one cotyledon removed, to show plumule and radicle: C, mature seedling: D. partially shrivelled cotyledons, from an older seedling. showing attachment to base of plumule: E. the same from the side with a completely shrivelled cotyledon: F. first stage in germination: in cotyledon hy., hypocotyl (part of stem below cotyledons): p., plumule M. stalk of cotyledon r., radicle: t., testa.

float the two corks on water, and after about a day put them again on the balance. The cork bearing the seeds with the micropyles dipping into the water is now much heavier than the other one.

Germination of the Runner Bean. - If some soaked Runner Beans are placed in damp sawdust, you will find that they soon begin to germinate. The testa splits near the micropyle, and the radicle begins to grow **downwards** (Fig. 36, F). A little later, the plumule starts lengthening in the **upward** direction. During its growth, the tip which bears the young leaves is sharply bent, as in Fig. 38. It is therefore the older part of the plumule which forces its way upwards through the soil, whilst the tender young leaves at the tip are drawn after it.

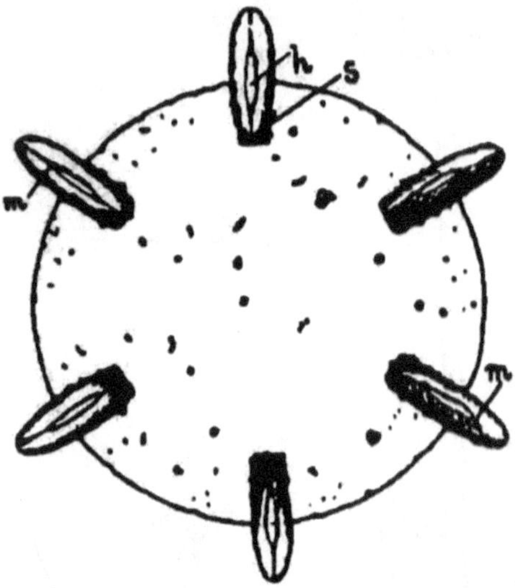

FIG. 37. - Slotted cork bearing Beans with the micropyles all facing upwards (after Osterhout). See description in text. h., hilum; m., micropyle s., slot in cork.

The plumule remains bent until, on reaching the surface of the soil, it comes into the light. Thereupon it soon straightens out. The small leaves at its tip now grow and become the **first green leaves of the plant** (Fig. 36, C).

The nourishment of the young seedling. - All this time, the cotyledons stay within the seed. The food which they contain nourishes the young plant. The latter is unable to manufacture food for itself, since both plumule and radicle at first grow beneath the soil. The young plant, therefore, depends on the **food** already **present in the seed**. In a full-grown seedling, the shriveled remains of the cotyledons are found still enclosed in the testa (Fig. 36, D and E).

The older seedling. - As the plumule lengthens, the radicle grows into the main root (Fig. 36, C), which very soon forms branches. When the plumule first begins to grow, you can recognize that the cotyledons, like the later leaves of the Bean plant, are attached to the stem of the plumule by short broad stalks (Fig. 38, c.s.). These are difficult to see before the seed sprouts, but elongate during germination, and in this way **help to free the plumule** from the seed-coat (Fig. 38).

Germination of the French Bean. - In many cases, as for example in the French Bean, the cotyledons do not remain permanently below

FIG. 38. - Illustration of the method of escape of the plumule in the Runner Bean. c., cotyledons; C.S., coty. ledon-stalk h., hypocotyl; P., tip of plumule r., radicle; t., testa.

the surface of the ground, but become spread out as the first green leaves of the plant. The seeds of the French Bean are smaller but otherwise like those of the Runner Bean. They germinate in a somewhat different way. A part of the stem situated between the cotyledons and the root, and known as the **hypocotyl**, grows very rapidly soon after the radicle has penetrated the soil. As a result, this part of the seedling becomes arched. Later, when the arch straightens out, the cotyledons get drawn out of the testa (compare Fig. 41, A, p. 61).

Summary. - A seed, therefore, contains an embryo or young plant, consisting of plumule, radicle, and cotyledons. When supplied with warmth, moisture, and oxygen, it germinates, the first step being the absorption of a large amount of water, mainly by way of the micropyle. The radicle is the first part of the embryo to escape from the split seed-coat, and this is followed by growth of the plumule. The cotyledons, in the seeds of the Bean, are storehouses of food for the growth of the young seedling. In the Runner Bean, they remain below the soil; in the French Bean, they are brought above it.

PRACTICAL WORK

1. Sow seeds of the following plants: Pea, Marrow, Shepherd's Purse, Sunflower, Cress. Note the method of germination and draw at least three stages in each case.

2. Collect a number of seedlings from a hedgebank or wood, and group them according as the cotyledons remain below or come above the soil.

3. Place ten soaked seeds of the Runner Bean to germinate. When the radicles have grown out of the seeds, carefully cut away *both* cotyledons from five of the seedlings. After one or two weeks, make draw-

ings to scale of a seedling from which the cotyledons were removed, and of one in which they were left attached. What do you conclude from the result of your experiment?

QUESTIONS

1. In what respects does a Potato differ from a seed? Point out the features which enable the Potato to act as an organ of reproduction.

2. What is the difference between a seed and a seedling? Make a drawing of a seed and a drawing of a seedling, and name the parts.

3. Describe, with drawings, the way in which the seed of a Runner Bean germinates.

CHAPTER XII

THE GERMINATION OF SEEDS (continued)

Monocotyledons and Dicotyledons. — In one of the two groups of Flowering Plants, the **Dicotyledons**, there are two cotyledons in the embryo. The Runner Bean and French Bean belong to this group. In the **Monocotyledons**, on the other hand, the embryo has but a single cotyledon. All the Grasses and most bulbous plants, such as the Hyacinth and Narcissus, are Monocotyledons.

The grain of the Maize. — As the grains of most of our wild Grasses are rather small, we will examine those of a cultivated Grass, the Maize. The grains of this plant are usually yellow, with a tough skin, and bear a number of small scales (the chaff) at their pointed ends. An oval whitish patch on one of the flat sides marks the position of the **embryo** (Fig. 39, A, e.). This is seen more clearly in a soaked grain, after the skin has been peeled off.

The part of the grain not occupied by the embryo consists of cells filled with **food-substances**. This food-storing tissue outside **the embryo** is termed the **endosperm** (Fig. 39, F, Y and W). The part of the endosperm next to the embryo is white (W) and contains starch, as you can see by painting the cut surface with iodine. The remainder of the endosperm is yellow and horny (Y), and contains another food-substance, sugar. This does not turn blue with iodine.

The embryo. — Soak a grain in water for twenty-four hours, and place it for a day or two on damp cotton-wool. After peeling it, you will recognize three parts in the embryo (Fig. 39, B). The larger part is a folded **cotyledon** (c.). This has a slit down its middle, out of which projects a small peg, the **plumule** (p.). At the pointed end of the grain, the white **radicle** will already have begun to grow (Fig. 39, C, r.).

The seedling. — A seedling that has been sprouting for some days (Fig. 39, G) will show you that the plumule grows **straight up** into the air. The plumule is enclosed in a hard pointed covering (t., see also Fig. 39, C), which protects the young leaves inside and easily pierces the soil. It is not until the surface is reached that the green leaves escape from this covering and spread out to the light (Fig. 40). The radicle is helped in its work by a number of adventitious roots that soon sprout out from the base of the stem (Fig. 39, G, and 40, A.R.). The grain attached to one of these older seedlings has **shriveled**, because the food in the endosperm has been taken up by the growing plant (Fig. 40).

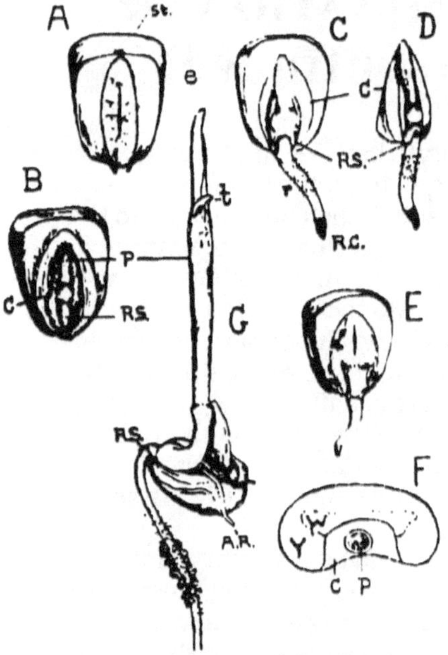

FIG. 39 – Structure of the grain and germination in the Maize (all figures slightly enlarged).
A, entire grain showing outline of embryo; B, grain, with envelope removed and edges of cotyledon rolled back, to show plumule and radicle; C, early stage in germination, envelope removed; D, the embryo, cut out of the last; E, first stage in germination; F, a grain, with envelope removed, cut crosswise; G, late stage in germination, showing escape of foliage leaves from the seed. a. embryo; b. plumule; c. radicle; d. rootcap; e. adventitious root; f. cotyledon; g. endosperm; p. plumule; i. radicle; k. rootcap; t. sheath round top of root; m. a tip of sheath round plumule; n. starchy part of the endosperm; o. sugary part of the endosperm.

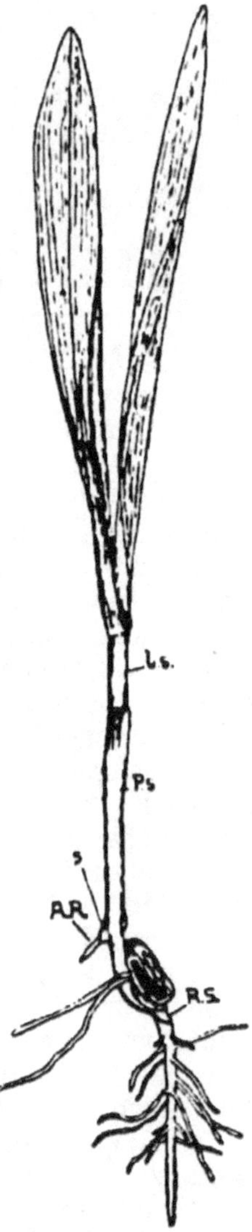

FIG. 40 – Older seedling of the Maize (slightly reduced). A.R. adventitious root; L.s. leafsheath; l.f. sheath that protects the young plumule; P.s. sheath that protected young radicle; s. sheath round base of secondary root.

Albuminous and exalbuminous seeds. — The grain of the Maize then differs in two ways from the seed of the Runner Bean. It possesses but a single cotyledon and has a special food-tissue, the **endosperm**, outside the embryo. When the latter is present, the seed is said to be albuminous. Seeds, like the Runner Bean and French Bean, which have no endosperm, are described as **exalbuminous**.

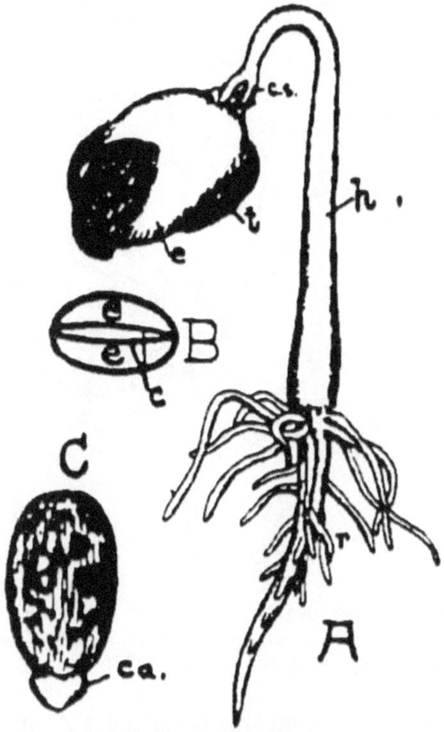

FIG. 41.-Seed and germination of the Castor Oil (slightly reduced). A, young seedling B, seed cut across; C, entire seed: c., cotyledons; ca., spongy swelling at one end of the seed; C.S., cotyledon-stalk i., endosperm; 4., hypocotyl; T., radicle and its branches; t., testa.

The seeds of Dicotyledons may, however, also be albuminous, for instance, those of the Buckwheat and the Castor Oil (Fig. 41, B, C). When these seeds germinate, the cotyledons at first **remain within the testa** (Fig. 41, A). In a young seedling, you will find them surrounded by a white mass, which is the endosperm (Fig. 41, A, e.). It is not until all the food in the latter has been absorbed that the cotyledons are dragged out of the seed, to become the first green leaves of the plant. Here, as in the French Bean, the cotyledons become released **by the growth of the hypocotyl** (Fig. 41, A, h.).

The general course of germination. — Seeds, as bought at a seed-merchant's, are dry and contain very little moisture, whereas the full-grown plant is quite juicy. It is natural, therefore, that the first step in germination is the sucking up of a large quantity of water. The tip of the radicle **always lies** just beneath the opening of the micropyle. The radicle is thus the **first part** of the embryo to receive water and to grow out of the seed (Fig. 36, F, Fig. 39, E). Sometimes the micropyle is covered over, as in the Castor Oil, where there is a little swelling at one end of the seed which sucks up water like a sponge (Fig. 41, C, ca.).

After the root has become fixed in the soil, the plumule in its turn

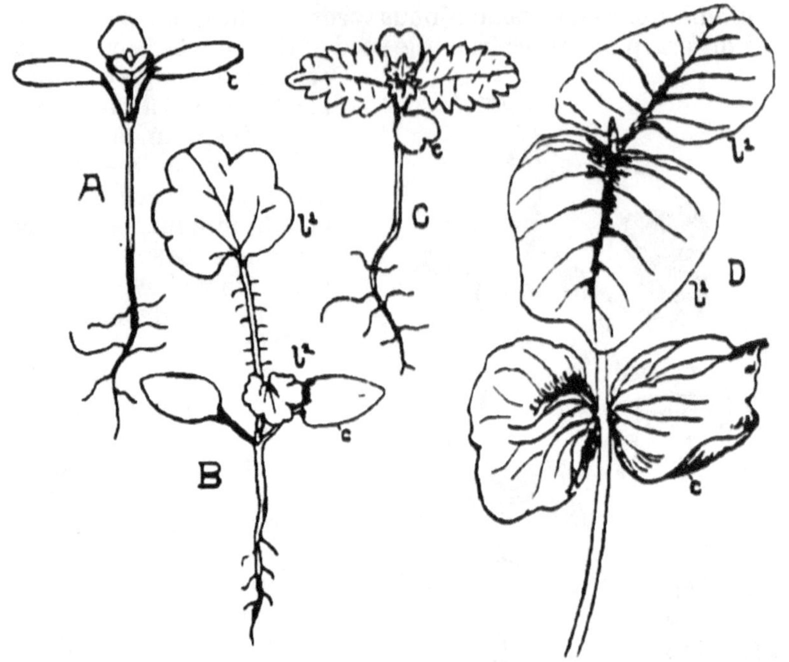

FIG. 42. - Different types of Dicotyledonous seedlings (all natural size). A, Garden Spurge; B, Greater Celandine: C, Stinging Nettle; D, Beech C., cotyledons; 1.1 and 1.2, first and second foliage-leaves.

escapes from the seed. You have learnt that this takes place in **three** different ways: either by the growth of the stalks of the cotyledons (Runner Bean, Fig. 38, Pea, etc.), by the direct growth of the plumule (e.g., Maize, Fig. 39, G), or by the lengthening of the hypocotyl (French Bean, Castor Oil, Fig. 41, A, Buckwheat).

In making its way to the surface of the soil, the **tip of the plumule** is **protected** in various ways. Thus, in the Runner Bean, the plumule itself is sharply curved (Fig. 38). In the Castor Oil, French Bean, and Buckwheat, it is the hypocotyl that is curved, whilst the young tip is further protected by the cotyledons between which it lies (Fig. 41, A). In the Maize, the plumule grows straight up but is covered by the hard and pointed tip of the outermost leaf (Fig. 39, G). Where the cotyledons are brought above the surface, their shape differs from and is simpler than that of the subsequent foliage-leaves (Fig. 42).

At the same time as seeds are germinating, the shoots of perennial herbs with underground stems are beginning to grow up to the surface. The young shoots are **protected** in a similar way to the plumules. Thus, those of the Lily of the Valley and Solomon's Seal (Fig. 29) are stout and pointed, whilst in the Dog's Mercury and Wood Anemone, the tips are sharply bent.

Summary. - You can therefore group seeds as albuminous and exalbuminous. Whether the food is stored up within or outside the embryo, it is always used up in the growth of the seedling. The embryo always consists of three parts, viz., the plumule, the radicle, and one (Monocotyledons) or two (Dicotyledons) cotyledons. The radicle is always the first part to grow out of the seed, whilst the plumule escapes in different ways.

PRACTICAL WORK

1. Examine a number of different seeds (e.g., Broad Bean, Castor Oil, Acorn, Beech, Wheat, Date, Buckwheat, and Onion. and group them as albuminous or exalbuminous.

2. Test the cut surfaces of the cotyledons or endosperm of the same seeds and see whether starch is present.

3. Squeeze a piece of the endosperm of the Castor Oil or Brazil Nut on a piece of thin white blotting paper, and note that a greasy spot is left. This is due to the oil, which is the form of the chief food reserve in these seeds.

QUESTIONS

1. How would you distinguish an albuminous seed from one that is exalbuminous? Describe the structure of any seed you may have examined, and explain to which of these classes of seeds it belongs. (Oxford Local Junior..

2. Describe carefully the way in which the shoot comes up from the ground in the germination of *three* different seeds, showing in each case how the delicate parts are protected from injury.

3. Compare the structure and germination of the seed in any Dicotyledon and any Monocotyledon.

4. Describe the manner of formation and the position of the stores of food, by means of which the first growth of any *three* of the following takes place in spring: Wood Anemone, Cuckoo Pint, Wild Hyacinth, Shepherd's Purse, Yarrow.

CHAPTER XIII

HERBS IN SPRING

WHEN shoots first appear above ground in spring, they are often exposed to wind and cold. Perhaps this is the reason why the young leaves are often densely clothed with **hairs** (e.g., Primrose, Barren Strawberry). These, as in biennials (p. 42), will prevent too much transpiration. The axillary buds also require protection, and in many cases are sheltered by the leaf base.

Bud protection. - In the Beaked Parsley, a very early spring plant, the base of the leaf broadens out into a **sheath**, which encloses part of the internode above and protects the axillary bud. The same feature is seen in the Hogweed and the Burnet Saxifrage (Fig. 43, C). In Grasses (Fig. 40), the blade spreads out from the top of a long sheath (l.s.), closely surrounding the stem for some distance above the node. This sheath is the much-enlarged leaf base, which forms a shelter for the younger leaves, and particularly for the flower buds. Where the blade and sheath join, there is a little scale-like ridge (Fig. 18, G, 1.). In the Docks, the Sorrels, and the Persicaria (Fig. 43, E), there is a membranous outgrowth from the leaf base. This forms a sheath around the axillary bud and the portion of the stem just above the leaf.

When a leaf has stipules, these are situated on either side of the axillary bud (Fig. 43, A and B), and so shield it. The larger the stipules, the more protection they afford.

Leaf arrangement. - The leaves of young shoots, when they first come above the ground, are generally crowded together. In this way, they protect one another to some extent from the wind, which, since the young leaves have but a **thin surface skin**, might cause too much transpiration. As the leaves get older, this skin **thickens**, so that the risk of losing too much moisture is no longer as great. By this time, the stem has lengthened, and most of the leaves have spread out to the light and air.

The leaves of a plant, looked at from above, are usually seen to be arranged so as only to **overshadow one another very slightly**. This is quite plain in many leaf rosettes (e.g., those of the Plantain and Daisy, Fig. 44), and especially in plants growing in shady places (Fig. 153, p. 184). When the leaves are arranged singly at the nodes (i.e.,

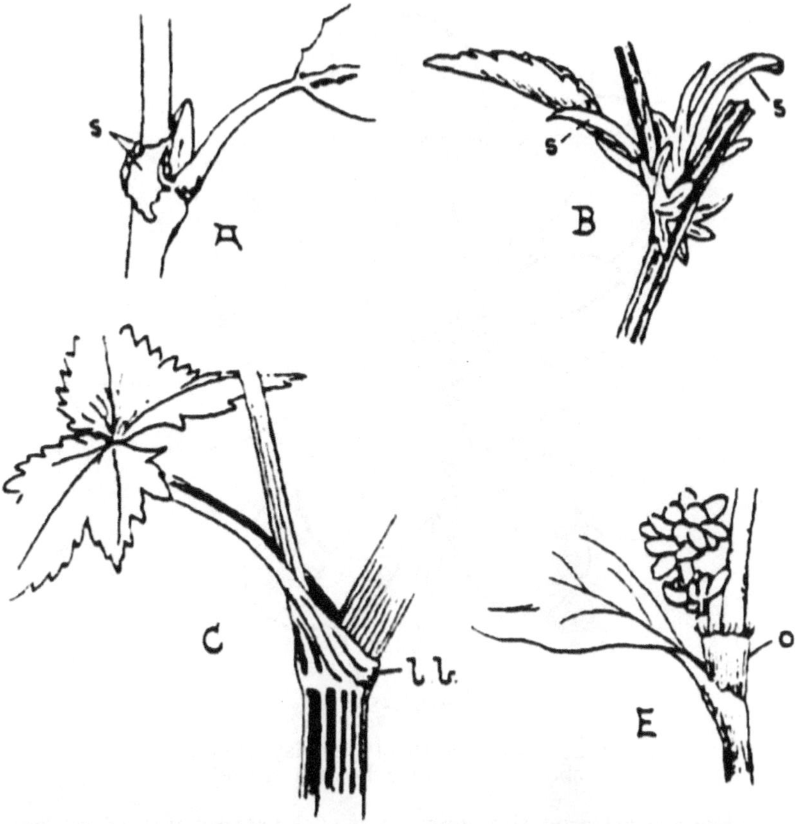

FIG. 43.- Leaf-bases and stipules of various plants (all about natural size). A, Willow, summer-shoot B, Pansy: C, Burnet Saxifrage; E, Persicaria: lb., leaf-base; o, sheath above the node in the Persicaria; S., stipule.

are **alternate**, p. 38), you can often count as many as five internodes between two leaves situated vertically above one another (e.g., in the Dog-rose, Fig. 45). Even in plants with **opposite** leaves (p. 38), the successive pairs are at right angles to one another (e.g., White Dead-nettle, Horse Chestnut, Fig. 25). The blades themselves are generally so placed that the rays of light strike the surface **at right angles**.

The shoot and light. - You learnt in Chapter V. that the shoot, in the majority of plants, is **upright**, so that its leaves are easily spread out to the light. We will now find out why the shoot thus stands erect. Grow some Peas in four pots, until the stems have reached a height of four or five inches. Put two of the pots in a dark cupboard, one upright and the other on its side. Of the remaining two, place one in the open air and the other indoors close to a window.

Fig. 44. - Leaf-rosette of the Daisy, seen from above (about twice the natural size).

After a short time, the upper parts of the stems of the Peas, next to the window, will have **curved over towards the light** (Fig. 46, B), so that the rays of the sun again strike the leaf blades at right angles. On the other hand, the Peas outdoors, which are equally lighted all round, have grown straight up. The shoot of an erect plant, then, curves in the direction from which stronger light comes. In nature, where the light is often equally strong on all sides, the stem usually grows upright.

The shoot and gravity. - In the case of the Peas placed in darkness, the shoots of those in the upright pot **show no curvature**. Those in the pot laid on its side, however, have bent so that their ends are **again erect** (Fig. 46, A).

The result of this experiment will remind you of what happens to a root when it is placed horizontally. It will be clear that the only distinction between the plants in the two pots was in their position. Gravity has, indeed, a peculiar **effect on the direction of growth**, both of roots and shoots. This is the reason why the plant placed on its side in the dark curved upwards. Whilst the main stem grows erect, its

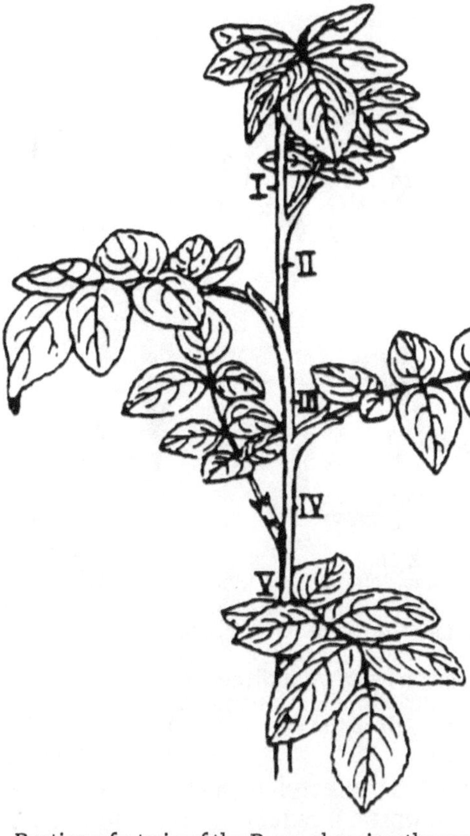

FIG. 45. - Portion of a twig of the Rose, showing the way in which the alternate leaves are arranged. The successive internodes are numbered I.-V.

branches, like those of the root, are not influenced in the same way by gravity, and are more or less horizontal. In creeping plants, only the flowering shoot generally grows erect (Fig. 15).

How herbs keep erect. - The combined effects of light and gravity thus cause the shoot to grow upwards, but we have still to find out how the plant is able to **remain erect**. A human being keeps upright owing to the support of the skeleton within his body. Plants also have a skeleton, although this consists, not of bone, but of **woody fibre**. In herbs, this skeleton is not strong enough to bear the weight of the plant. For, as soon as a herb withers for want of water, it becomes limp and bends over, being unable to support itself. Such withered plants generally recover, however, when placed in water. The shoots of shrubs and trees, before they become woody, behave in the same manner.

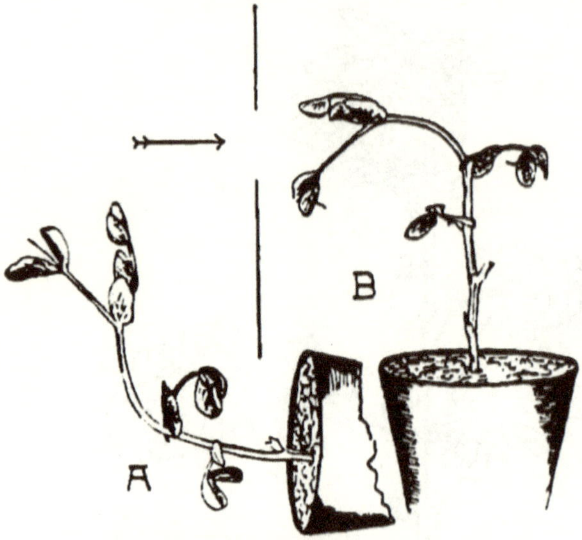

FIG. 46.
A., seedling of a Pea which has been placed horizontally in the dark, showing the shoot bending upwards under the influence of gravity: B, a similar seedling, which has been exposed to light coming from one side (as indicated by the arrow), showing how the shoot curves over towards it. (About one-third the natural size.)

On any hot summer's day, you can see the same thing in the garden. When the drooping plants are watered, they too revive. Evidently then, **unless a plant is well supplied with water**, it becomes limp. Most of the little cells which build up the plant (p. 5) are like tiny balloons inflated with water, but when there is not enough of the latter, they collapse and the plant droops.

Summary. - The axillary buds are often protected by an enlarged leaf-base. The leaves of plants are not borne irregularly on the stem, but show a definite arrangement, whereby they shade one another very little. Light and gravity act together to cause the shoot of the ordinary plant to grow erect. The stems of herbs can only keep upright when supplied with sufficient water.

PRACTICAL WORK

1. Examine plants of the Willow, Plane-tree (or Syringa), Beaked Parsley, and Wayfaring Tree, and notice how the buds are protected.

2. Look at the arrangement of the leaves in the Hazel, a Grass, a Sedge, the Hedge Woundwort, and the Plantain. Draw in outline the leaves as they appear when looked at from above, paying special attention to the direction of their midribs.

3. Perform the experiments described on p. 61-62 with Sunflower or Marrow seedlings.

4. Take two young shoots of the Elder (in winter, the flowers of the Daffodil will do as well), place one with its lower end in water, and

let the other wither. Next day, holding each at its lower end, compare their powers of remaining upright.

QUESTIONS

1. Describe, with the aid of diagrams, the different ways in which axillary buds are protected.
2. Describe carefully how the leaves are arranged on a branch of a Beech Tree.
3. Describe experiments by which you would show how (a) light and (b) gravity affect the direction of growth of shoots.
4. Explain, as fully as you can, why an herbaceous plant droops on a hot summer's day.

CHAPTER XIV

TREES AND SHRUBS IN SPRING

WHILST herbs are pushing through the soil in spring, the buds of trees and shrubs are bursting into leaf. First, the buds swell, then the bud-scales are pushed apart, and finally, the young folded leaves appear.

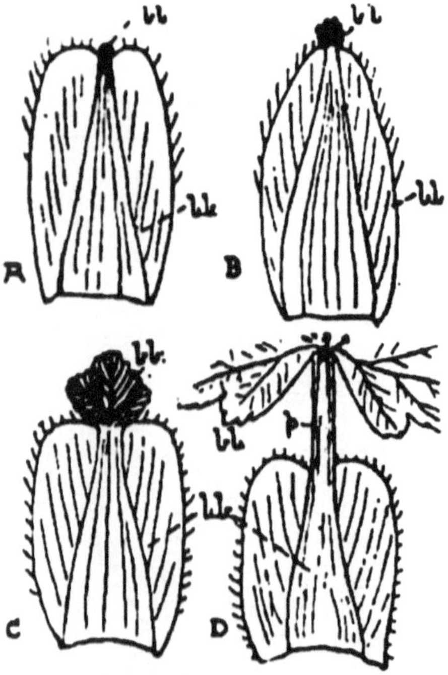

FIG. 47. - A.C. Three bud-scales of the Flowering Currant A and B Flowering Currant taken from near the outside of the bud: C, from the inside; D, lower end of one of the foliage-leaves from the same bud; bl., the blade of the leaf: lb., the leaf-base; p., the petiole. (All the figures are enlarged.)

The Bud-Scales. - Pick an opening bud of the Flowering Currant. Then, starting from the outside, pull off the bud-scales one by one and lay them in a row before you. The outermost are small and thick and end in a tiny black tip (Fig. 47, A, bl.). The scales farther in are larger and thinner, and the dark tip is bigger (Fig. 47, B). Some of the innermost often show a small green blade in place of the black tip (Fig. 47, C, bl.). This small blade is lobed in the same way as the green leaf of the Flowering Currant.

The young foliage-leaves within the bud have a broad leaf-base, looking like one of the inner bud-scales (Fig. 47, D). Here, however, a large folded blade is borne at the end of a short petiole, so that all three parts of the leaf are present. In the bud-scales, whilst the **leaf-base** is **very much enlarged**, the petiole and the blade are very small or absent. The little black tip (Fig. 47, A and B) on the outermost scales is all that represents the blade.

Similar bud-scales, consisting of enlarged leaf-bases that show the same gradual change to the foliage-leaves, are found in the Sycamore, Ash, and Rose. If, however, you lay out scales and leaves from an opening bud of the Lilac or Privet in the order of their removal, you will find it difficult to say where the bud-scales stop and the foliage-leaves begin. In this case, therefore, the bud-scales are not leaf-bases only, but **entire leaves** which remain small and have a dark green color.

Stipules as Bud-Scales. - The bud-scales of the Beech and Elm are formed by **stipules**. In an opening bud of the former, you will find that the inner scales arise in pairs, one on either side of the base of each foliage-leaf. As the latter unfolds, the scales appear plainly as narrow brown stipules, which fall off soon after. The leaves to which the outer pairs of bud-scales belong are often absent. You may notice that the buds of the Beech are further protected, when they first open, by a dense fringe of hairs along the edge of each leaf-blade.

FIG. 48. -Twig of the Apple bearing spur-shoots (Sp.) (slightly reduced). Note the closely crowded leaf-scars on these spur-shoots. The bud at the end of one of the upper spurs is bursting into leaf.

The Sprouting of Buds. - Soon after the buds open, the internodes between the foliage-leaves begin to **grow rapidly**. At the same time, the bud-scales drop off. The part of the stem from which the latter arise does not lengthen, so that their scars remain crowded together. Such a group of **bud-scale scars** or "**ring-scars**" (Fig. 25) is formed each year when the terminal bud sprouts. The interval between two successive groups represents one year's growth. You can, therefore, tell the age of the different parts of a twig by counting the number of groups of "**ring-scars**" between any part and the tip.

The growth in length of the new season's shoot is accomplished in a very short time. During the greater part of the summer, the woody plant is forming buds for next year's growth.

As the leaves become separated, the blades enlarge and the folds, which they showed in the bud, are gradually smoothed out. When the young leaves emerge from the bud, they are sometimes covered with a **down of hairs**, which is white in the Horse Chestnut and brown in the Plane Tree. These hairs, like those of the Beech, lessen the risk of too much transpiration during the cold winds of spring. Later, when the outer skin of the blade has thickened, many of the hairs fall off.

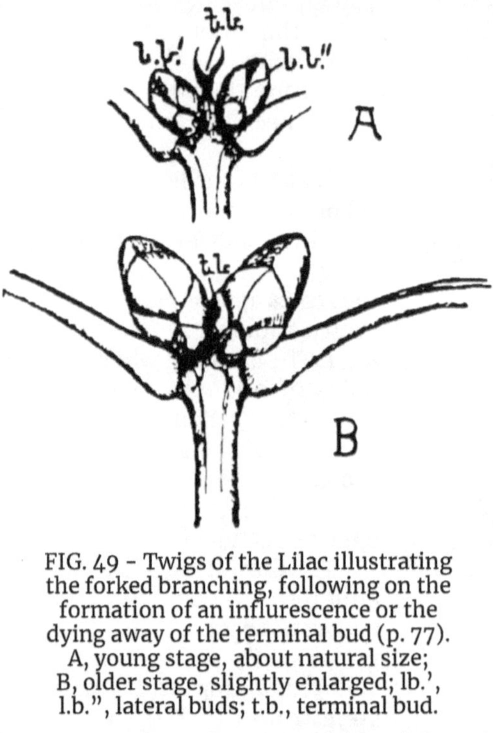

FIG. 49 - Twigs of the Lilac illustrating the forked branching, following on the formation of an influrescence or the dying away of the terminal bud (p. 77). A, young stage, about natural size; B, older stage, slightly enlarged; lb.', l.b.", lateral buds; t.b., terminal bud.

The Branches of the Shoot. - At the same time as the large buds at the ends of the branches add to their length, some or all of the axillary buds grow out into side-twigs. In fruit-trees, the internodes of the side-branches often scarcely lengthen at all, so that the leaves remain crowded together. Such shoots are spoken of as **spur-shoots** (Fig. 48). When the branch merely forms a stump, it is called a **dwarf-shoot**. These are plainly seen in the Larch and the Scotch Fir. All the side-branches of the stem arise **from the surface** (Fig. 21, C-D) and not from the interior, as in roots.

Flowers within Buds. - The winter-buds of many trees and shrubs (Horse Chestnut, Lilac) already contain the future flowers. These, like the young foliage-leaves, were therefore really **laid down in the previous season**. Soon after the leaves unfold, the big inflorescence of the Horse Chestnut appears. The flowers open, fruits are formed, and later in the year, the whole structure falls off.

The growth then, of a Horse Chestnut branch, is brought to an end after an inflorescence has been formed. In the next season, **one of the side-buds** immediately below the scar of the inflorescence carries on the growth (Fig. 25). The inflorescence of the Lilac also occupies the end of a branch, but here it is the **pair of buds**, situated just below, that grow out in the next season (Fig. 49). The two lengthen almost equally, so that the shrub as a whole shows a repeated forking of its stem.

The food for the sprouting bud. — In its early growth in spring, the bud lives on the food-materials which, as you have seen, are **stored up just below it** (p. 51). Most of the structures that emerge from the bud are already present in miniature before it opens. Consequently, the growth, as well as the crop of flowers and fruits, produced in any season, often depends upon the weather and the vigor of the plant in the previous year. An unfavorable summer in one year, as a result, is often followed by a poor harvest of fruit in the next.

Summary. — Bud-scales may be leaf-bases, stipules, or entire leaves. The part of the stem which bears them does not lengthen, so that their scars remain crowded together at the base of each season's growth. When buds open, the internodes lengthen, thus separating the unfolding foliage-leaves. This growth takes place at the expense of food stored up in the shoot. When the bud contains an inflorescence, the growth of the main shoot is usually brought to an end.

PRACTICAL WORK

1. Draw the opening buds of the Maple (or Sycamore), Ash, Cherry, Privet, and Elm. In each case, treat the buds as described on p. 66, and determine the nature of the bud-scales.

2. Make drawings of the twigs of the Pear, Apple, and Scotch Fir.

3. Cut through a number of different winter-buds lengthwise and paint the cut surface with iodine.

QUESTIONS

1. Draw the terminal bud of a Horse Chestnut tree as seen in winter, and label the various parts. Draw the same bud as it appears when it has just opened in the following spring.

2. Describe the opening of the winter (resting) bud of a Beech tree. What features enable you to determine the positions of former winter-buds on a twig?

3. Compare, with diagrams, the method of branching of the root and shoot.

4. By means of a number of examples, show the different nature of bud-scales in different plants. What is the function of the bud-scales?

CHAPTER XV

PLANTS IN AUTUMN

IN the autumn, all nature is getting ready for the sleep of winter. Seeds are shed and leaves begin to fall. The annual gradually withers, whilst perennial herbs die down so that only the underground portions remain. Trees and shrubs shed all but their woody parts, unless they be evergreens with protected leaves. Most of the flowers are over, although a few plants begin to bloom in the autumn months (e.g. Michaelmas Daisy, Meadow Saffron). This, too, is the time of the year when Toadstools are most abundant.

The fall of the leaves. — When the leaves of woody perennials are shed, each breaks off at a **definite place** near the leaf-base (Fig. 50). After they have fallen, smooth **scars** (Fig. 50, C, b.s.) covered with cork (p. 39) remain. This corky layer is formed before the leaf actually falls and, until the leaf is shed, it is only connected with the stem by the slender strands of water-pipes. The latter are easily snapped across by the wind, or when the leaves become weighted with moisture from the air. This is why such showers of leaves fall on windy and misty days in autumn. The broken ends of the water-carrying strands appear as little dots on the leaf-scars (Fig. 25; Fig. 50, C, b.s.).

The branching of the Beech. — In the autumn, it is easy to follow the branching of woody plants. This takes place in one of two ways. The first method is illustrated by the twigs of the Beech (Fig. 27). These have a long pointed terminal bud, **without any leaf-scar immediately below** it. This bud will sprout in the next season and so add to the length of the twig; after that, a new terminal bud will be formed at its end. The branches of the Beech may thus go on lengthening year by year (Fig. 52, B). Side-branches grow out from the buds in the axils of the leaves (now represented by leaf-scars) of the main branch. All the lateral buds do not, however, develop into branches.

The branching of the Elm and Lime. — The second kind of branching is shown by the Elm and Lime. At the tip of a twig of either of these trees, you will find a large winter-bud (Fig. 51, B). In this case, however, there is a **leaf or leaf-scar just below** the

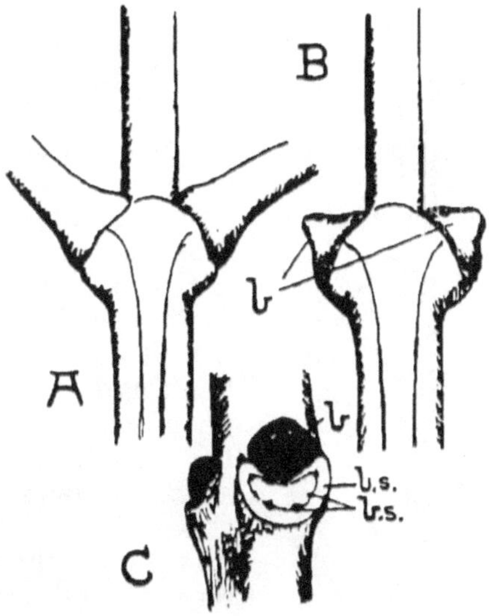

FIG. 50. — Diagrams illustrating leaf fall (all enlarged). A and B, Mock Orange; in A the leaves are shown attached, in B they have fallen off; C, Ash; b, axillary buds; b.e., broken ends of woody strands; l.s., leaf scar.

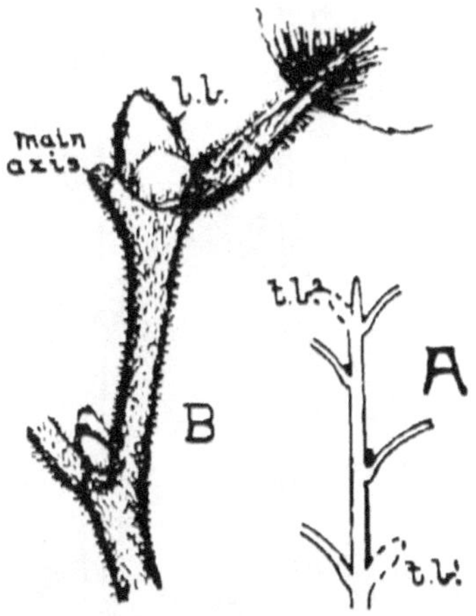

FIG. 51. — B, portion of a twig of the Elm in the autumn (somewhat enlarged). A, diagram to explain the behaviour of the terminal bud in the Elm or Lime; l.b., lateral bud; t.b.1. and t.b.2. in Fig. A, terminal buds of successive seasons which die away.

end-bud. On the opposite side, you will see a small withered bud (*main axis* in Fig. 51, B) which, in the Lime, often drops off leaving a scar. The withered bud is the true terminal bud of the twig. This is plain from the fact that it does not arise in the axil of a leaf-scar. The large bud found at the end of the branch, although it appears to be terminal, is really a **lateral bud** which has arisen in the axil of the leaf whose scar is just beneath it.

In the summer, the terminal bud stands out straight from the end of the branch. The lateral bud just below it grows much more rapidly, and thus gradually pushes the true terminal bud on one side. In the Lime and Elm, therefore, the tips of the branches regularly die away. The lengthening of the twigs during the following season is due to the growth of the lateral bud situated just behind them (Fig. 51, A; Fig. 52, E.).

The branching of the Lilac. — The branches of the Lilac often show a similar dying away of the terminal bud (Fig. 49); or, as you have seen, their growth ends with the production of an inflorescence which falls off after fruiting (p. 73). Whenever

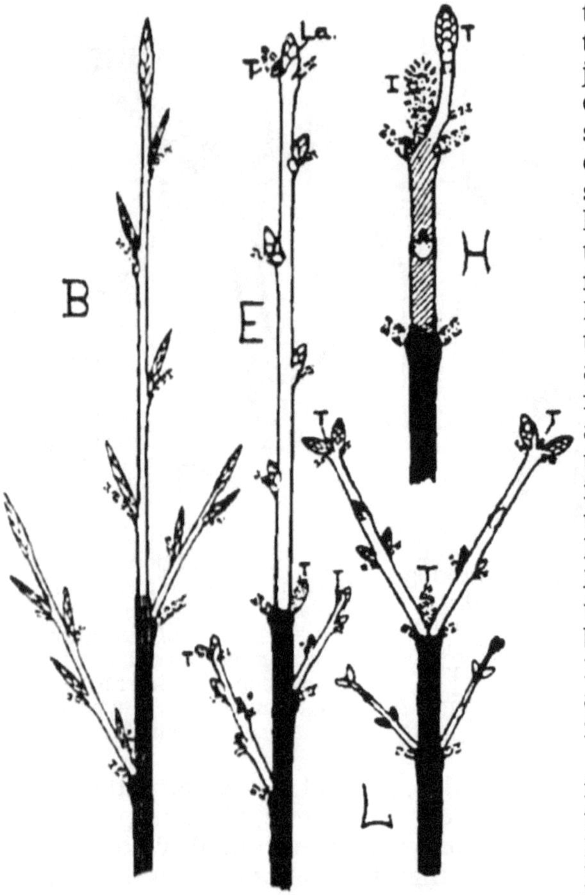

FIG. 52. - Diagrams to explain the methods of branching of B., the Beech, E., the Elm, H., the Horse Chestnut, L., the Lilac. In B., E., and L. the previous season's growth is shown black, in H. the previous season's growth is shaded, and that of two years back is shown black. Terminal buds and leaf-stalks, which have fallen off, are indicated by dots. I., inflorescence, La., lateral bud: T., terminal bud.

this occurs, the **two side-buds** just below the end of the twig sprout vigorously in the next season, so that it looks as though the branch had **forked** (Fig. 52, L.). It is plain that this does not always happen, for sometimes a branch has all three buds at its tip, namely a terminal and two lateral buds. The Mistletoe shows the same kind of branching as the Lilac, and here again the stem is repeatedly forked.

When not flowering, the twigs of the Horse Chestnut lengthen and branch (Fig. 52, H.) in the same way as in the Beech. But if an inflorescence is formed, the growth of the particular branch has been seen to come to an end (Fig. 52, H., upper part). Then, as in the Lime, a lateral bud just below the tip carries on the growth in the next season.

The internal structure of the stem. - When the shoots of plants have reached their full size in the autumn, their internal structure is easily studied. If you cut across a stem of the Vegetable Marrow, you

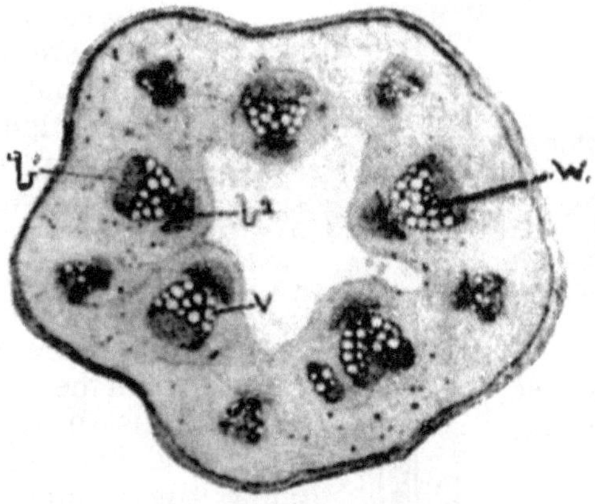

FIG. 53. - Photograph or a thin slice obtained by cutting across the stem of the Vegetable Marrow (about three times the natural size). v, the water-carrying tubes which form the greater part of the water-conducting strands, w; b1, b2, other parts of these strands which serve to carry food-substances from one part of the plant to the other.

will first notice that it is hollow in the center (Fig. 53). Situated around this space are the strands of **water-conducting tubes** (w), which form several groups arranged in an irregular ring. Some of the tubes are so large that they appear as tiny round holes to the naked eye (Fig. 53, v). The water-carrying strands will be found to be arranged in the same way if you cut across a stout stem of the Buttercup (Fig. 54, A) or the tip of the stem of the Sunflower. Outside each woody strand, there is a mass of softer tissue (Fig. 54, A), which serves to convey food-substances, such as sugar, from one part of a plant to another.

The stem of woody plants. - The three plants just mentioned are all Dicotyledons. Most of these show such a ring of strands in their **young** stems. In the woody members, the number of water-conducting tubes

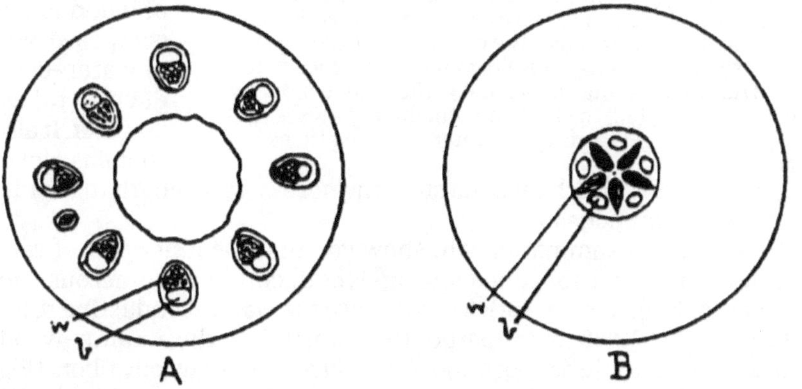

FIG. 54. - Appearance of sections cut across the stem (A) and the root (B) of the Buttercup. v. the water-carrying part; b, the food-carrying part of the strands.

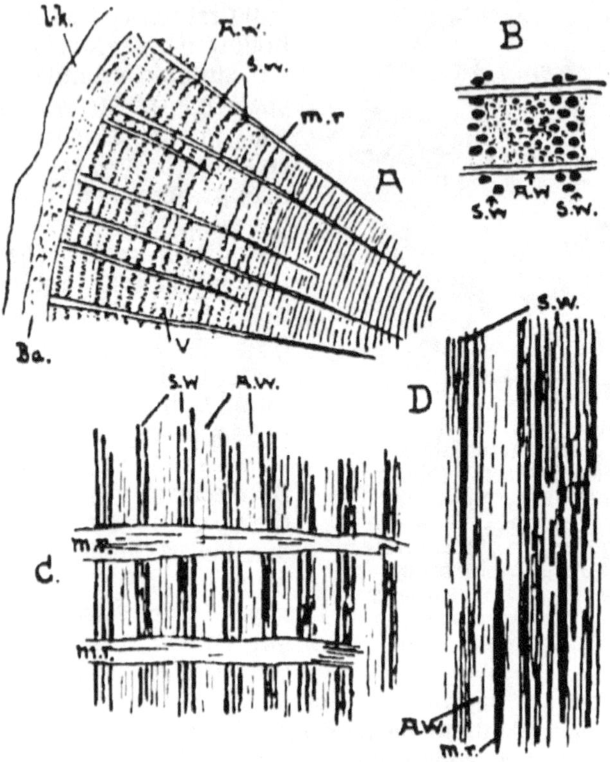

FIG. 55. - Structure of a woody trunk (somewhat enlarged).
A, appearance of a cross-section; B, a small part of the same, more enlarged; C. a section cut lengthwise through the middle of the trunk; D, a section cut lengthwise through the surface of the trunk A.W., autumn-wood Ba., the food-conducting region; bk., the bark m.r., medullary rays; s.w. spring-wood; V, the water-carrying tubes.

is increased as the stems become older, and a continuous **ring of woody tissue** is formed. Each year, a fresh ring is added on the outside of that of the previous season, and this is why the branches gradually get thicker.

When a tree trunk or one of the thicker branches is cut across, the wood is seen to consist of a series of such rings. These are called **annual rings** (Fig. 55, A). The mass of wood is not composed only of water-conducting tubes, however. It also contains a lot of **woody fibers**, which give the stem the necessary strength to bear its numerous branches.

A careful examination will show you that the inner part of each annual ring, the so-called **spring-wood**, contains numerous tiny holes looking like pin-pricks. These are the water-conducting tubes (Fig. 55, A, V). The outer part of the annual ring, the autumn-wood, has very few of these tubes and is chiefly formed of woody fibers (Fig. 55, A and B, A.W.). Extending in from the edge of the wood, like the spokes of a wheel, are a large number of fine lines, the medullary rays, which consist of soft cells (Fig. 55, A, m.r.).

The stems of Monocotyledons. - The stems of Monocotyledons, when cut across, show very **numerous** woody strands, which appear **irregularly scattered.** This is well seen in the Maize. No matter how old the stem you cut across, you will notice the same structure. Monocotyledons, therefore, do not, like woody Dicotyledons, add new rings of wood each year.

Summary. - Leaves become detached in autumn at definite places, leaving scars covered with cork. In woody perennials, two chief kinds of branching can be recognized. In one, the terminal bud, formed at the end of each season, continues its growth in the next (Beech). In the other, the terminal bud either withers or forms an inflorescence (Elm, Lilac); next year's growth is due to a lateral bud, which, as it grows, takes the place of the withered terminal bud.

The young stem of a Dicotyledon, when cut across, shows a ring of separate woody strands. As the stem grows older, complete rings of new wood are added each year outside the original strands. The stems of Monocotyledons do not thicken in this way but always show a large number of separate and scattered woody strands.

PRACTICAL WORK

1. Examine twigs of the Lime, Oak, Poplar, Willow, Hornbeam, and Lilac. Determine the method of branching in each case and look at the leaf-scars.

2. Cut across the stems of the following plants: Hogweed, Groundsel, Dead-nettle, Reed, Bulrush, Hyacinth. Draw a diagram of the arrangement of the woody strands in each.

3. Examine, if possible, the cut stumps of one or more trees. By counting the number of annual rings, determine their age.

QUESTIONS

1. Describe carefully the structure of a leaf-scar of any one plant, and say how it has been formed.

2. Draw and describe a branch of any tree with which you are familiar. Describe the way in which the branch would grow from year to year.

3. Compare the way in which growth is carried on from year to year in (a) the Lime or the Elm, and (b) the Horse Chestnut.

4. In what ways does the stem of an oak (or other forest tree) resemble and differ from that of a bean (or other herbaceous plant)?

CHAPTER XVI

THE PLANT AND THE SOIL

YOU have already learnt that plants not only obtain moisture, but also an important part of their food, from the soil. If, therefore, you are to understand how plants live, you must know something about the ground in which they are rooted.

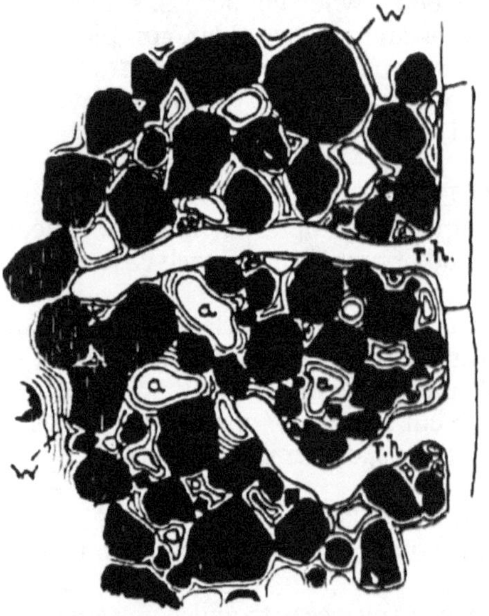

FIG. 56. - Diagram of a soil showing two root-hairs (r.h.) (very much magnified) pushing their way between the particles. The latter are shown black. Each particle is surrounded by a film of water (70.), whilst in between are numerous air-spaces (a.).

How soil is formed. - Soil is formed as a result of the gradual breaking up of rocks by the action of rain, frost, etc., a process that is called **weathering**. In this way, exposed rock becomes split up into small particles which often collect at the surface. If the ground slopes, however, they are mostly washed away by rain and carried into streams. This is why the latter look so muddy after heavy rains. Lower down in their course, streams generally become sluggish, and here the mud sinks down onto the bed or gets deposited as fine **silt**. Such **alluvial soils** are frequently found near the mouths of rivers.

Different kinds of soils. - The particles of a soil are generally of various kinds and of very different sizes. A **sandy soil** consists almost entirely of small flinty fragments. These are rather loosely packed, so that a large amount of air is present between them. In **clayey soils**, the particles are much finer and closer together, so that there is less

FIG. 57. - Photograph of the side of a cutting to show the dark soil (a) with humus, and the lighter-coloured subsoil (b) below. The strip of white paper represents a length of I foot. (Photo, E. J. S.)

air between them. Soils with densely packed particles, since they are difficult to dig, are said to be "**heavy**."

Soils containing a large amount of sand are, on the other hand, easy to dig, and are described as "**light**." One of the commonest light soils is **loam**, in which there are almost equal amounts of clayey and sandy particles.

Humus. - In a freshly dug ditch, the earth at the surface appears darker (Fig. 57). This is because the upper layer of the soil contains the decaying remains of plants which once grew upon it. These remnants are called **humus**. The amount of humus varies very much in different soils. Those which contain very little generally support only a poor growth of plants. In gardens and on other cultivated land, the supply of humus is kept up by the constant addition of **manure**.

How to separate the soil particles. - Place about an egg-cup full of soil in as large a medicine bottle as you can find. Fill up the bottle with water and shake thoroughly. Then let the bottle stand for a short time. Most of the soil collects on the bottom, but a small part, the humus, floats to the top. The soil at the bottom is sorted out into par-

FIG. 58. - Experiment to show the effect, upon seedlings of the Maize, of growth in distilled water, and in water to which soil has been added.

ticles of very different sizes, the larger (sandy) particles below, the finer ones above. If you shake up a number of different soils in this way, you will find that they vary in the amounts of coarse and fine particles and in the quantity of humus.

The position of the water. - The moisture in the soil forms a thin film around each particle (Fig. 56, 20). After a piece of firewood has been dipped into water, it is seen to be covered with a wet film. Now cut it into two pieces and dip these in. The two pieces clearly pick up more water than the one, since there is now a film over the freshly cut ends as well. So that the more you cut up the firewood, the larger the quantity of water that will cling to its pieces. In the same way, if we take two lumps of soil of equal size, the one which has more particles (i.e., the one in which they are smallest) will hold the greater amount of water. A clayey soil is therefore **usually wetter** than a sandy one.

In summer, when there has been no rain for some time, the plants gradually use up the moisture in the surface layers. The soil, however, does not dry completely, because water is sucked up from the damp earth below. This suction is not as strong in a coarse-grained as in a fine-grained soil. In summer, a sandy soil will therefore **become dry more quickly** than a clayey one.

The food substances in the water. - The water absorbed by roots, as you have learnt, contains various **substances in solution**. You can prove that these are necessary for the nourishment of the plant in the following way. Fill a large jam-jar with distilled water (or rainwater), and another with distilled water in which a lot of soil, previously baked in an oven, has been stirred up. The latter therefore contains the same mineral substances as the soil-water. For each jar, cut out a cardboard lid, in the middle of which you make a small hole. With

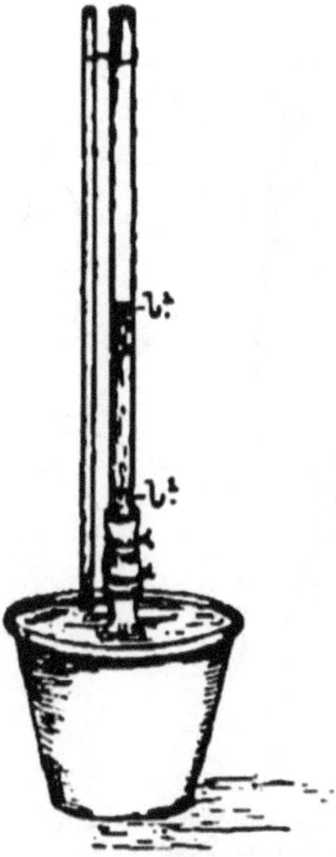

FIG. 59. - Experiment to show root-pressure, see the text. L1, L2, the successive levels of the water-column.

a pair of scissors, cut a slit in each lid extending from the margin to the central hole (Fig. 58, s.). Bend apart the edges of the slits and push an equal number of healthy Maize seedlings into the central hole of each lid. Then place the lids on the jars and prop up the seedlings with cotton-wool, so that the roots reach into the contained liquid, whilst the shoots are outside (Fig. 58).

If you watch the seedlings for some weeks, you will find that those in the soil-water are **growing much better** than those in the distilled water (Fig. 58). In fact, the latter will probably sooner or later die away.

Root pressure. - The water taken up from the surface of the soil particles by the root-hairs (Fig. 56) is gradually passed **into the central core of the root** (p. 32, Fig. 54, B, W.). From here it travels into the water-carrying tubes of the stem, and is distributed from them to the leaves. When the roots are absorbing plenty of water, the latter is sometimes forced up the stem with considerable pressure. This **root pressure** is shown in the following experiment (Fig. 59).

Cut off the stem of a Fuchsia, which has been well watered, a little above the level of the soil. To the cut end, attach a long piece of narrow glass tubing by a short length of rubber tube. Twist wire round the joints so that they are air-tight. Push a long stick upright into the soil, near the plant, and tie the glass tubing to it. After a few hours, or on the next day, you will see that a column of liquid is gradually being forced up the tube (Fig. 59).

The pressing out of liquid water by plants. - It is only when there is plenty of moisture and the soil is warm that the water rises in this way. The pressure of the liquid in the water-carrying pipes may then become so considerable that, in some plants, it is forced out from the ends of the finer veins in the form of **little drops** (Fig. 60). These are easily seen after a warm, moist summer's night, looking like beads of dew on the tips of Grass leaves (Fig. 60, A) or round the edges of the leaves of the Garden Nasturtium (Fig. 60, B).

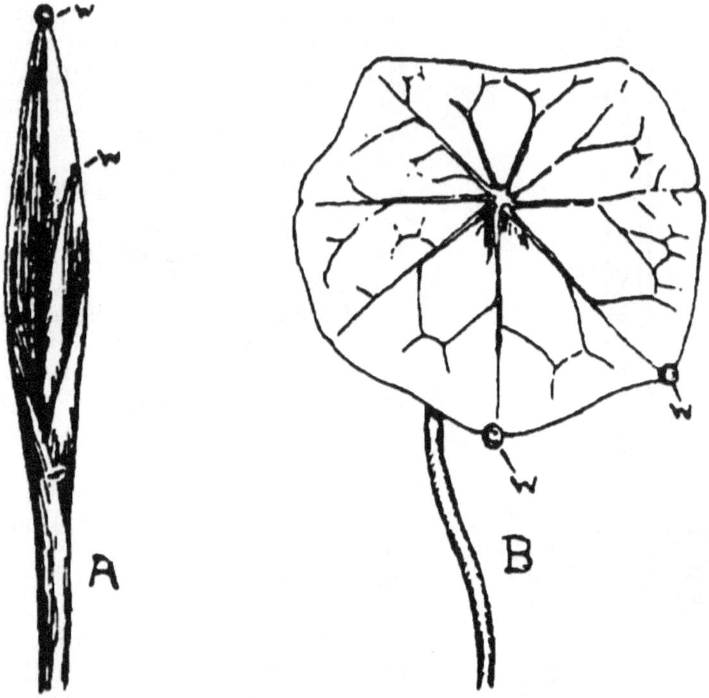

FIG. 60. - Leaves of A. the Maize, and B, the Garden Nasturtium, showing drops of water (W.) which have been forced out.

Summary. - Soils are composed of small particles of rock mingled with plant remains or humus. They are heavy or light according as they consist mainly of fine or coarse particles. The fertility of a soil greatly depends on the amount of humus present. The soil contains both air and water, the amount of the latter being largest in fine-grained soils. The water which the root takes up is a **weak** solution of mineral substances without which the plant cannot thrive.

When roots are absorbing actively, the water may be forced up the tubes in the stem with considerable pressure. If this be very great, part of the water may in some plants be forced out as drops of liquid.

PRACTICAL WORK

1. Shake up a number of soils, as described on p. 83, and note the amounts of coarse, fine, and humus particles.

2. Take two small tins and punch holes through the bottoms. Fill one with damp clay and the other with damp sand. Stand each for an hour in a saucer full of water. Allow the surplus to drain off, and then

weigh each tin. Now let the soils dry and, after a week or so, weigh them again. Note that the sandy soil dries first and contains less water.

3. Place a quantity of garden soil on a shovel and heat it strongly, for some hours, over a hot fire. Compare its colour before and after heating. Explain the cause of the change in colour.

4. Perform the experiments described on p. 78-79.

QUESTIONS

1. Name several different kinds of soil and compare the relative amounts of air, water, and humus in each.

2. Describe how you would show that a soil is built up of particles of different sizes.

3. Why does a pea seedling grown in water at first flourish and then gradually die? How may its death be prevented?

CHAPTER XVII

HOW PLANTS FEED

The uses of water to the plant. - In Chapter II, you were told that the mineral substances, brought in with the soil-water, remain in the plant when the water is given off in transpiration. This process of evaporation causes a suction which probably helps to draw up more water.

Plants do not, however, give off all the water which they absorb. Quite a large amount **remains behind**. This can be easily proved by comparing the weight of a fresh plant with its weight after it has been dried. Cut up the fresh plant into small pieces, place these in a saucer, and then weigh the whole. Afterwards, put the saucer near a hot stove, and weigh again after a day or two.

Assimilation. - You have also learnt (Chapter III) that plants obtain another part of their food from the carbonic acid gas of the air. This gas consists of carbon and oxygen. It is split up in the plant, and the carbon is used to form **starch**. The oxygen is liberated, and may be collected in quantity in the following way.

Take a bunch of Canadian Pondweed, or of some other water plant, and put it in a cylinder (or large jam-jar) full of water (Fig. 61, c.). Over the cut ends of the stems place a glass funnel (f.), upside down. Fix this by means of wire, so that the whole is under water (Fig. 61). Next, fill a test-tube (t.) with water, and, placing your thumb over the open end, invert it over the stem of the funnel, as in the figure.

Bubbles of gas soon begin to rise from the cut ends of the Pondweed and pass up into the test-tube. There they take the place of the water and collect in the upper end (Fig. 61). After a day or two there will be no water left in the test-tube. Now lift up the tube and quickly push a glowing splinter of wood into it. The latter immediately bursts into flame, and this shows at once that most of the gas in the tube is **oxygen**.

The conditions of assimilation. — You can use this same experiment (Fig. 61) to find out how outside conditions affect assimilation. Thus, when the apparatus is taken out of the sun into the shade, the bubbles rise much more slowly. When put in the dark, they almost stop. This shows you that **the weaker the light, the slower** the process of **assimilation**, since the rate at which the bubbles rise depends on how quickly assimilation is going on.

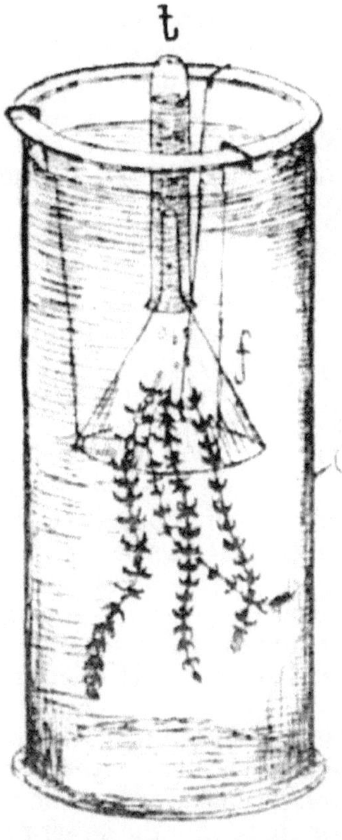

FIG. 61. - Apparatus to show that an assimilating water-plant gives off oxygen. Description in the text, p. 82.

Next, keep the apparatus in sunlight, but add a little warm water. The bubbles come off quicker. Then, drop in a handful of powdered ice, and, after a short time, the bubbles are much less frequent. So, the **temperature** of the water (or of the air in the case of land-plants) also has a great effect on the **rate of assimilation**. Even evergreens, therefore, assimilate very little in winter.

Fit up the same experiment as before (Fig. 61), but, instead of ordinary water, use some which has been boiled and allowed to cool. Such water no longer contains any carbonic acid gas. As a result, no bubbles of gas pass up into the test-tube, even in bright sunlight. If, however, you add some soda-water, which contains a lot of carbonic acid gas, bubbles of oxygen begin to rise almost at once. The more you add, the faster the gas collects. This last experiment shows that **the more carbonic acid** gas there is, the **quicker** the plant assimilates.

Assimilation, therefore, depends on the presence of **carbonic acid gas**, and of sufficient **light** and **warmth**.

Light and assimilation. — There is another simple way of showing the importance of light. Cut out two pieces of cardboard of the same shape as one of the green leaves of a plant. In the middle of one piece, make a circular hole, about an inch wide. Place this on the upper side of the leaf (which should be left on the plant), and the uncut piece on the lower side; the two can be kept in position by spiral paper-clips.

Leave the plant in bright sunlight for a day or two. Then, if possible late in the afternoon, pick off the leaf. Remove the green color in the way described on p. 11, and paint with iodine. The circular hole stands out dark against a light background (*compare* Fig. 62). This result shows that **starch is only formed** where the leaf was not shaded.

Chlorophyll and assimilation. — You have been told (p. 12) that the green coloring matter of the plant (called **chlorophyll**) is also necessary for assimilation. In **variegated** leaves, there is **no chlo-**

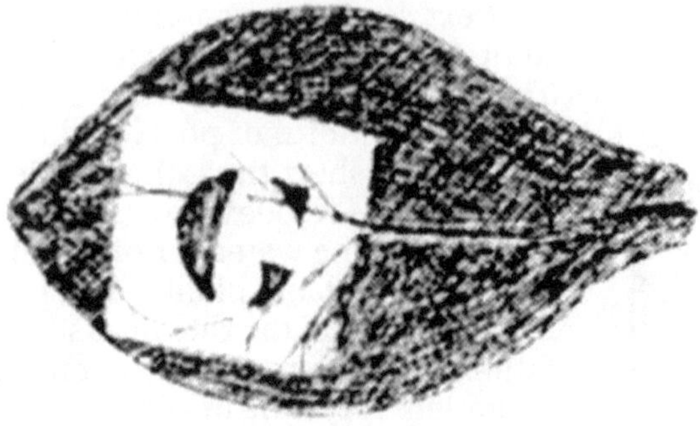

FIG. 62. - A so-called starch-print. The leaf has been covered with a stencil plate bearing the letter G, exposed for some hours to sun, light, then decolourised, and painted with iodine.

rophyll in the parts which are not green. These parts, therefore, do not form starch. Make a careful sketch of a leaf of the variegated Privet, showing the arrangement of the green patches. Then decolorize it and paint with iodine. Starch will only be found in those parts that contained chlorophyll.

Starch-formation. — When a photographic plate is exposed, the light falling upon it brings about a **chemical change**. In a similar way, the light that falls on the green parts of plants probably brings about the **chemical changes** that lead to the formation of starch **in** assimilation. The materials that are acted upon are the **carbonic acid gas** from the air and the water from the soil. The former consists of carbon and oxygen, and the latter of hydrogen and oxygen.

Starch is built up of carbon, hydrogen, and oxygen. Since the carbonic acid gas and the water between them furnish more **oxygen** than is required to form starch, the rest is **given off** during assimilation. A little of this oxygen is used in respiration (p. 13), but the larger part escapes into the air.

Starch and other similar compounds (e.g. sugars), formed in assimilation, are gradually built up by the plant into the very complicated substances which form its living body. These, besides carbon, hydrogen, and oxygen, also contain nitrogen, sulfur, phosphorus, etc., all of which are supplied in the soil-water. Although four-fifths of the air consists of nitrogen, most plants obtain all of it from the nitrogen-compounds in the soil. The substances formed in assimilation accumulate in the leaves during the daytime but are removed to other parts of the plant during the night (see item 4 of the practical work).

By the feeding-processes of the plant, the materials are produced from which new leaves, branches, flowers, etc., are formed. When a plant breathes, however, some of this food is used up, and, with the oxygen, forms the carbonic acid gas which is given out (p. 12). Thus, in assimilation there is a **gain in weight**, in respiration a **loss of weight**. As a result, if a plant is grown in darkness, its weight gradually decreases.

Summary. — Plants take in water and mineral salts from the soil, and carbonic acid gas from the air. By means of their chlorophyll, when exposed to light, the carbon in the carbonic acid gas is used to make starch, whilst the oxygen is liberated. Such assimilation depends on a sufficient supply of carbonic acid gas and sufficient heat and light. It only takes place in the green parts of plants.

PRACTICAL WORK

1. Cut up, into small pieces, (a) a number of seeds of the Runner Bean, (b) a Potato, and (c) a number of seedlings of the Runner Bean. Place each set in a saucer, and weigh them as described on p. 82. Keep them next to a stove for some days, and compare the amount of water lost by each in drying. What do you conclude from the result?

2. Repeat the experiments on p. 82 and p. 83.

3. Test a variety of variegated leaves for starch, and notice that its distribution corresponds with that of the chlorophyll.

4. Compare the color, when painted with iodine, of the leaves of a Runner Bean or Privet (a) gathered in the early morning, and (b) in the late afternoon of a sunny day. Explain the result.

QUESTIONS

1. State how outside conditions affect the process of assimilation.

2. What is starch? How do you recognize it? How and where is it formed?

3. Describe experiments by which you could show what gases are taken in and given out by leaves (a) in the dark, and (b) in the light; and state briefly what is the importance to the plant of these processes.

4. Describe an experiment to show that chlorophyll is necessary for the formation of starch.

CHAPTER XVIII

SPECIAL WAYS OF OBTAINING FOOD

The feeding of plants and animals compared. — The experiments you have already performed have shown that plants feed on simple chemical substances, such as water, carbonic acid gas, and minerals taken up from the soil. Animals would be quite unable to live on such a diet, and all of them really **depend on plants** for their food. Even those animals which are flesh-eating feed on others whose food consists of plants. Animals, as well as human beings, therefore, really live on substances like sugars, fats, proteids, etc., manufactured by plants from simple chemical compounds.

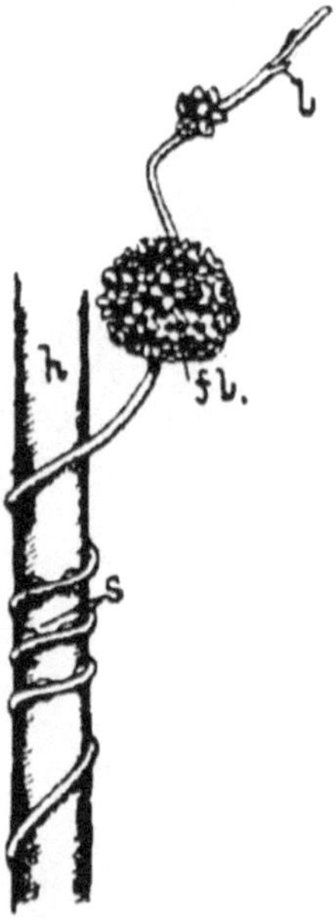

FIG. 63. -Small part of a plant of the Dodder, showing the method of entwining the stem of the host (slightly enlarged). fl., flowers: h., stem of host; l., leaf; s., suckers.

Plants that are not green. — Plants are able to feed in the way they do, owing to the chlorophyll which they contain. A certain number of plants, however, are **not green**. Consequently, like animals, they have to live on complicated chemical substances (e.g., sugars, fats, proteids, etc.). These are obtained either from living plants and animals, or from their decaying bodies.

The Dodder. — The Dodder attacks Clover-crops and the plants growing on heaths, obtaining its food from their living bodies; in other words, it is a **parasite**. It consists of numerous yellowish thread-like stems, bearing tiny colorless leaves at wide intervals. In the height of the summer, it forms bunches of pale pink flowers (Fig. 63, A.).

The stem of the Dodder twines round that of the plant on which it preys (the **host**, Fig. 63, h.). At certain points, the coils are wound very tightly. If you pull these off, you will find that they were attached by a number of little **suckers** (Fig. 63,

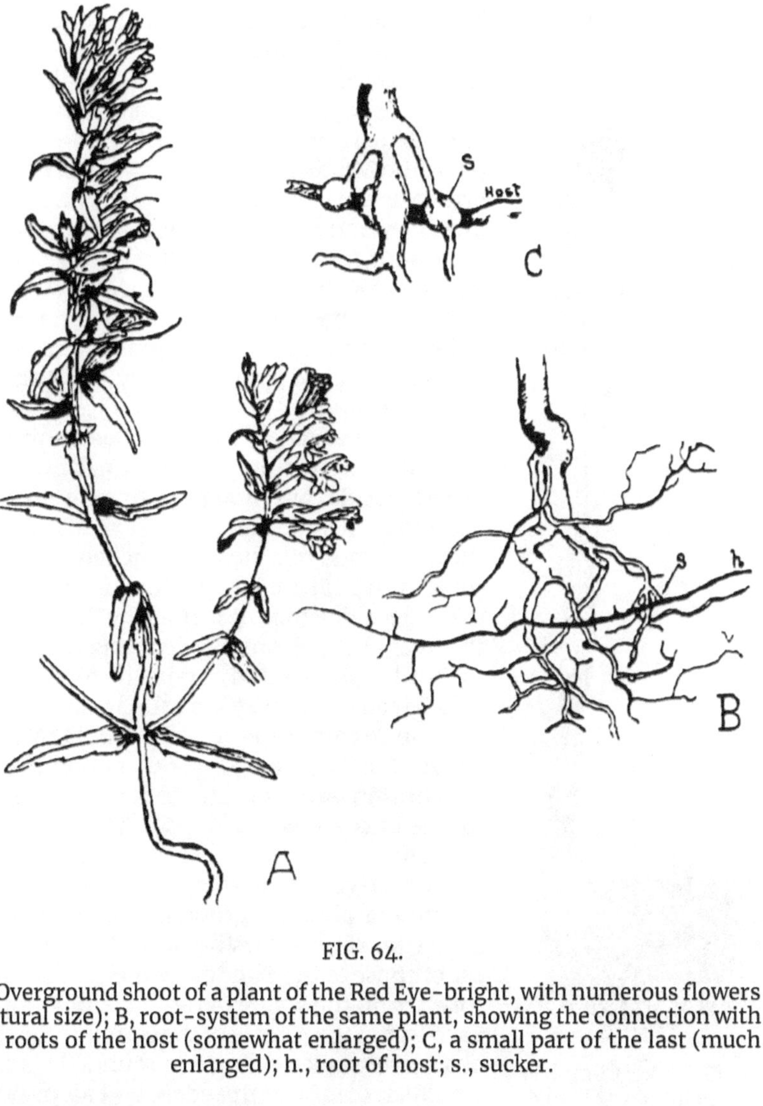

FIG. 64.

A, Overground shoot of a plant of the Red Eye-bright, with numerous flowers (natural size); B, root-system of the same plant, showing the connection with the roots of the host (somewhat enlarged); C, a small part of the last (much enlarged); h., root of host; s., sucker.

S.) which had pierced their way **into the stem of the host**. Through these suckers, the parasite takes up nourishment.

The Dodder, like all parasites, forms numerous flowers and large **quantities of seed**. This is necessary because many of the seeds will fall and germinate in places where there is no suitable host, so that they soon die.

Other British parasites. — Other parasitic flowering plants found in England are the Toothwort and the Broomrapes, but these are much rarer than the Dodder. They live on the **roots of the host**, so that their suckers can only be found by careful digging.

There are some parasitic flowering plants which contain chlorophyll. They, therefore, depend on the host only for **part of their food**. A common example is the Mistletoe, which grows aloft on the branches of trees and sends peg-like suckers into the wood of the host. Certain herbs found in meadows, such as the Yellow Rattle and the Red Eye-bright (Fig. 64, A), have small green leaves. But they obtain most of their nourishment from the roots of the grasses, to which they are attached by suckers (Fig. 64, B and C).

FIG. 65. - Complete plant of the Bird's Nest Orchid (about half the natural size). A., flower: l., leaf: n., the underground nest-like portion.

Saprophytes. — The Bird's Nest Orchid (Fig. 65), frequently found in Beech-woods, is another flowering plant that has no green leaves. In this case, however, there is **no connection** with any other plant. Beneath the soil, the stem ends in a richly branched structure (the "nest," Fig. 65, n.), which is embedded in the decaying humus formed by the leaves of the trees above. From this decaying substance, the Bird's Nest Orchid obtains its food. Plants which feed in this way are called **saprophytes**.

The many kinds of Toadstools, Mushrooms, Puffballs, etc. (Fig. 66), so common in the autumn, are saprophytic plants belonging to one of the lower groups of the Vegetable Kingdom.

Insectivorous plants. — A very peculiar method of obtaining food is shown by a few plants growing in marshy places. The commonest of these is the Sundew, which forms little rosettes on the spongy Bog-moss of swamps. Each leaf of the rosette of the common Sundew has a long stalk, ending in a rounded blade of a reddish color. On the edge, and all over the upper surface of the blade, are a number of large hairs, each bearing a little **sticky knob** (see Fig. 67).

Small insects settle on the blades, attracted by the brilliant color of the leaves and the glistening knobs at the ends of the hairs (Fig. 67, ins.). They are unable to fly away again because they stick to the knobs. After a short time, the hairs around

FIG. 66. - Photograph of a group of seven Puffballs and one Toadstool. (Photo, F. J. S.)

the insect begin to **curve inwards**. In this way, they grasp its body, which gradually becomes almost completely surrounded. Then digestive juices pass out of the hairs, and by slow degrees the soft parts of the insect are dissolved and taken up into the leaf. After a day or more, the hairs return to their original position, ready for another victim.

The Sundew thus obtains part of its food **from the insects** which it entraps. If plants of the Sundew are kept under a jam-jar, so that no insects can reach them, they grow much less vigorously. Moreover, they produce fewer flowers and fruits. The Butterwort, which is common on moorlands, also feeds on the bodies of insects. These are caught on the upper sticky surfaces of the yellowish leaves.

The Pitcher-plant, often cultivated in greenhouses, is an insect-catching plant that grows in the Tropics. At the ends of its leaves, there are large brightly colored "**pitchers.**" Flies and other insects, falling into them, become drowned in the fluid, which half fills the pitcher. The soft parts of their bodies are then gradually absorbed by the plant.

Summary. — Green plants live on simple chemical substances. Animals live on complicated ones, previously formed by plants. Plants which are not green are either parasites or saprophytes. Some parasitic plants have green leaves and so are partly independent.

FIG. 67.- Photograph of two plants of the English Sundew, in which the blades of the leaves are oval. On one of the leaves of the left-hand plant an insect (ins.) has been caught.

Yet other green plants supplement the food they themselves manufacture by entrapping insects and digesting their bodies.

PRACTICAL WORK

1. Carefully dig up a plant of the Yellow Rattle or Red Eye-bright, with the soil around its roots. Wash the soil carefully away, and make out the attachment of the parasite to the roots of the host.

2. Examine the different kinds of plants described in this chapter growing in their wild state. (N.B. — As most of these plants are uncommon, do not uproot them.)

3. Strongly heat a little starch or sugar in a test-tube, and notice that it becomes black. This is due to the carbon in these substances.

QUESTIONS

1. Describe an example of a common British parasite and of a common British saprophyte. Explain how they differ in their method of obtaining food.

2. Compare, as far as you can, the feeding and breathing of plants and animals.

3. Describe carefully how the Sundew obtains its food. What would be the effect of growing specimens of this plant beneath a jam-jar?

CHAPTER XIX

HOW PLANTS GROW

DURING the warmer months, such large quantities of food are formed that there is a surplus. This is stored up for future use in seeds, tubers, bulbs, rhizomes, etc. Some of the food-substances manufactured by plants are, however, at once used **to carry on growth**.

How to measure growth. — The growth of plants, like that of animals, takes place so slowly that it can only be followed if you magnify it. A simple way of doing this is by using a "**growth-lever**," like that shown in Fig. 68. The lever consists of a long wooden rod (l.), pierced near one end by a pin (p.). At this point, it is attached to an upright support, so that it can move up and down quite easily over the surface of the scale.

First, wrap a small piece of cotton-wool round the tip of the stem of some plant, whose growth is to be measured, and round this securely tie a piece of cotton thread. The other end of this thread is fastened to the short end of the lever, so that the latter slopes slightly upwards (Fig. 68). You then make a note of the position of the tip of the lever on the scale. A day later you will find that the tip **has dropped**. This must be due to the plant's growth, which, however, has been much magnified.

To find out how much growth is made in a certain time, lay a ruler against the plumule of a seedling and make a mark on it with Indian ink, at a distance of two inches from the tip. After a day or two, again measure the distance between ink-mark and tip. It will now be more than two inches, and the increase gives you the **amount of growth**.

In the same way, mark the radicle of a bean-seedling at a distance of one inch from the tip. Then allow it to grow vertically downwards in a jam-jar, as described on p. 33. Here again, the increase in the length of the piece marked off shows the amount of growth.

The effect of warmth and darkness on growth. — Measure the growth of two plants of the same kind (e.g., two bean-seedlings), one of which has been left in a warm room and the other in a cold one. You will find that **warmth increases** the rate of **growth**. There is also a difference in the amount of growth of the stem in light and in darkness.

This is easily seen in seedlings (e.g., of peas) or sprouting potato-

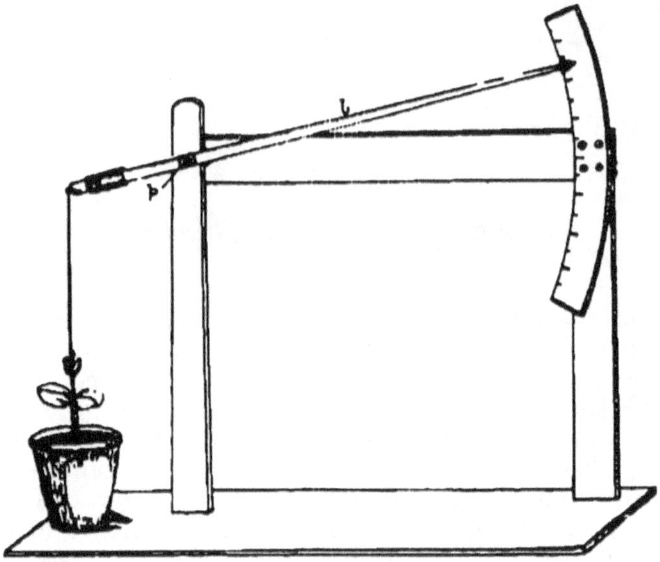

FIG. 68. A growth-lever. For description, see the text, p. 91.

tubers. Some of them are allowed to grow from the very first in darkness, whilst others are left in the light. After the same length of time, the plants in the dark produce **a much taller** stem than those in the light (Fig. 69). Moreover, the leaves are smaller and more widely separated, and the whole plant is colorless. Such plants are said to be **etiolated**.

This experiment teaches you **three things**: (a) that chlorophyll is not formed in darkness, (b) that the stem grows much more rapidly in the dark than in the light, and (c) that in the dark, the leaves remain small. If, before they die of starvation, etiolated plants are brought into the light, they become green and grow quite normally. When plants having rhizomes or root-stocks are kept in darkness, their **petioles** generally grow very rapidly. This fact is made use of in producing the long fleshy leaf-stalks of the rhubarb, celery, and sea kale.

Growth and breathing. — Germination, in other words, the early growth of the plant, has been seen to take place only when the temperature is sufficiently high and when there is enough water and oxygen. The older plant likewise only grows when these conditions are satisfied. **Oxygen** is as **necessary** for the **growth** of plants as for that of animals, because, when breathing ceases, all the life-processes are brought to a standstill.

Curvatures during growth. — You have previously learnt that light, gravity, and moisture **influence the direction** in which the different parts of the plant grow. A root, for instance, placed horizontally, curves

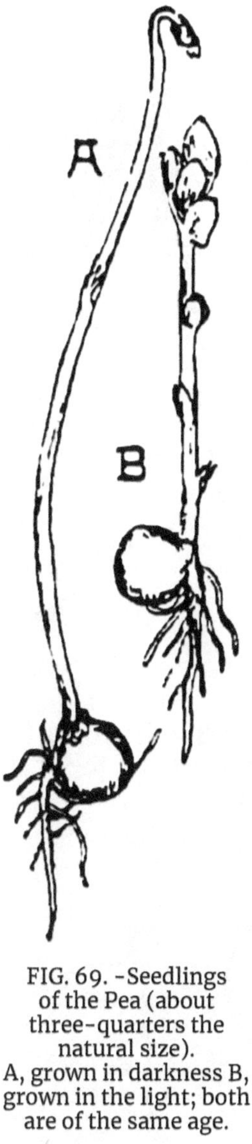

FIG. 69. -Seedlings of the Pea (about three-quarters the natural size). A, grown in darkness B, grown in the light; both are of the same age.

until it again points vertically downwards. Such curvatures are due to the two sides of the curving root or shoot growing **at different rates**.

Tendrils, like those of the White Bryony (Fig. 14) and Sweet Pea, curve when they merely rub against a rough object. Thus, if you gently stroke the underside of a young straight tendril of the White Bryony (Fig. 14, A) near its tip, the latter **begins to curve** after a few minutes. Similarly, tendrils very soon coil round an upright stick, if it is placed so that they touch it. In this way (see p. 22), tendrils help to support climbing plants. In stem-twiners (p. 21), however, rubbing has nothing to do with their coiling around a support. This is due to other complicated causes.

Other movements. — You thus see that many parts of plants can alter their position (i.e., **move**) as a result of **outside influences**. In the Sundew, also, you have learnt that the hairs on the leaves curve when touched by a fly. Further examples of plant movements are shown by many flowers. Those of the Poor Man's Weather-glass (Pimpernel) close about mid-day or in dull weather. The flowers of the Tulip and Crocus open widely in warm sunshine, whilst those of the Wood Anemone not only close, but also droop down at night.

The compound leaves of the Wood Sorrel and the Dutch Clover shut up at dusk, just like flowers. In the Wood Sorrel (Fig. 70) each of the three leaflets folds along its midrib and sinks down, so that all three lie close together against the petiole.

Summary. — The growth of plants is influenced by temperature, light, and darkness, and the supply of water and oxygen. Plants grown in darkness become etiolated, i.e., are colorless, and form long stems and small leaves. The parts of plants are able to move, but, unlike animals, the ordinary plant does not move as a whole from place to place.

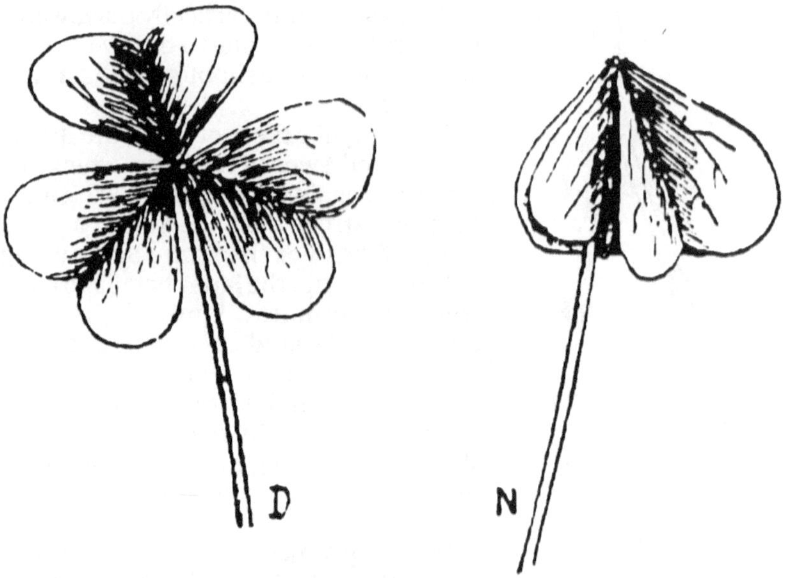

FIG. 70. - Two leaves of the Wood Sorrel (natural size). D., in the day-position; N., in the night-position.

PRACTICAL WORK

1. Beginning at the tip, make marks on the radicle of a young Bean seedling, at equal distances from one another and as near together as possible (Fig. 71, A). Place the seedling in a damp jam-jar, as described on p. 33. After a day or two, make a sketch of the root, showing the new positions of the different marks. You will see that growth has been most rapid at a short distance behind the tip (see Fig. 71, B).

2. Mark a plumule of a young Bean seedling in the same way as described in (1). After a day or two, make a sketch of the plumule, showing the new positions of the different marks. You will see that growth takes place over a wider region

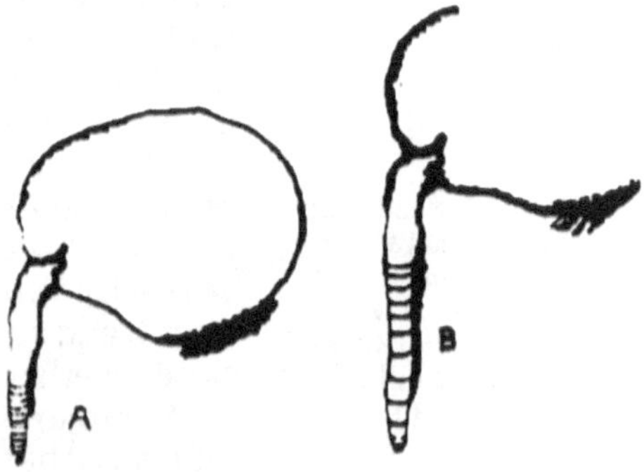

FIG. 71. Illustration of the experiment in the first item of the practical work. room, and then again in a cold room. A, Bean seedling showing the method of marking the radicle; B, the same, forty-eight hours later.

than in the case of the root, and that the most rapidly growing portion is farther away from the tip.

3. Repeat the experiments with tendrils, described on p. 93.

4. Put some flowers of the Tulip or Crocus in water. Place them first in a cold room, then in a warm room, and then again in a cold room. Note the result.

QUESTIONS

1. Two Bean seeds are allowed to germinate, one in the dark and the other in the light. Describe how the two seedlings will differ (a) in appearance and (b) in weight. Explain these differences as far as you can.

2. Compare the method of growth and the branching of a stem and a root.

3. "Plants are living creatures." What reasons can you give for the truth of this statement?

4. Describe carefully, with diagrams, one example to show that plants can move. Illustrate your answer by means of an experiment.

CHAPTER XX

PLANTS THAT GROW IN DRY PLACES

A SOIL containing a large number of sandy particles, such as that of a sandy common or of a dune beside the sea, does not, as you have seen (p. 80), hold very much moisture. Since transpiration is always going on, the plants growing in such soils must **economize their water-supply** as far as possible. They do this in many different ways.

FIG. 72. - Portion of a plant of the Horsetail Fern, showing the minute leaves (l) which are joined to form sheaths at the nodes.

The leaf and transpiration. – Plants, which grow in soils holding plenty of moisture (e.g., those found in an Oak wood or in a meadow), have **large, thin leaves**. They thus expose a large surface from which water is rapidly lost in transpiration. The loss is much reduced when the **leaves are small**, as in the Arbor Vitae and Cypress.

Plants also lessen the amount of water-vapour given off from their leaves by **thickening the surface-skin**. You can see how effective this is if you use cobalt-paper (p. 9) to compare the rates of transpiration from a leaf of an ordinary Cherry and from that of a Cherry Laurel or Holly. The result will show that the leathery leaf of the evergreen gives off moisture much more slowly than that of the Cherry.

Reduction of the leaves. – Many of the plants growing in dry places have a very small leaf-surface. For instance, the Furze or Gorse has small spiny leaves (Fig. 77, B, l.sp.), whilst those of the Scotch Fir are needle-like and have a very thick skin. In other cases, the leaves are **mere scales**, whilst the stem is green and carries on the assimilation of the plant. Good examples are furnished by the Horsetails (Fig. 72).

The Butcher's Broom. – A very peculiar case is seen in the Butcher's Broom (Fig. 73, B). In this plant, the flat oval structures that look like leaves are **not leaves** at all. If you examine the plant closely, you will find that all of them arise in the axils of little brown scales (Fig. 73, B, l.), which are the true leaves. This shows that each flat green structure is a very curious kind of **branch**. This is also proved by the fact that one (the upper) surface of these branches bears a scale (Fig. 73, B, s.) and sometimes even a flower (Fig. 73, B, f.).

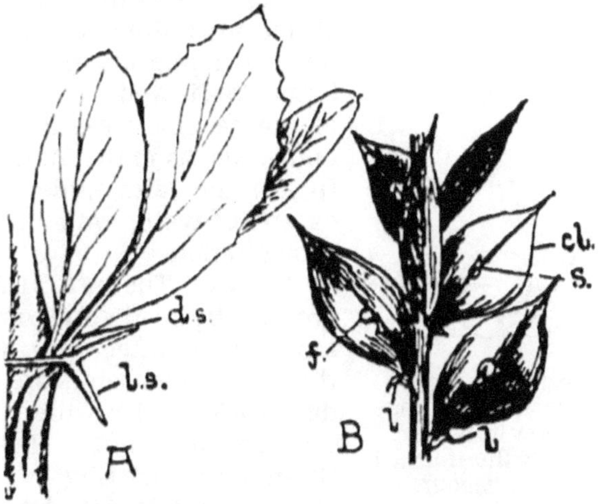

FIG. 73.
A, small portion of a branch of the Barberry, showing the three- branched leaf-spines (1.5.) (natural size); the foliage-leaves arise from a dwarf-shoot (it.s.) in the axil of the spine: B, branch of the Butcher's Broom (natural size): cl., the leaf-like B, f.). s., the sealy leaves on the leaf-like branches.

Rolled leaves. – Many of the Grasses growing in dry places (e.g., Sheep's Fescue, Marram Grass) appear to have narrow thread-like leaves. The blades are really like those of other Grasses, but are usually **rolled up** like a tube (Fig. 75). The small holes (pores) through which the water-vapour escapes are, in such leaves, situated on the surface which lines the inside of the tube. There are none on the outer surface, which has a very thick skin (Fig. 75, c). The air within the tube will thus be laden with moisture (Fig. 75, s.ch.), and this will only escape slowly from the rolled-up leaf to the outside. In the Heather, the small leaves are rolled up much in the same way (Fig. 74).

The storage of water. – All the plants mentioned in this chapter are able to exist on dry soils because their rate of transpiration is slow. But there is another way of providing against an insufficient supply of water, and that is by storing it up during periods of rain. Examples are the Houseleek (Fig. 76, B), often found growing on roofs, and the Yellow Stonecrop (Fig. 76, A), common in many dry places. In both plants, the leaves are fleshy or **succulent** owing to the storage of water within them. Such plants can live for a long time without any but

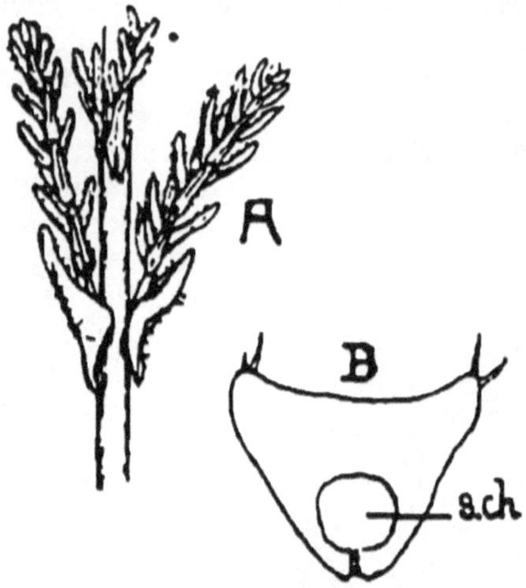

FIG. 74. A, small portion of a plant of the Heather B, a leaf of the same cut across to show how it is rolled up; s.ch. the inner cavity thus formed which is full of water-vapour.

their own supplies of water. If a Houseleek is kept on a dry shelf for several weeks, it will probably grow quite well when again planted.

Hairs. – Plants in dry situations quite commonly have a dense clothing of **hairs**. This is well seen in the Mouse-ear Chickweed and the Cudweeds. As in the Mullein (p. 42), the hairs hinder the escape of water-vapour in transpiration.

Spines. – The bushes that grow on dry heaths and commons are very often spiny, but the spines themselves are of different kinds. Thus, the long pointed spines of the Hawthorn or the Sloe (Fig. 77, A) arise in **the axils of the leaves** and are therefore really branches. Indeed, not uncommonly they bear leaves and resting buds (Fig. 77, A). In other cases, however, the spines are leaves which have lost their flat shape and become stiff and pointed. This is the case in the Gorse (where the branches are also spiny, Fig. 77, B) and the Barberry (Fig. 73, A). In these plants, the spines are recognized as leaves because **branches arise in their axils.**

Prickles. – You must not confuse such spines with the **prickles** of the Rose and the Bramble, which are merely outgrowths of the surface-skin (Fig. II, B, p.). The prickles of a Rose are quite easily broken off, leaving only a **surface-scar** and not a deep wound, as in the case of a spine. The prickles of these plants are also quite irregularly scattered, and show no definite arrangement with reference either to leaves or branches.

FIG. 75. A leaf of the Sheep's Fescue, cut across to show how it is rolled. c, the thick outer skin; s.ch., the inner cavity which is filled with water vapour, v.b., the water carrying strands.

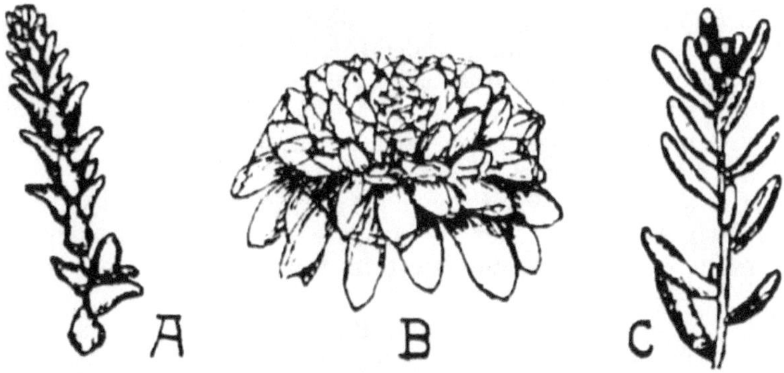

FIG. 76. - Examples of succulents (all natural size).
A, Yellow Stonecrop or Wall-pepper: B, Houseleek; C, White Stonecrop.

The habit of plants in dry places. – Another feature commonly shown by plants in dry places (e.g., heaths) is the **uniform level** to which they grow. In this way, the plants protect one another. Shoots which project above the general level usually die owing to excessive transpiration. The growth of all such plants generally goes on very slowly.

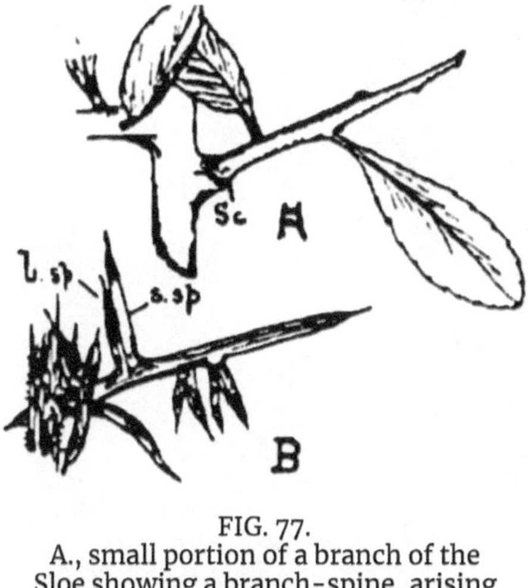

FIG. 77.
A., small portion of a branch of the Sloe showing a branch-spine, arising in the axil of a leaf-scar (sc.) and bearing two leaves: B, small portion of a branch of the Gorse showing both leaf- (l.sp.) and stem-spines (s.sp.).

Summary. – Plants, which get little water from the soil, reduce the rate of transpiration by (1) a thick surface-skin, (2) hairs, (3) the formation of small leaves, (4) rolling of the leaves, (5) low growth. Such plants often store up water and thus become succulent. The leaves or branches are frequently changed into spines.

PRACTICAL WORK

1. Examine as many of the following plants as you can obtain, and determine the method of reducing transpiration: Heather, Broom, Bilberry, Horse-tail Fern, Needle Furze, Marram Grass, Stonecrop, Saltwort, Sheep's Fescue, and Holly.

2. Examine, with a magnifying glass, the hairs on the leaves of the following: Mullein, Cudweed, Garden Stock, Mugwort, Sea Buckthorn, Mouse-ear Chickweed. Find out whether the hairs are simple or branched.

3. Compare, by means of cobalt-paper, the rates of transpiration of the Laurel, the Hazel, and the Mullein.

4. Draw the prickly outgrowths of the following plants and determine whether they are leaf-spines, stem-spines, or prickles: Sloe, Bramble, False Acacia, Spiny Rest-harrow, Barberry.

QUESTIONS

1. Describe briefly the various devices which enable plants to grow in dry situations.

2. Sketch and briefly describe a branch from a Gorse bush, explaining the nature of the spines. How do the spines of this plant differ from the thorns of a Bramble?

3. Make a drawing of a branch of the Butcher's Broom. Label the different parts, giving your reasons for naming them as you do.

4. How would you compare the rates of transpiration in a hairy leaf, an evergreen leaf, and a deciduous leaf? State what results you would expect to get.

CHAPTER XXI

PLANTS THAT GROW IN WET PLACES

YOU have probably noticed that some plants, such as the Milkmaid, Marsh Marigold, and Rushes, are always found in wet places. Others, like the Water Lily, Water Buttercup, and Pondweeds, grow in or even under the water itself. These plants are called **aquatics**, whilst those which live in very wet soil are known as **marsh-plants.**

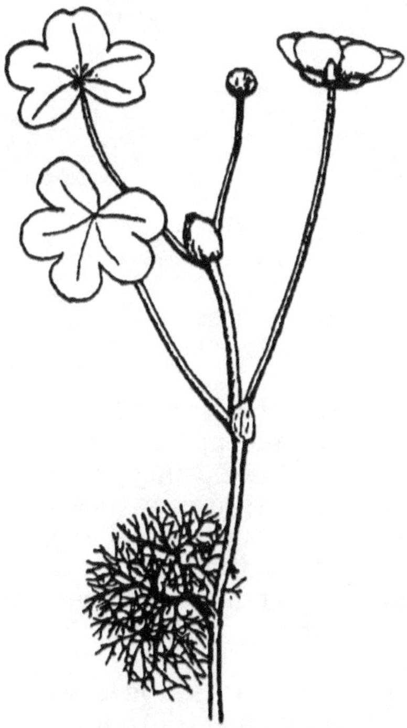

FIG. 78. - Portion of a plant of the Water Buttercup (about two-thirds the natural size), showing floating and submerged leaves.

Marsh-plants. – At the edges of streams and ponds, where the banks slope gently, there is generally a belt of marsh-plants. Here you will find such familiar flowers as the Marsh Forget-me-not, Brooklime, Water Mint, and Ragged Robin. Growing in the shallow water beyond are a great variety of plants, many of which are tall. The most striking are the Spearwort, Water Plantain, Iris, and various Grasses and Sedges. In all these, the blades of the leaves stand straight up, instead of spreading out like those of the ordinary land-plant.

Floating and submerged plants. – In the deeper water, you will find the aquatics, which are of two chief kinds. Some, like the Water Lily (Fig. 79) and the Water Buttercup (Fig. 78), have

FIG. 79.-White Water Lily growing amongst Reeds, Wicken Fen, Cambridge. The floating leaves and flowers of the former are seen.

leaves **floating** on the surface, in addition to those which are under the water. In others (Water Milfoil, Fig. 82), the **whole plant**, except the flowers, is **submerged**.

The leaves. – The leaves under the water are generally separated by long internodes, and are either very much **cut up** (Figs. 78 and 82) or else very thin (e.g., Canadian Pondweed). The **floating leaves** usually differ very much in form from the submerged ones. Thus, in the Water Buttercup (Fig. 78), they are reniform and have but a slightly cut margin. The submerged leaves, on the contrary, are divided up into a number of **thread-like segments**. In other cases, the floating leaves have a perfectly smooth margin (e.g., Water Lily, Fig. 79, Floating Pondweed).

The stems and roots. – Most of these aquatics have long white rhizomes which produce the slender shoots that trail out into the water. The rhizomes bear roots, but these are unbranched and not very numerous. As a matter of fact, their main purpose is to **fix the plant** in the mud. They are not required for the absorption of water, since this can pass through the thin skin all over the surface of the plant. Some aquatics, such as the Hornwort, have no roots and are not fixed in any way.

The breathing of water-plants. – If you cut across the petiole

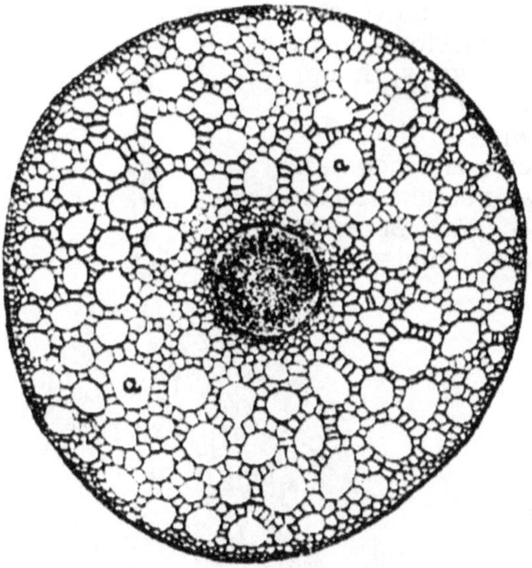

FIG. 80. - Stem of the Mare's Tail cut across to show the numerous air spaces (a.) (considerably enlarged).

of a Water Lily or the stem of the Bulrush or Mare's Tail (Fig. 80), you will find that the cut surface looks something like a honeycomb. This is because there are numerous **air-spaces** (Fig. 80, a.) which are of great importance to the water-plant. In the first place, the large quantity of air which they contain makes the plant light. Its shoots are thus able to **float upright** in the water, although the supporting skeleton is very weak.

When water-plants assimilate, the oxygen which is produced does not escape into the water, but collects in the air-spaces. The latter are therefore **storehouses for the oxygen** which is required for breathing. In studying the way in which plants feed, you performed an experiment (p. 87) in which you collected the bubbles of oxygen escaping from the air-spaces in the stem of the Canadian Pondweed (Fig. 61).

This saving up of oxygen is necessary because the air dissolved in the water contains **too little** of this gas for the needs of the plant. Water holds much more carbonic acid gas, so that assimilation goes on rapidly. The submerged parts of water-plants do not, however, have pores in the surface-skin, like those through which the air enters in land-plants. As a result, even the carbonic acid gas is absorbed rather slowly, although the deep division of the leaves creates a **very large surface** through which it can be taken up.

Growth of aquatics. – Everything is generally favorable for the rapid growth of water-plants. There is no lack of water and mineral salts, and the temperature is fairly uniform. Moreover, you have seen that the structure of the aquatic is such as to lessen most of the disadvantages of life in water. Many aquatics **grow so quickly** that they sometimes choke up streams and canals. Fragments, which break off, readily take root and grow into new plants, so that there is abundant **vegetative reproduction**. In a mild winter, many water-plants continue to grow, though more slowly than in summer.

Land-forms. – Owing to their thin leaves, the absence of pores, and their weak skeleton, water-plants are not suited for life on dry land. Sometimes the Water Buttercup and the Water Starwort are found growing

FIG. 81. — Water-form (W) and Land-form (L) of the Water Starwort (natural size).

FIG. 82. — Portion of a plant of the Water Milfoil, showing the inflorescence which is supported by the parachute-like group of leaves just below (about the natural size).

on the damp mud round the edges of ponds, but they are then very small (Fig. 81).

Flowering. – In most cases, the flowers of aquatics open **above the surface** of the water, for instance, those of the Water Buttercup (Fig. 78) and the Water Milfoil (Fig. 82). There are a few water-plants, like the Hornwort, in which even the flowers are submerged. The **seeds** of aquatics, unlike those of land-plants, are not harmed by water, and often float for a long time before they sink.

Free-floating aquatics. – A large amount of the light which falls on the surface of a pond or river is **reflected**, so that only part reaches the submerged plant. As the water gets deeper, the light near the bottom becomes weaker. In the deepest water, there is **very little light**, and only very few plants live there. Where the water begins to get deeper, we find fewer plants sending their leaves into the air. Here are plants that are not attached at all, but **float freely** on the surface of the water. Good examples are furnished by the Duckweeds, in the commonest of which the plant consists merely of a small oval

FIG. 83. - Plant of the Common Duckweed, showing the hanging roots. Above, a plant seen from the upper surface (somewhat enlarged).

green plate, with a slender root dangling down from the underside (Fig. 83).

Summary. – The plants of wet places can be divided into (1) marsh-plants, (2) plants growing in the water, but with most of their leaves in the air, (3) those which have floating leaves, (4) those which are free-floating, and (5) those which are completely submerged. The aquatic plant has numerous air-spaces which contain oxygen for breathing and give it buoyancy. The submerged leaves are thin or deeply divided. The roots serve only for attachment. The flowers are generally produced above the surface. Vegetative reproduction is extremely common.

PRACTICAL WORK

1. Examine the Water Buttercup, Arrowhead, Canadian Pondweed, Starwort, Water Milfoil, Water Lily, and Duckweed. Make drawings of the leaves of each plant and label them as submerged or floating. In the Starwort, compare the length of the internodes in the submerged and floating parts of the stem.

2. Cut across the stem of the Reed and that of the Floating Pondweed, and note the air-spaces.

3. Cut a stem of the Canadian Pondweed into short lengths and place these in water, with a little soil at the bottom. Note how each grows into a new plant.

4. Compare the Land- and Water-forms of the Starwort and Water Buttercup.

QUESTIONS

1. Compare the Water Buttercup with an ordinary Field Buttercup, and point out how the differences between the two are related to the conditions in which each lives.

2. Describe three examples of water-plants, pointing out those features which fit each for its life in the water.

3. Water-plants always contain a large number of cavities. What purposes do these fulfill? Mention any experiment in support of your statements.

CHAPTER XXII

THE FLOWERING PARTS OF PLANTS

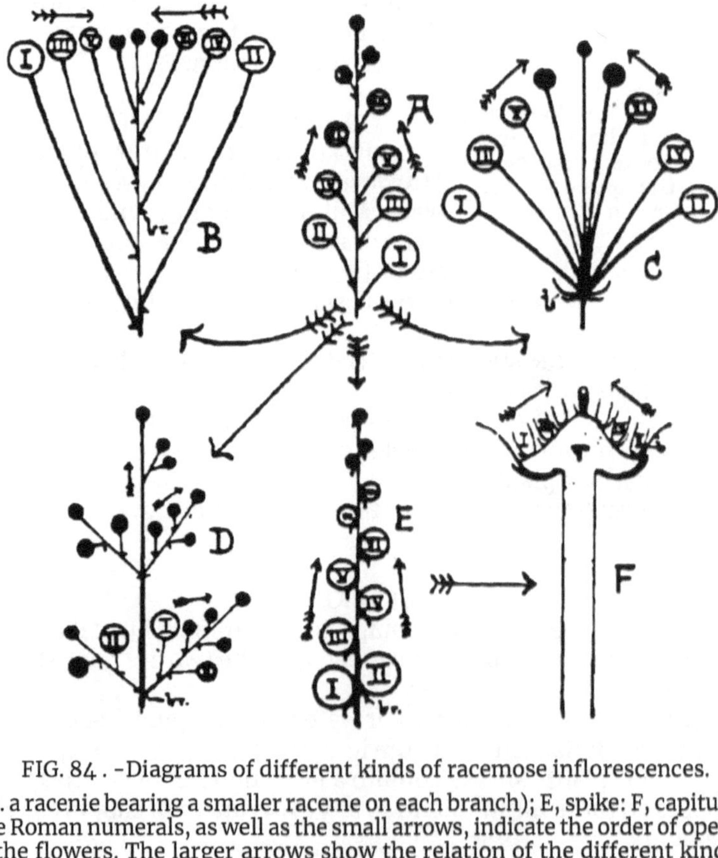

FIG. 84 . -Diagrams of different kinds of racemose inflorescences.

(i.e. a racenie bearing a smaller raceme on each branch); E, spike: F, capitulum. The Roman numerals, as well as the small arrows, indicate the order of opening of the flowers. The larger arrows show the relation of the different kinds of inflorescences to one another. br., bracts; i., involucre; r., receptacle of the capitulum.

Racemose inflorescences. – The flowers of the Shepherd's Purse and of the Wallflower are collected together towards the ends of the branches. Such groups of flowers you have learnt to call an **inflorescence** (Fig. 1, fl.). As the flowers of these two plants ripen into fruits, the main stalk or **axis** of the inflorescence (Fig. 1, a.i.), lengthens. It is then evident that the oldest flowers are towards the base and the youngest at the top. The flowers thus open in a definite order, **from below upwards**, and this is the distinguishing feature of what is called a **racemose** inflorescence (see also Fig. 84, A).

FIG. 85. - Inflorescence of the Candytaft (natural size). showing the enlarged marginal outer flowers often have larger petals flowers.

A, simple raceme; B, corymb; C, simple umbel; D, compound raceme Other examples of such racemes are seen in the Currant, Lupine, and Germander Speedwell. Here the young flowers are not crowded as in the Wallflower, and the axis scarcely lengthens after pollination. In these three plants, and indeed in many others, the flowers arise in the axils of small scale-like leaves termed bracts (Fig. 84, A). Sometimes the flower-stalk or peduncle itself bears minute leaves or bracteoles, as in the Violet.

The corymb. - In the Candytuft (Fig. 85) the lower flowers have longer stalks than the upper ones, so that all the flowers lie at about the same level. This kind of raceme is called a **corymb** (Fig. 84, B). In this inflorescence the outer flowers often have larger petals than the inner ones (Fig. 85).

The simple and compound umbel. - In the Cowslip and the Cherry, all the flowers arise close together from the top of the stem. Their bracts form a ring or **involucre** around the bases of the peduncles. A raceme of this kind is termed a **simple umbel** (Fig. 84, C). More commonly, as in the Hogweed and Carrot, the top of the flower-bearing stem forms several branches, each of which produces a small umbel at its tip. We therefore have an umbel of umbels or a **compound umbel**. Here too the outermost flowers often have enlarged petals. An involucre is often present, not only around the base of the smaller umbels, but also around that of the whole umbel.

The spike. - The flowers of the Plantain or Ribwort and of the Pondweeds (Fig. 86) are not stalked, and such a raceme of sessile flowers is called a spike (Fig. 84, E).

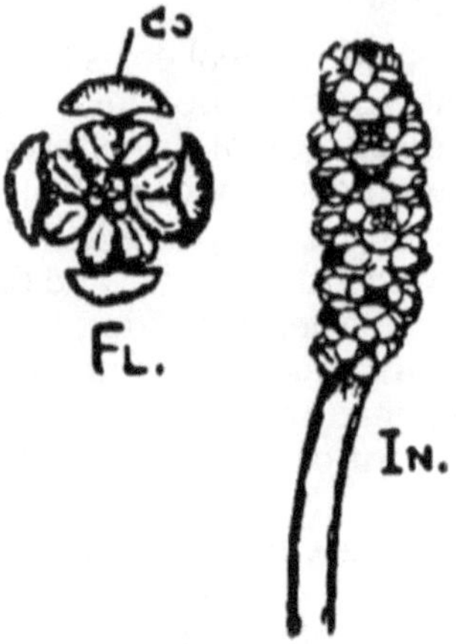

FIG. 86. - Flower (FL) and inflorescence (In.) of the Floating Pondweed (the flower enlarged, the inflorescence natural size): co., an enlargement of the part of the stamen joining the two anther-lobes (connective).

The capitulum. - A peculiar kind of racemose inflorescence, called a **capitulum**, is found in the Sunflower and Daisy. Here numerous small sessile **flowers** are borne on the much-enlarged and flattened end of the inflorescence-stalk (Fig. 84, F, r.). The flowers are of **two kinds**, tiny yellow ones in the middle and larger ones, with curious petal-shaped corollas, at the edge. The outer flowers thus show the same enlargement as in the umbel and corymb. Outside the whole group of flowers is an **involucre** (Fig. 84, F, i.) of dark green bracts. In the Sunflower, where the parts of the capitulum are much larger, it is evident that the outer flowers **open first**, whilst those in the middle are still in bud.

Cymose inflorescences. - In the Buttercup, the **first** flower to open is that situated **at the end** of the main axis of the inflorescence (Fig. 87, A, I.). The next flower that opens is borne at the end of a side-branch (Fig. 87, A, II.). This branch may in its turn bear a third flower which opens still later (Fig. 87, A, III.). In this case, therefore, the **oldest flower is at the top** of the main axis, whereas in a racemose inflorescence it is at the bottom. The inflorescence of the Buttercup is an example of what is called a **cymose** inflorescence. Other instances of the same kind are seen in the Poppy (Fig. 88) and the Herb Bennett.

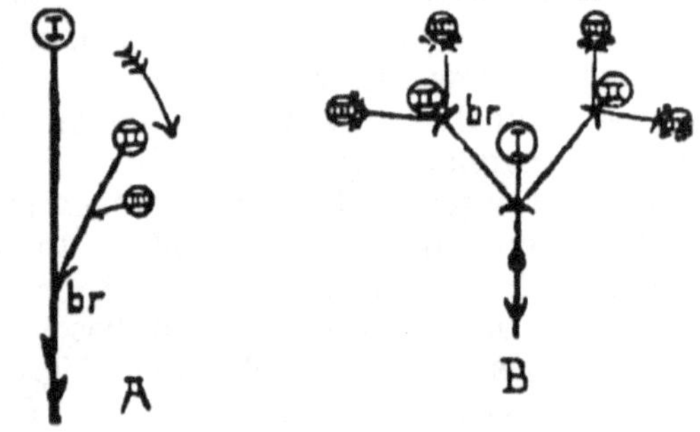

FIG. 87. - Diagrams of cymose inflorescences. A, simple cyme. B, dichasial cyme. The Roman numerals and the arrow in A indicate the order of opening of the flowers; br., bracts.

When a plant has opposite leaves (e.g. Campion), the first flower of the cymose inflorescence is, as before, formed at the end of the main axis (Fig. 87, B, I.). Then, however, the **two** flowers which end the pair of branches, arising just below the first flower, open at

FIG. 88. - Cymose inflorescence of the Poppy (about one-half the natural size). The end of the main axis bears a fruit (d), whilst the flowers at the ends of the side branches lower down are still in bud (a and b): c shows an open flower from behind.

the same time (Fig. 87, B, II.). After this pair of flowers has opened, a new pair comes into bloom below each (Fig. 87, B, III.). In this kind of cymose inflorescence (known as a **dichasial** cyme) the **oldest** flowers are plainly **in the centre**, and the youngest towards the outside. This is just the reverse of what is found in a racemose inflorescence.

The position of the flowers. - The flowers of an inflorescence are always placed in a **definite position** towards the main axis. The side of the flower that is next to the axis is called the **posterior** side, whilst that which is away from it and towards the bract is the **anterior** side. Thus, in the Flowering Currant, one of the five sepals faces towards the axis, whereas the bract lies opposite the gap between the two front sepals. In the Wallflower there are no bracts, but you can still distinguish that two of the sepals lie at the sides of the flower, whilst the other two are placed at the front and back.

Summary. - There are two main kinds of inflorescences, namely the racemose, in which the order of opening is from below upwards, and the cymose, in which the flower at the end of the main axis is the first to open. Racemose inflorescences are either racemes, corymbs, umbels, spikes, or capitula, whilst cymose inflorescences are either simple or dichasial. Each flower occupies a definite position, so that we can distinguish a posterior side towards the axis, and anterior one away from it.

PRACTICAL WORK

1. Look at a number of inflorescences, such as those of the Plantain, Chickweed, Dandelion, Stock, Jack-by-the-Hedge, Snapdragon, Beaked Parsley, Mignonette, etc. Determine the nature of the inflorescence in each case.

2. Make line-diagrams of two or more of these inflorescences to show the order of flowering and indicate the position of the bracts.

3. Pull off the outer petal-shaped flowers from all the capitula of a Sunflower or Marguerite plant. Compare the number of insects visiting this plant with the number visiting another of the same kind, that has not been so treated.

QUESTIONS

1. Make diagrams of the inflorescences of (a) the Currant or Lupine, and (b) the Buttercup or Pink. Show by numbers the order of opening of the flowers, and explain the difference between the inflorescences of the two plants you select.

2. Describe carefully, with diagrams, the inflorescence of the Dog Daisy or Marguerite. Why is it called a racemose inflorescence?

3. What do you understand by the terms bract, posterior, axis of inflorescence, peduncle, corymb, involucre?

CHAPTER XXIII

MORE ABOUT FLOWERS

The perianth. - Flowers differ amongst one another in numerous respects. The complete flower of a Dicotyledon consists, as in the Wallflower, of calyx, corolla, stamens, and ovary. In some Dicotyledons, however, the flowers have **only one set** of floral leaves, all of which are coloured alike. Examples are the Marsh Marigold and Winter Aconite (Fig. 113, p. 138), where they are brightly coloured, and the Hellebore, where they are green. In these cases, in which it is impossible to distinguish a calyx and corolla, the floral leaves are collectively called the **perianth**.

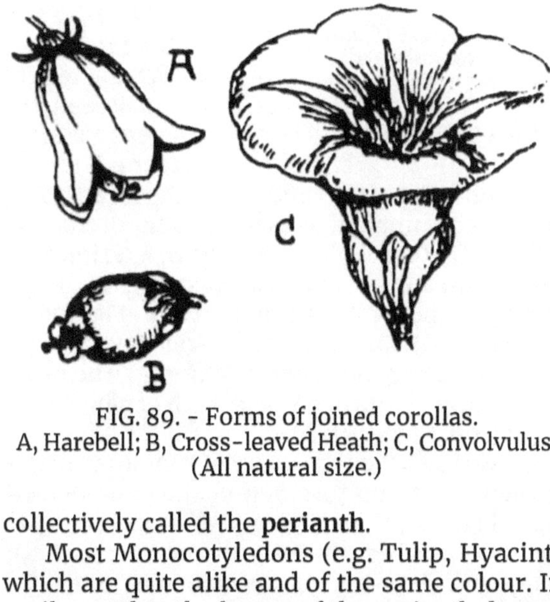

FIG. 89. - Forms of joined corollas.
A, Harebell; B, Cross-leaved Heath; C, Convolvulus.
(All natural size.)

Most Monocotyledons (e.g. Tulip, Hyacinth) have floral leaves which are quite alike and of the same colour. In this group, you can easily see that the leaves of the perianth do not all arise **at the same level**. For instance, in the Tulip, they are arranged in two sets or **whorls** which alternate with one another.

The calyx and corolla. - In many Dicotyledons, such as the Wallflower (Fig. 116, p. 141), Geranium, and Stitchwort (Fig. 120, B, p. 144), the corolla, as well as the calyx, each consist of four or five **separate** floral leaves. But quite commonly all the sepals are **joined** so as to form a tube (Fig. 120, A). In many flowers the petals are united in the same way (Fig. 89). This is quite clear in the Primrose and Convolvulus (Fig. 89, C). In such flowers, you can tell how many sepals or petals are

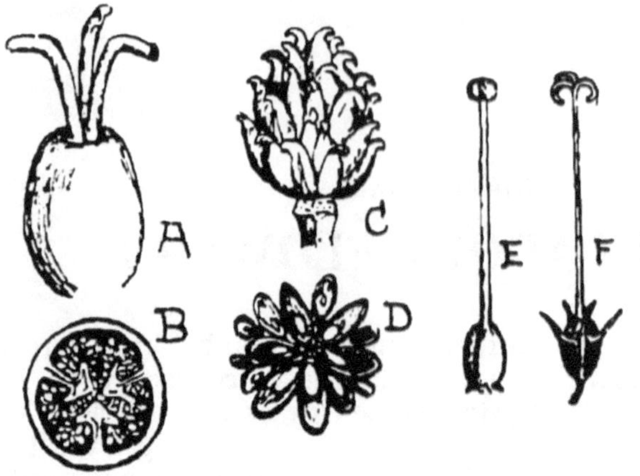

FIG. 90. - Ovaries and their structure (E and F natural size, the other figures enlarged).
A, Ovary of the St. John's Wort; B, The same cut across; C. Ovary of the Buttercup; D, The same cut across; E, Ovary of the Foxglove; F. Ovary of the Canterbury Bell.

present by counting the number of teeth on the calyx or the number of lobes on the corolla.

The stamens. - There are often as many, or twice as many, stamens as there are petals. Thus in the Primrose there are 5, in the Willow-herb 8 (Fig. 94), and in the Stitchwort 10. When the petals are joined, the stamens are often attached to the inner side of the corolla-tube (Fig. 93, A) and not to the receptacle.

The ovary. - Many of our common flowers have a **single** structure in the centre forming the ovary (e.g. Wallflower, Fig. 8, A, Primrose). Its top is often drawn out into a long stalk, the **style** (Fig. 90, E and F), bearing the **stigmas** at its end, although in the Tulip (Fig. 106, p. 130) and the Wallflower (Fig. 8, B), for instance, the style is very short. In other flowers, like the Buttercup and Marsh Marigold, the ovary consists of a number of **separate** parts or **carpels**, each of which ends in a stigma of its own (Fig. 90, C, Fig. 91, A).

The structure of the ovary. - When the ovary of a Violet or Primrose is cut across, it is seen to have only a single chamber or **loculus**. That of the Snapdragon (Fig. 140, D, p. 163) or Wallflower (Fig. ,D), on the other hand, has two chambers. In the Tulip or Narcissus the ovary contains three, in the Willow-herb or Fuchsia four, and in the Mallow or Hollyhock many chambers.

When the ovary has more than one loculus, each is generally **formed from a single carpel**. So that the ovary always consists of carpels which, like the sepals and petals, may **either be separate** (e.g. Buttercup, Fig. 90, C), **or joined** together. In the latter case, the number of loculi usually shows the number of carpels composing the ovary.

When there is only a single chamber, the ovary may actually consist of but one carpel; this is the case in the Pea and Bean. But a one-chambered ovary may also be f**ormed of several joined carpels,** as for instance in the Campion and Pink. Here you can tell the number of car-

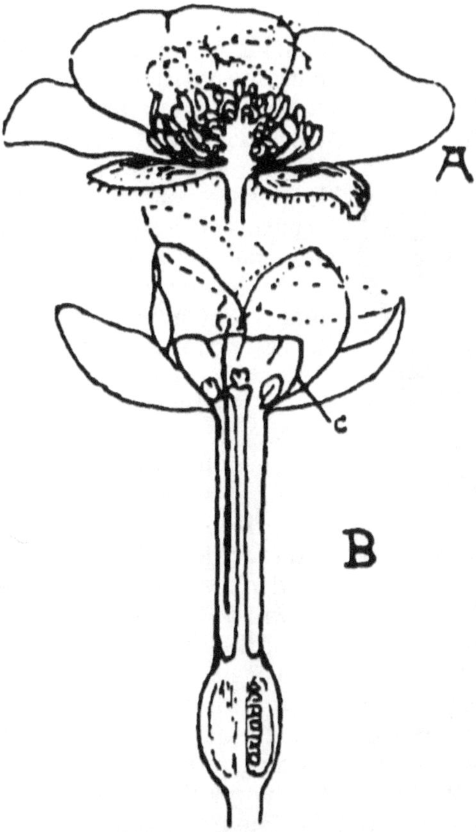

FIG. 91. - Sections cut lengthwise through the flowers of A, a Buttercup (open flower), and B, the Pheasant's eye Narcissus (tubular flower), showing a superior and inferior ovary respectively. The body of a pollinating insect is shown by dotted lines, its tongue being indicated by a continuous line. c., outgrowth (corona) of the corolla.

pels by counting the styles at the top of the ovary. In the Campion, there are five, and in the Pink, two. In the St. John's Wort, the three styles at the top (Fig. 90, A) show that there are three carpels in the ovary.

Very often, even the styles are joined together, but then the number of separate stigmas or lobes to the stigma is generally the same as the number of carpels (e.g., the Wallflower, Fig. 8, B, and the Canterbury Bell, Fig. 90, F).

Within the ovary, there are always one or more ovules, which are frequently present in very large numbers (Fig. 90, B). They are not arranged irregularly, but, as you will learn, are attached to **definite points**, either on the ovary wall or on the partitions between the loculi.

Superior and inferior ovaries. - In most of the flowers mentioned, the sepals, petals, and stamens are borne on the stalk below the ovary (Fig. 91, A), so that the latter can only be seen by looking **into** the flower. In the Narcissus (Fig. 91, B) or Apple, however, the petals and stamens arise from the top of the ovary, which forms a swelling **below** the flower. In this case, the ovary is said to be **inferior**, whilst where it arises **above** the other parts of the flower, it is described as **superior**.

The floral diagram. - The best way of representing the structure of a flower is to make a plan, called a **floral diagram**, like that shown in Fig. 92. First, five concentric circles are drawn with a pair

FIG. 92. - Floral diagram of the Herb Robert. Description in the text. a., axis of inflorescence; b., bract; P., petal S., sepal.

of compasses. Near the outermost circle, a dot (a.) is put to mark the position of the main axis of the inflorescence from which the flower arises. Next, on the outermost circle, mark the position of the sepals (s.) by means of heavy lines, taking care that the posterior sepal or sepals are put in correctly, **nearest the axis**. In the Herb Robert and most Dicotyledons, for instance, you will find that **one** of the five sepals is **posterior**. The five petals (p.) are shown in the same way, **alternating** with the sepals, on the next circle. If the sepals or petals are joined, this is indicated in the diagram in the way shown in Fig. 138 (p. 162).

Of the ten stamens of the Herb Robert, the **outer** five stand opposite the petals, and the **inner** five opposite the sepals. These are indicated in the floral diagram in their correct positions on the next two circles, as in Fig. 92. Within the last circle, draw a plan of the ovary, as it appears when cut across. In doing this, you will notice that the five chambers are **opposite** the petals. The bract (b.), in whose axil the whole flower arises, is shown by a heavy line on the side away from the axis.

Insects and flowers. - You have already learned that insects play an important part in the pollination of flowers (p. 14-15). One of the chief means of attracting insects is the **honey**. This is usually produced near the base of the flower, often in special structures called **nectaries**. When the flower has free petals (as in the Buttercup and Stitchwort), the corolla generally forms an **open cup** (Fig. 91, A). Almost any insect visiting such a flower, even if it has a very **short tongue**, can reach the honey.

When the petals are joined, the lower part of the corolla often forms a **long tube**, at the top of which the lobes spread out (Fig. 91, B). Insects are unable to enter the tube and can only suck honey from their position on the spreading part of the corolla, which serves as an alighting platform (Fig. 91, B). As a consequence, it is only insects that have **long tongues** (e.g., Bees, Butterflies) that

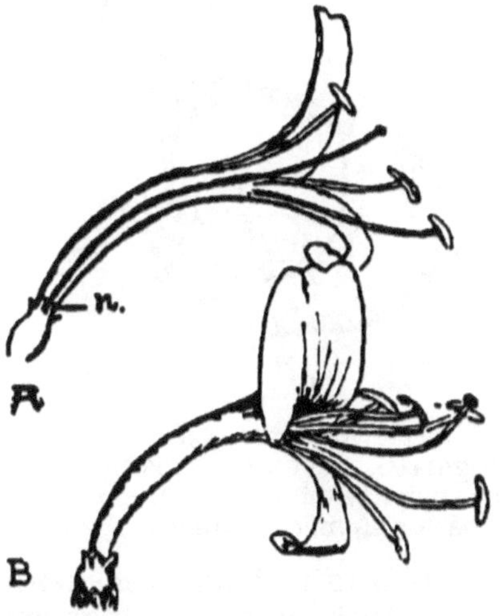

FIG. 93. — Irregular flowers of the Honeysuckle. A, cut through lengthwise; B, entire flower seen from the side; n, nectary. (Both figures natural size.)

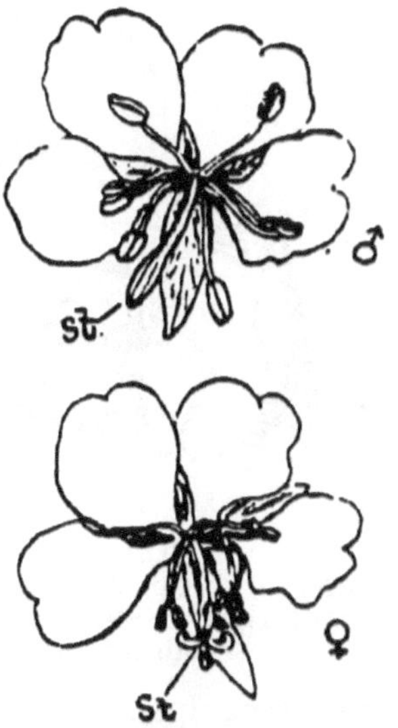

FIG. 94. — Two flowers of the Rose-bay Willow-herb. (Natural size.) In the upper, the stamens are alone ripe, the four lobes of the stigma being closely pressed together. In the lower, the stamens have withered, whilst the lobes of the stigma have spread out. st., stigma.

can reach the honey. The Primrose and the Wallflower (Fig. 116, p. 141) are good examples of such **tubular** flowers.

Regular and irregular flowers. - If a flower of the Buttercup or Tulip is halved lengthwise, by cutting through the middle of **any one of the floral leaves**, the two halves will be quite alike. Such a flower is therefore symmetrical all round, and is said to be **regular**. Flowers like the Dead-nettle and the Honeysuckle (Fig. 93), on the other hand, owing to the shape of their corolla, can be cut lengthwise into two equal halves only **in one direction**, namely, from the posterior to the anterior side. In these **irregular** flowers, the number of stamens is often fewer than that of the petals.

In the case of a regular flower, an insect can alight and suck honey from every side, but in an irregular flower, it can **only alight in one way** if it is to obtain honey. Only a few kinds of insects with sufficient intelligence, like Bees, will therefore be able to visit such flowers with success.

Self- and cross-pollination. - In a few flowers, the stamens and

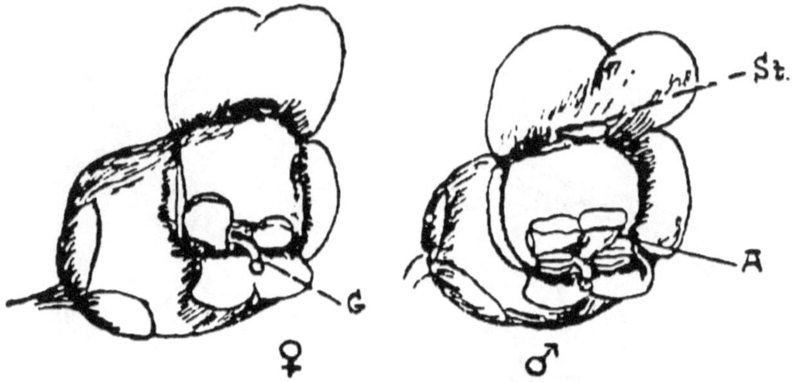

FIG. 95. - Two flowers of the Figwort (enlarged).
The left-hand flower shows the ripe stigma (G), but the stamens have not yet opened. The right-hand one shows the stigma withered, but the stainens (A) shedding their pollen. St., a barren stamen (staminode).

the stigma ripen at almost the same time (e.g., White Dead-nettle). When this is the case, pollen may be carried by an insect to the stigma of the same flower; in other words, **self-pollination** may occur.

Usually, however, the stamens and the stigma **ripen at different times**. Thus, in the Willow-herb (Fig. 94) and the Canterbury Bell, the stamens begin to wither before the branches of the stigma spread out. On the other hand, in the Figwort (Fig. 95), the stigma ripens first. In all such cases, the stigma will usually receive pollen from stamens in another flower of the same kind; that is, **cross-pollination** takes place. This usually appears to lead to the production of more vigorous seeds than self-pollination.

Summary. - The floral leaves are either all alike and form a perianth or are distinguished as calyx and corolla. The whorls of sepals and petals are either free or joined. The ovary is composed of carpels, which are either separate or united into one structure. In the latter case, the ovary may be superior or inferior, may consist of one or many carpels, and may have one or many chambers. Flowers may be distinguished, according to the shape and arrangement of the floral leaves, into open or tubular, and regular or irregular. The stamens and stigma often ripen at different times, so that cross-pollination is the rule and self-pollination rather rare.

PRACTICAL WORK

1. Make floral diagrams of some of the following flowers: Wallflower, Primrose, Tulip, Convolvulus, Stitchwort, Crown Imperial, Potato, Poppy.

2. Take flowers of the Tulip, Buttercup, Narcissus, Hogweed, and

Fuchsia. Carefully halve each of them lengthwise, so that your section passes from the posterior to the anterior side of the flower, in other words, make a *longitudinal section.* Then represent in a drawing the form of the actual cut surfaces of each, but show none of the body of the flower behind (see Fig. 96). Your drawings should show the shapes of the floral receptacles and the way in which the different parts of the flowers arise from them. Note also whether the ovary is superior or inferior.

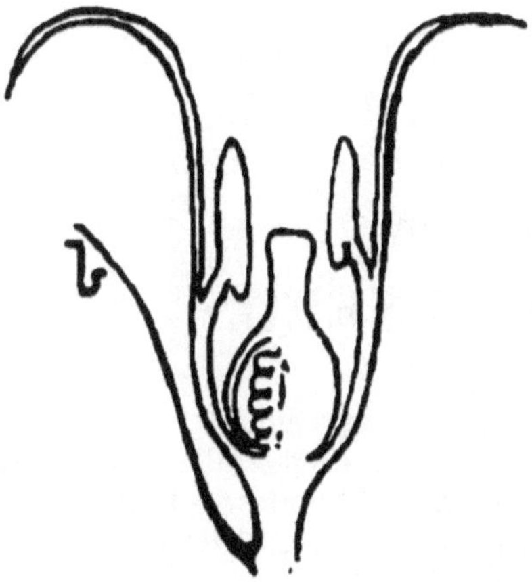

FIG. 96. - Drawing of a longirudinal section of the flower of the Hyacinth, to explain item (2) in the practical work.
b., bract.

3. On a bright sunny day, watch several regular and irregular flowers. Note the insect-visitors and how they settle on the flowers.

4. Examine flowers of the Campion, Canterbury Bell, Figwort, Plantain, and Foxglove. See whether stamens or stigma ripen first.

QUESTIONS

1. Illustrate by descriptions and drawings (a) an ovary composed of separate carpels, (b) a one-chambered ovary composed of a single carpel, (c) a one-chambered ovary composed of several carpels, and (d) a several-chambered ovary.

2. Draw from memory longitudinal sections of the flowers of (a) a Buttercup or Stitchwort, and (b) a Primrose *or* Narcissus. Explain, in each case, how the form of the flower affects the kind of insects visiting it.

3. In the flowers of many plants, the stamens ripen before the stigma. What is the significance of this fact? Give a brief account of the life of some flower which possesses this peculiarity.

4. What do you understand by the terms carpel, inferior, irregular, cross-pollination, loculus?

CHAPTER XXIV

FRUITS AND SEEDS

As a result of changes due to pollen having reached the stigma, the ovary ripens to form the **fruit** and the contained ovules develop into **seeds**. This you have already noticed in the Shepherd's Purse and the Wallflower. The other parts of the flower wither, although the sepals often remain as a **protection** for the fruit.

Dry and succulent fruits. - A little observation in the autumn shows that there are many different kinds of fruits. Some, like the Plum and the Blackberry, are fleshy or **succulent**, whilst others, like the Pea-pod and the fruit of the Shepherd's Purse, are hard and **dry**. If dry fruits contain several seeds, they split open when ripe to let the seeds escape, that is, they are **dehiscent**. But dry fruits containing only a single seed usually remain closed (e.g. the Hazelnut), that is, they are **indehiscent**. As a consequence, the seed is only freed **after the decay** of the fruit-wall. Nearly all succulent fruits are indehiscent.

Follicles and legumes. - Dehiscent fruits vary much in form and open in many different ways. In the Marsh Marigold, each of the separate carpels forming the ovary splits open when ripe, along **one** edge (see also Fig. 97, b). A fruit produced from a single carpel and splitting in this way is called a **follicle**. When a follicle, for instance that of the Monkshood, has dehisced (Fig. 97, b), it looks like a small **folded leaf**, with the seeds borne on the two split edges. As a matter of fact, the seeds, in nearly all fruits, are borne in this position **on the margins** of the carpels. The pod or **legume** of the Pea is also formed by a single carpel, but splits along **both** its edges (Fig. 97, c).

The siliqua. - When the pod-like fruit of the Wallflower (Fig. 9, A) is cut across, it shows two compartments, each with two rows of seeds (Fig. 8, D). Since, as you have just learnt, the seeds are borne along the margins of the carpels, the fruit of the Wallflower evidently consists of two carpels joined edge to edge. Such a fruit is called a siliqua. When ripe, it splits open along both its edges, from below upwards, exposing the thin partition to which the seeds remain attached (Fig. 97, d, Fig. 9, B).

Capsules. - The siliqua is merely a special kind of **capsule**, a term employed for all dehiscent fruits containing several seeds and com-

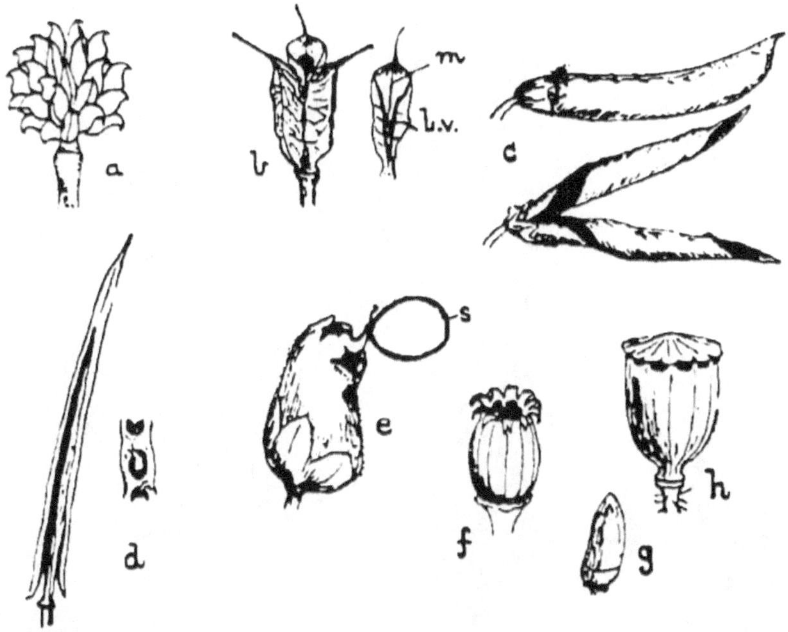

FIG. 97 - Examples of dry fruits (a somewhat enlarged, others slightly reduced). a. Buttercup (group of achenes) b. Monkshood (three follicles): m., midrib of carpel; l.u. lateral vein of same: c. Tare (legume) the lower figure shows the pod after dehiscence; d, Wallflower (siliqua), the right-hand figure shows a portion of the membrane to which the seeds are attached: i, Snapdragon (capsule opening by pores near the top): S., style; f. Campion (capsule opening by teeth) g. Plantain (capsule opening by a lid); h, Poppy (capsule opening by holes just beneath the top).

posed of **more than one carpel**. Later on, you will get to know several other kinds of capsules, but for the moment it will be enough to notice that the fruits of the Snapdragon (Fig. 97, e), the Campion (Fig. 97, f), and the Poppy (Fig. 97, h) **are** all varieties of capsules, opening in the different ways shown in the figures.

Fruits that split into one-seeded portions. - Some fruits in which each compartment contains but a single seed break up, when ripe, into **one-seeded** indehiscent **portions**. Thus, in the Garden Nasturtium (Fig. 98, E), the fruit splits into three, and in the Beaked Parsley (Fig. 98, A) into two pieces. In the Mallow (Fig. 98, C) and Hollyhock, it breaks up into a large number of one-seeded parts.

Dry indehiscent fruits. - There are two common kinds of dry indehiscent fruits, both usually one-seeded. These are the **achene**, in which the fruit-wall is thin but tough, and the **nut**, in which it is rather thick and woody. Achenes are formed by the Buttercup (Fig. 97, a),

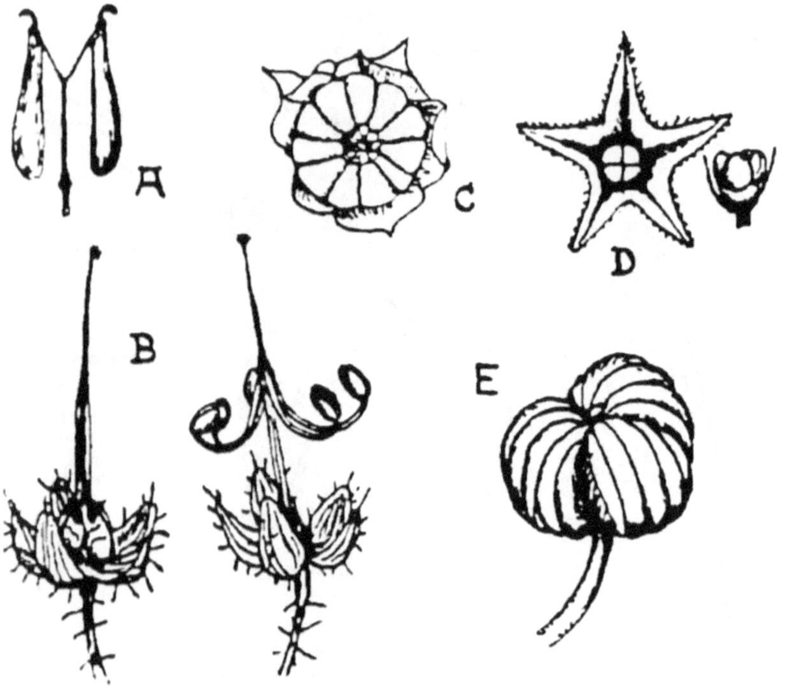

FIG. 98. - Fruits that split, when ripe, into one-seeded portions (A enlarged, other figures natural size).
A, Beaked Parsley; B, Crane's Bill, left-hand figure before, right-hand figure after, splitting into achenes: C: Mallow: D, White Dead-nettle, right-hand figure shows fruit, with calyx removed, in side-view; E, Garden Nasturtium.

where one is produced from each carpel of the ovary. The Hazel and the Acorn furnish good examples of nuts. Many fruits called "nuts" in everyday life are not nuts in the botanical sense.

Berries and drupes. - Most of the indehiscent fruits are fleshy, and are then classed either as berries or drupes. **Berries**, like those of the Gooseberry (Fig. 99, A-B), Tomato, and Bittersweet (Fig. 99, C-D), usually contain several seeds. These have a **hard** covering, formed by the **testa**, while the whole wall of the fruit is **fleshy**. The Date is a berry containing only one seed, whilst the Vegetable Marrow and Cucumber are huge berries of a peculiar kind.

Drupes generally contain only a single seed. This is enclosed in the "stone," which is the **hard** inner part of the **fruit-wall**. The most familiar drupes are the Plum, Apricot, and Cherry (Fig. 99, E-F). In the Blackberry (Fig. 99, G-H), each carpel of the ovary develops into a small drupe, so that the fruit consists of a **cluster of drupelets**. The

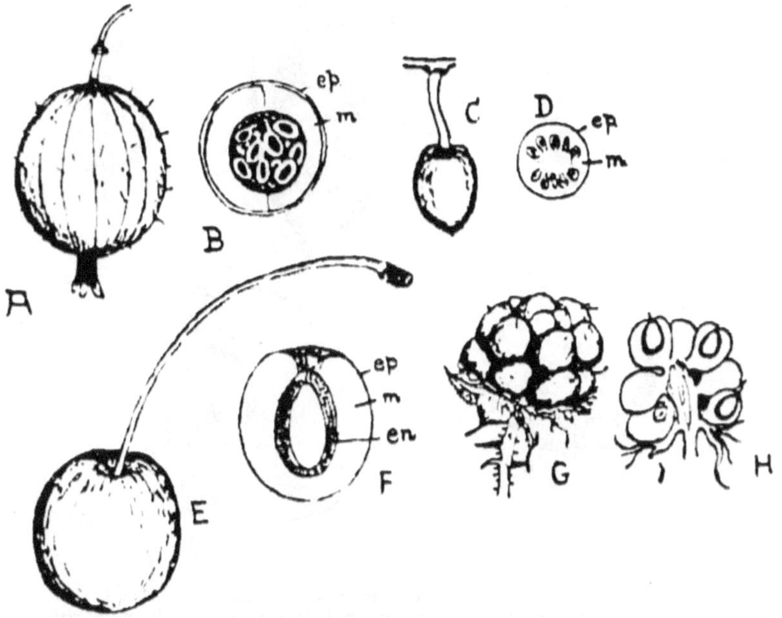

FIG. 99. - Examples of fleshy fruits (slightly reduced).
A B. Gooseberry, entire and cut across: C.D. Bittersweet (berry), entire and cut across E.F. Cherry (drupe). entire and cut through lengthwise; G-11, Blackberry (collection of drapes). entire and cut through lengthwise; PN, stony part of fruit-wall; ep, surface skin of fruit-wall: m fleshy part of fruit-wall.

Walnut and the Almond are drupes, from which the fleshy part of the fruit-wall is generally removed before they are placed on the market.

False fruits. - In some cases, the fleshy part of the fruit is formed not merely from the ovary-wall, but from the neighbouring parts of the flower as well. In this case, the fruit is said to be **false**. Thus, in the Strawberry, the floral receptacle (p. 16) enlarges very much in the fruit and forms the edible part. The pips borne on its surface are the true fruits (achenes, Fig. 100, D,a.).

In the Mulberry (Fig. 100, A), the so-called fruit is formed from an **entire inflorescence**. It consists of a number of achenes, each enclosed in four fleshy structures. These, before ripening, formed the floral leaves (Fig. 100, A, p). The fruit of the Fig likewise consists of a whole inflorescence, but here the true fruits line the hollow inside.

How to distinguish fruits and seeds. - One-seeded indehiscent fruits must be carefully distinguished from true seeds. In such fruits, there is a **second envelope** (the fruit-wall) outside the seed-coat. The simplest way of distinguishing seeds and fruits is by examining the scars. A seed has but **one scar** (the hilum, p. 54), where it was attached

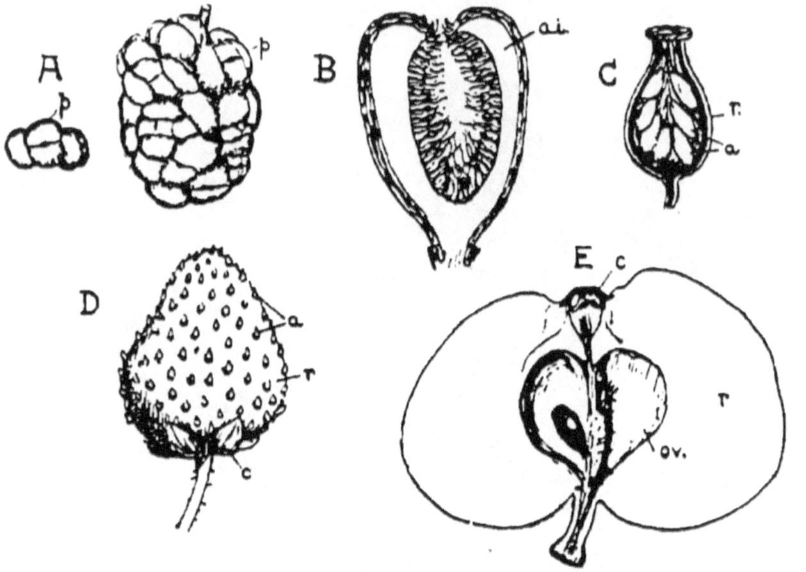

FIG. 100. - Examples of false fruits (slightly reduced).
A, Mulberry, a single fruit is shown on the left: t. the floral leaves around the fruit: B, Fig cut through lengthwise: a.i., the axis of the inflorescence: C, Hip of the Rose (p. 156) cut through lengthwise: D, Strawberry; E, Apple (p. 156) cut through lengthwise. a., achenes; c., calyx; ov., ovary: r., receptacle of flower.

to the fruit-wall. A fruit, on the other hand, has **two scars**, the one where it was attached to the flower-stalk, and the other marking the position of the stigma. The latter may, however, have shriveled without dropping off.

The Maize and other Grasses have a one-seeded fruit (achene), in which the fruit-wall and testa are so **closely joined** together that they cannot be separated in the ripe condition. The fruit of the Sunflower shows a similar structure.

Summary. - Fruits can be classed as dehiscent and indehiscent, as dry and succulent. The chief kinds of dehiscent fruits are the follicle, legume, siliqua, and capsule. Indehiscent fruits, when dry, are usually either achenes or nuts. In some cases, fruits split up into one-seeded indehiscent portions (Hollyhock). Soft fruits are either berries, with a hard testa and a fleshy fruit-wall, or drupes, in which the inner part of the fruit-wall is stony and the outer part fleshy. False fruits are those in which other parts of the flower, in addition to the ovary, contribute to the formation of the "fruit." In the Mulberry and Fig, the whole inflorescence becomes fleshy.

PRACTICAL WORK

1. Examine fruits of the following plants: Poppy, Foxglove, Cress, Shepherd's Purse, Chickweed, Vetch, Crane's Bill, Shepherd's Needle, Pimpernel. Make out the way in which the seeds are liberated, and state to what class the fruits belong.

2. Examine the so-called "seeds" of the following: Maize or Wheat, Broad Beans, Sunflower, Acorn, Hazel-nut, Avens, Marrow. State in each case whether the structures are really seeds or fruits, giving your reasons.

3. Examine fruits of the following plants: Cherry, Sloe, Apple, Grape, Rose, Currant, Raspberry, Tomato, and Greengage. Determine in each case (a) whether the fruit is a true or false one, and (b) in the former case, whether it is a berry or drupe.

QUESTIONS

1. Describe the form of the fruit, and the way in which the seeds are liberated, in any *five* of the following: Pimpernel, Holly, Blackberry, Hogweed, Damson, Campion, Honesty, Marsh Marigold, Lesser Celandine. Illustrate your answer by drawings.

2. Distinguish carefully between the fruit and the seed of a plant. Illustrate your answer by a description of a plum.

3. Describe carefully what happens as a result of pollination to the flowers of the Wallflower, Strawberry, and Mulberry.

CHAPTER XXV

HOW FRUITS AND SEEDS ARE SCATTERED

Why dispersal is necessary. - Plants of the same kind require the **same** sort of food. If they grow close together, they will therefore **interfere with one another**, and few, if any, will grow vigorously. On the other hand, different kinds of plants can often grow side by side without harm to one another (see item (1) of Practical Work), because they require different food and have root-systems reaching to different depths. If, therefore, the seeds of a plant are **widely scattered**, they will be much more likely to grow into robust plants than if they come to lie close together. It is thus very important, not only that seeds should be carried far away from the parent, but also that they should be widely separated from one another. Hence the necessity for a good means of **dispersal**.

It is plain that in **vegetative reproduction** (p. 48), the offspring usually develop **close to the parent**, and may compete with it and with one another. Plants reproducing mainly by seeds do not usually suffer from this disadvantage.

In Flowering Plants possessing dehiscent fruits, the latter remain attached to the parent-plant. The seeds, which are generally numerous, get scattered in different directions. Indehiscent fruits, except berries, usually contain only one seed, and here the fruit falls off as a whole. The contained seed, in the case of dry fruits, only becomes free by the gradual **decay** of the fruit-wall or by its being burst open during germination.

Indehiscent fruits and the seeds of dehiscent fruits get scattered in various ways. Most commonly, they are carried away **by the wind**. The small seeds of a large number of plants (e.g. Foxglove), owing to their powdery character, are easily blown some distance by gusts of wind. But in other cases, the seeds or fruits, as the case may be, are provided with special outgrowths that **serve to make them light**.

Winged fruits and seeds. - Many dry indehiscent fruits are constructed so that they readily float on the breeze for some time. In the Ash (Fig. 101, A) and the Elm, for instance, the fruits are provided

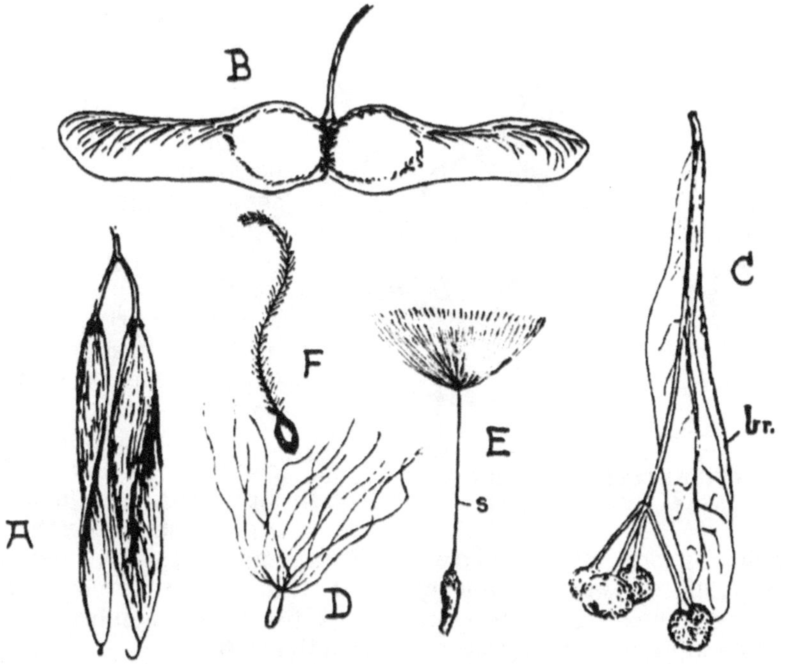

FIG. 101. - Winged and plumed fruits and seeds (all natural size). A, Ash (winged achenes); B, Sycamore (fruit splitting into two winged achenes): C, Lime; the wing here is formed by a bract (br.). which is joined to part of the inflorescence stalk; L', plumed seed of the Willow-herb; E, Dandelion (achene with a pappus arising from the top); S., a stalk that develops between the fruit and the pappus; F, Old Man's Beard or Clematis (achene with a feathery style).

with a broad wing. Those of the Maple and Sycamore (Fig. 101, B), when ripe, split into two one-seeded portions, each with a wing. **Winged seeds** are more rare, but are found in the Honesty, the Field Spurrey (Fig. 102, B), and the Scotch Fir (Fig. 102, A).

Plumed fruits and seeds. - Many seeds and fruits are made light, in proportion to their size, by **hairs** which arise from the fruit-wall or the seed-coat. A well-known example is the parachute-like tuft of hairs (or **pappus**) at the top of the fruit of the Dandelion (Fig. 101, E) or Thistle. Another kind of **plumed fruit** is found in the Old Man's Beard (Fig. 101, F). Here the style grows out into a long feathery structure as the fruit ripens. In the Poplar and Willow-herb, the seeds are plumed and become blown out of the capsules after they have split open.

Dispersal of fleshy fruits. - Fleshy fruits are generally distributed **by animals**. Birds are attracted by the bright colours and the

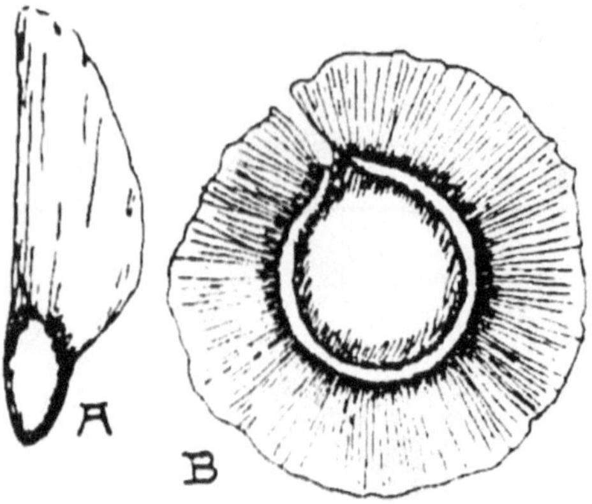

FIG. 102. - Winged seeds.
A, of the Scotch Fir (about twice the natural size); B, of the Spurrey (very much enlarged).

prospect of feeding on the soft parts. Sometimes, they simply peck at the fruits, but then the seeds commonly stick to their beaks, and so get carried some little distance away before being rubbed off (Mistletoe). Larger fruits, like the Cherry and Plum, are frequently **carried off bodily** to some place where the bird can eat the flesh in comfort.

The small seeds of berries are often **swallowed** with the fruit, and, after passing through the animal's body, get deposited with its droppings. In this way, the seeds may fall to the ground some miles away from the parent-plant. The hard envelope around the seed protects the contained embryo from being injured by the digestive juices of the animal.

Burr-fruits. - Fruits may, however, be distributed by animals in another way. In this case, the fruits bear **small hooks** which catch onto the hairy body of passing animals, and thus get carried long distances away from the parent-plant. For example, in the Herb Bennett (Fig. 103, D), each of the achenes ends in a long claw formed from the style. Other instances are furnished by the fruits of the Goosegrass and Enchanter's Nightshade (Fig. 103, B), in which the whole surface is covered with small hook-like hairs.

Explosive fruits. - As the legumes of the Gorse ripen and dry, the fruit-wall contracts unequally. In this way, a tension is set up, so that the slightest touch causes the fruits to open **with great vigour**. The parts of the fruit-wall curl up suddenly, and the contained seeds are shot out with some force. Similar **explosive fruits** are found in the Touch-me-not, whose name is due to this characteristic of the fruits.

Dispersal by water. - Apart from wind and animals, water may also serve to distribute fruits and seeds. This is particularly the case in those plants which grow at the water's edge.

Summary. - The scattering of fruits and seeds is necessary so that there should not be competition between the offspring. This dispersal is effected by wind, animals, or water. Wind-distributed fruits and seeds are usually very small or possess wings or plumes. Those which are distributed by animals are either soft and edible or dry and possess hooks.

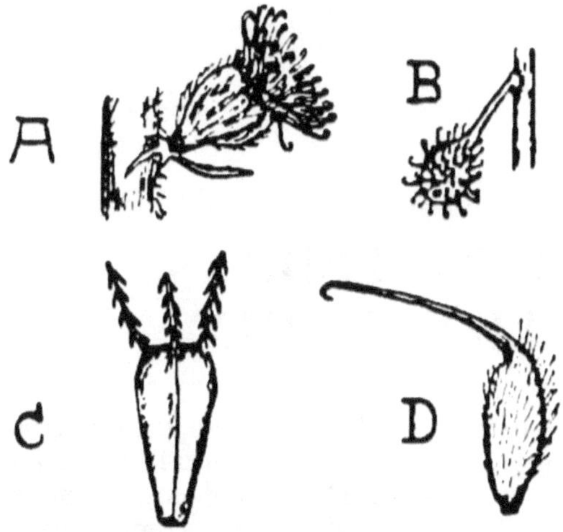

Fig. 103. - Burr-fruits (A and B natural size, C and D somewhat enlarged).
A, Agrimony (hooks on the floral receptacle,: B. Enchanter's Nightshade (hooked fruit); C. Burr Marigold (hooked calyx, p. 175); D, Herb Bennett (hooked style).

PRACTICAL WORK

1. In three pots, sow (a) fifty seeds of the Cress, (b) ten seeds of each of the following: Cress, Mustard, Poppy, Clover, and Wheat, and (c) ten seeds of the Cress. When the shoots in any one of the pots have grown to a height of about ten inches, compare the number and size of the plants in each.

2. Examine the seeds of the following plants: Mullein, Snapdragon, Sandwort Spurrey, Poplar, Willow-herb, Scotch Fir. Say how they are dispersed, and mention in each case any peculiarity that helps towards this end.

3. Note how the following fruits are suited for distribution: Raspberry, Currant, Herb Bennett, Elm, Burr Marigold, Woodruff, Wood Sanicle, Cuckoo Pint, Salsify, and Sow-thistle.

QUESTIONS

1. Describe and draw two fruits whose seeds are dispersed by the wind, and two whose seeds are dispersed by animals.

2. Give *four* examples of fleshy fruits. Describe in each case the nature of the fleshy part and show how it is of use to the plant.

3. Name *three* common weeds and mention any facts connected with their seed-dispersal which you think might explain why they are so abundant.

4. Compare the advantages and disadvantages of vegetative reproduction and of reproduction by seeds. Illustrate your answer by reference to one example of each kind.

CHAPTER XXVI

MONOCOTYLEDONS: THE LILY-FAMILY

The Monocotyledons. - In the preceding Chapters, the two groups of Flowering Plants, namely, Monocotyledons and Dicotyledons, have been frequently mentioned. To the **Monocotyledons** belong the Grasses, Rushes, Sedges, Lilies, Hyacinths, Orchids, and, amongst cultivated plants, the Palms and many bulbous forms.

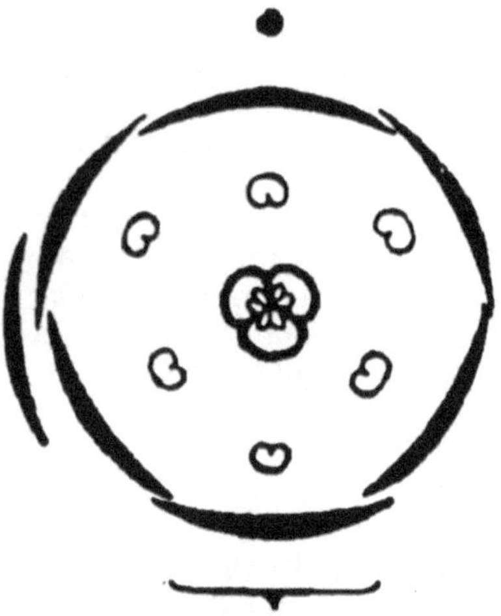

FIG. 104. - Floral diagram of the Liliaceae.

You have already learnt that this group of Flowering Plants usually shows **the following characters**: (a) an embryo with but a single cotyledon, (b) simple undivided leaves, generally linear or lanceolate in form and with a smooth margin, (c) several prominent parallel veins, (d) a fibrous root-system, (e) numerous scattered woody strands in the stem, and (f) flowers showing no distinction between calyx and corolla.

The flower of the Tulip. - We will now study Monocotyledonous flowers more fully, and, as a first example, we will take the Tulip. Here the six leaves of the **perianth** are, as usual, all alike, being coloured like petals. When their method of attachment to the top of the peduncle (i.e., the floral receptacle) is examined, three are seen to arise **at a slightly lower level** than the other three (Figs. 104 and 106), whilst the two sets or **whorls** alternate with one another (Fig. 104).

The six **stamens** are similarly arranged in **two whorls of three** (Fig. 104). Each consists of a filament and a long anther, which opens by **two slits** (Fig. 105, S.) to set free the yellow pollen. If you cut through an anther, before it splits open, you will find inside four small spaces, the **pollen-chambers** (Fig. 105, P.C.), filled with pollen (P.G.). These are placed in pairs on either side of the anther, and are joined together by the upper part of the filament or connective (Fig. 105, C.). The same structure is to be found in the young stamens of nearly all Flowering Plants.

The green **ovary** in the centre of the flower has three pale ridges at the top, which are the **stigmas** (Fig. 106, ST.). With a sharp knife, cut the ovary across and examine the surface with a magnifying glass. You can then see that it contains three little loculi (i.e., it is **trilocular**), which are **opposite the gaps** between the three inner stamens (Fig. 104). In each chamber, there are a number of ovules attached to a little swelling near the centre (Fig. 104).

The parts from which the ovules arise are called the **placentas**. When the latter, as here, are in the centre of the ovary, they are said to be **axile**. Each chamber, as you know (p. 119), is formed from a single carpel, so that three carpels join together to produce the ovary of the Tulip. This is expressed by saying that the ovary is **tricarpellary**.

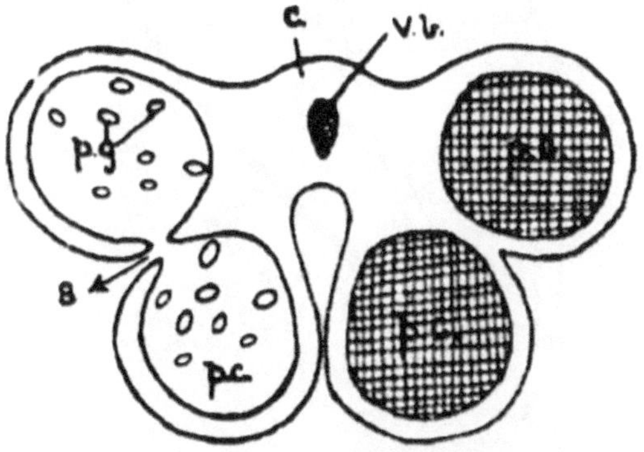

FIG. 105. - Diagram of a section across an anther of the Tulip (very much enlarged). On the right-hand side the pollen-chambers are shown as they appear in a young anther, ovary, they are said to be axile. on the left-hand side as in an old one; c., connective; p.c., pollen chamber; p.g., pollen grain; s., slit v.b., woody strand.

Longitudinal section of the Tulip-flower. - Now cut a **longitudinal section** (p. 124) of the flower, so that it passes through **the middle** of an outer petal on one side and of an inner petal on the other. You can then see that the **floral receptacle** is swollen (Fig. 106, R.). Of the two petals halved by the section, the outer (O.) will be found attached at a slightly lower level than the inner one (I., on the opposite side), whilst the stamens (I.S. and O.S.) arise still higher up.

The ovary is situated right at the top, and is therefore **superior**. The cut ovary shows very clearly the way in which the ovules are attached. In making a drawing of the longitudinal section, notice that the section passes **through a chamber** of the ovary on the one side (Fig. 106, I.) but **through the wall between** two chambers on the other side.

The families of Monocotyledons.—The flowers of most Monocotyledons are **constructed similarly** to those of the Tulip, that is to say, the parts are usually in threes, the floral leaves are six in number, and calyx and corolla are generally not recognisable. There are, however, by no means always six stamens, and the ovary is not always superior.

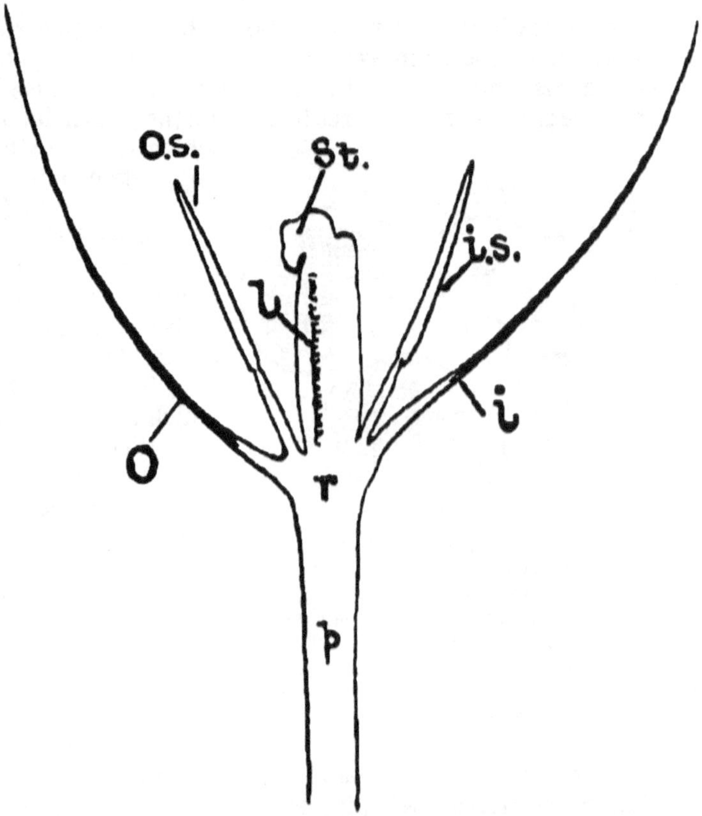

FIG. 106. - Longitudinal section of Tulip-flower.
o., outer perianth-leaf: i., inner perianth-leaf O.S., outer stamen: i.s., inner stamen; st., stignia; l., loculus of ovary showing ovules: p., peduncle; r., receptacle.

Flowering Plants are divided into a number of **families** or groups. The members of these groups **resemble one another** in many respects, especially in the structure of their flowers, and often in the form of shoot and root. The Tulip belongs to one of the families of Monocotyledons called the *Liliaceae*, whose special characters are as follows.

The Liliaceae. — The flowers are regular, with their parts usually in threes, although Herb Paris has its parts in fours. There are two whorls of stamens and a superior ovary with three compartments and axile placentas. The **inflorescence** is often a simple raceme, though single flowers (e.g. Tulip, Meadow Saffron) are not uncommon. **Honey** is formed in narrow slits in the wall of the ovary, and the flowers are generally pollinated by insects. The fruit is either a capsule splitting open by a number of long slits (Wild Hyacinth), or a berry (Asparagus). All the Liliaceae are **perennial herbs**, lasting through the winter by means of bulbs (Tulip, Hyacinth), rhizomes (Solomon's Seal), etc. As a rule, they do not fruit very freely, but multiply by **vegetative reproduction**.

Other plants belonging to the Liliaceae are the Lily, Onion, Star of Bethlehem, and Hyacinth. In the last, the floral leaves are slightly joined together at their base, and this is still more striking in the Lily of the Valley (Fig. 107). Here also, the filaments of the **stamens** are **joined to** the **petals** for the greater part of their length. When this is the case, the stamens are said to be **epipetalous**. Other Liliaceae show the same feature, but not to so marked an extent.

FIG. 107. - Single flower of the Lily of the Valley (about twice the natural size), showing how the perianth leaves are joined together.

Summary. — The *Liliaceae* are herbs with bulbs or rhizomes, regular flowers with their parts in threes, two perianth-whorls, two whorls of stamens, a superior trilocular ovary of three carpels, and with axile placentas. The fruit is a capsule or a berry.

PRACTICAL WORK

1. Examine flowers of the Hyacinth, Tulip, Lily, Onion, Solomon's Seal, and Lily of the Valley. Make floral diagrams in two cases, and cut through the stamens of several of these flowers.

2. Draw a longitudinal section through the flower of the Hyacinth and label its parts.

3. Examine fruits of as many Liliaceae as you can obtain, and notice whether they are capsules or berries.

QUESTIONS

1. How does the whole plant of the Tulip *or* Lily of the Valley differ from that of the Shepherd's Purse *or* Wallflower? Say which of the

characters you mention are shared by other Monocotyledons and Dicotyledons.

2. State, giving your reasons, whether the following plants are Monocotyledons or Dicotyledons: Cabbage, Potato, Grass, Violet, Crocus.

3. Describe, with the aid of drawings, the characters of the Liliaceae.

CHAPTER XXVII

OTHER MONOCOTYLEDONS

The Amaryllidaceae. — The flowers of the Narcissus family or *Amaryllidaceae* are very similar to those of the Liliaceae. The chief distinction is that the ovary in this family is **inferior**.

The most familiar member of the Amaryllidaceae is the Daffodil.

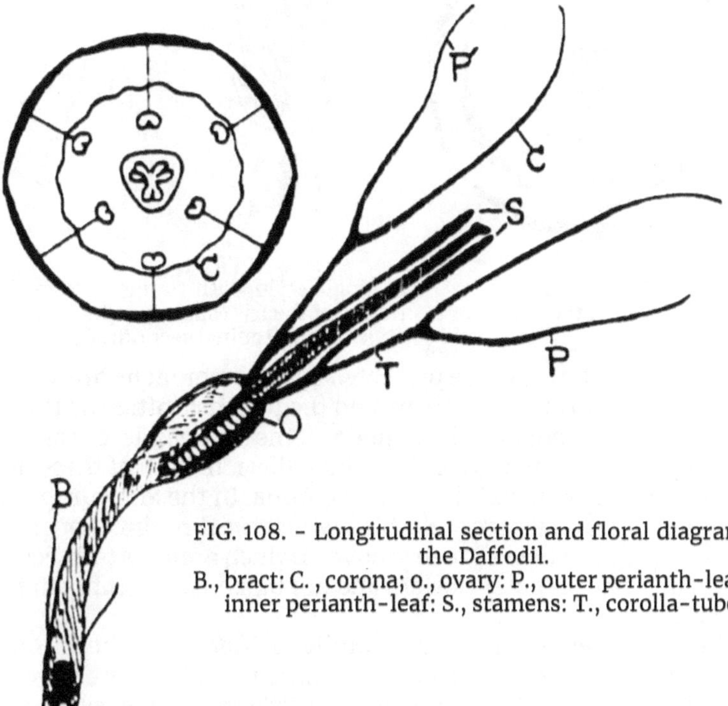

FIG. 108. - Longitudinal section and floral diagram of the Daffodil.
B., bract: C. , corona; o., ovary: P., outer perianth-leaf; P. inner perianth-leaf: S., stamens: T., corolla-tube.

Here you find the same **two whorls** of **perianth-leaves** (Fig. 108) as in the Tulip, but they arise from the top of the ovary and are partly joined together. At the top of the tube (Fig. 108, T.) formed by the joined floral leaves is a curious bell-shaped, bright-yellow outgrowth, the **corona** (C.). This is also seen in the Narcissus, but there the corona is much smaller (Fig. 91, B, C.). The **stamens** (Fig. 108, S.) are again six in number and are epipetalous (p. 139). The **inferior ovary** (Fig. 108, O.) appears as a green swelling below the flower, and, as in Liliaceae, is tri-carpellary and trilocular, with axile placentas.

The flowers of the Daffodil and Narcissus, whilst in bud, are protected by a membranous **bract** (Fig. 108, B.), which forms a sheath around the peduncle after the flower has opened. The other British members of the Amaryllidaceae are the Snowdrop (Fig. 144, p. 169) and the Snowflake. In both of these, the floral leaves are free, and there is no corona. In the Snowdrop, the three outer petals are large and white, whilst the three inner ones are much smaller and show a green groove in which **honey** is formed. All these plants have regular flowers and are bulbous, blooming in the early spring.

FIG. 109. — Floral diagram of the Crocus.

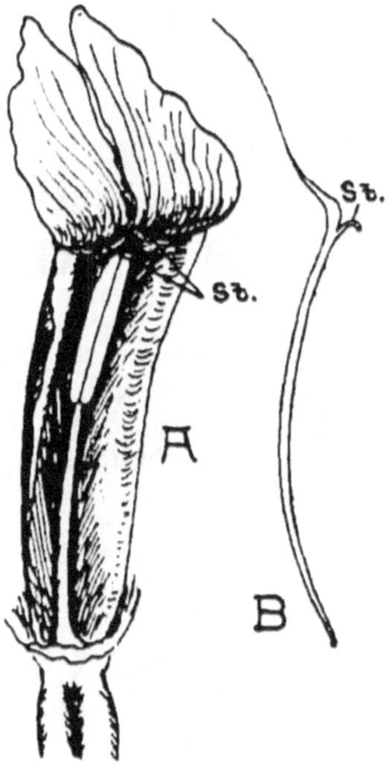

FIG. 110.
A, single style, with stamens, from the flower of the Iris (slightly reduced); B, a style in longitudinal section; st., stigma.

The Iridaceae. — In the Iris-family or *Iridaceae*, whose commonest members are the Iris and the Crocus, the flowers have an **inferior ovary**, as in the Amaryllidaceae. There are, however, **only three stamens**. In drawing a floral diagram of the Crocus (Fig. 109) you will notice that these three stamens lie opposite the gaps between the inner petals. The inner whorl of stamens, present in the Tulip or Narcissus, is therefore absent in this case, a fact that is shown in the floral diagram (Fig. 109) by representing the missing stamens by dots.

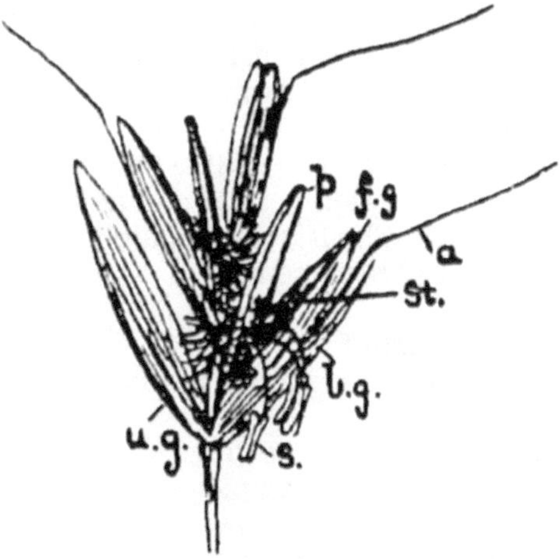

FIG. 111. - Group of flowers of the Wild Oat, forming a small spike.
S., stamen; st., stigma f.g. l.g., P. and u.g., different bracis of the inflorescence; a, bristle-like outgrowth.

In the Crocus, the petals are joined to form a **very long tube** (Fig. 30, A), so that the inferior ovary is below the ground. The flower of the Iris is unique in several ways. The styles (Fig. 110, A), which lie opposite the outer floral leaves, are **large and petal-like**. A stamen is included between each one of the outer petals and one of the three branches of the style. A little ridge (Fig. 110, st.) on the inner surface of each style represents the **stigma**, pollen being received on its upper surface. You will also notice that the inner floral leaves are much smaller than the outer ones.

The Iridaceae are perennial herbs, persisting by means of a corm in the Crocus and a rhizome in the Iris. In both these plants, the flowers are regular, but in the Gladiolus, which belongs to the same family, they are irregular. The **fruits** of all three are capsules.

Wind-pollinated Monocotyledons. — The Liliaceae, Amaryllidaceae, and Iridaceae all have conspicuous, **brightly coloured** perianth-leaves. Their flowers are visited by insects for honey, and the insects at the same time effect pollination. There are, however, a number of Monocotyledons, such as the Rushes, Sedges, and Grasses, in which the pollen is **carried by the wind**. Their flowers are quite **inconspicuous**, and either have no floral leaves or only a small scale-like perianth.

Grasses and Sedges. — The flowers of Grasses, when they open, are seen to possess three stamens (Fig. 111, s.). These have long slender filaments to which the large anthers are loosely hinged. The latter are easily swayed to and fro by the wind, and the dry **powdery pollen** is thus **shaken out of them**. At the top of the ovary there are two large, much-branched, **feathery stigmas**, which readily catch up the pollen wafted in the breeze. You will notice that the stamens and stigma of the same flower do not ripen at the same time, so that cross-pollination is usual.

The leaves of Grasses are arranged in **two rows**, and you will remember that they are peculiar in having a large sheathing leaf-base, with a little ridge at the top (Fig. 18, G). The stem is round, and often has hollow internodes. Sedges are easily distinguished from Grasses by the fact that the leaves are arranged in **three rows**. Moreover, their stem is usually three-cornered and solid.

Summary. — The *Amaryllidaceae* have flowers like those of the Liliaceae, but with an inferior ovary. The floral leaves are frequently joined and sometimes show a corona. The *Iridaceae* again have an inferior ovary, but only three stamens are present.

PRACTICAL WORK

1. Draw floral diagrams and longitudinal sections of the flowers of the Crocus and Snowdrop.

2. Compare the way in which the leaves of the Crocus and Iris are borne on the stem. In the latter, note how the older leaves ensheathe the younger.

3. Examine the leaves and stems of a Grass and a Sedge, and make a list of the differences.

QUESTIONS

1. Compare, giving a floral diagram of each, the flowers of the Liliaceae, Iridaceae, and Amaryllidaceae.

2. Mention all the differences you know between a Tulip *or* Lily of the Valley, and a Grass.

3. Describe carefully the flowers of the Iris and of the Daffodil. Illustrate your answer by longitudinal sections of the two flowers.

CHAPTER XXVIII

DICOTYLEDONS: THE BUTTERCUP-FAMILY

Dicotyledons. — The second group of Flowering Plants, the **Dicotyledons**, has been seen to possess: (*a*) an embryo with two cotyledons, (*b*) net-veined leaves, (*c*) a ring of woody strands in the stem, and (*d*) flowers usually showing calyx and corolla. Moreover, Dicotyledons frequently have the parts of their flowers **in fives**. The group includes a large number of families, many of which are well represented in Britain, for instance, the Buttercup-family, Wallflower-family, Chickweed-family, Rose-family, Daisy-family, etc. We may begin by studying the Buttercup family (*Ranunculaceae*), and, as a first example, will examine the common Buttercup.

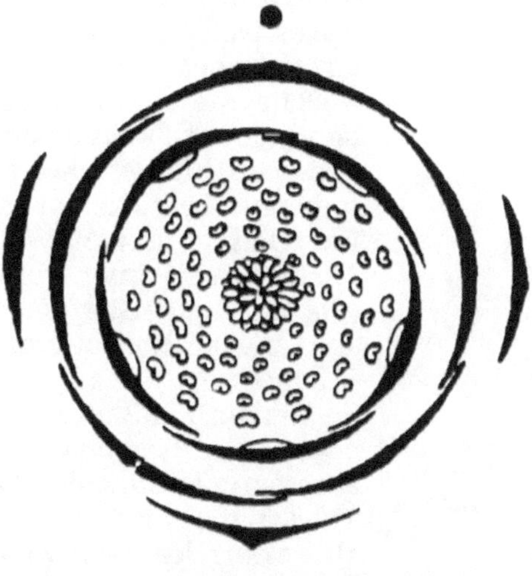

FIG. 112. - Floral diagram of the Buttercup. The two bracteoles are shown on either side of the flower.

The Buttercup. — The **inflorescence** of this plant was found to be a simple cyme (p. 115). Each flower (Fig. 91, A) has a green **calyx** consisting of five free sepals, and a **corolla** of five golden petals. The latter are likewise free, and are situated opposite the gaps between the sepals (Fig. 112). The **stamens** are very numerous and, though at first curved towards the centre of the flower, gradually spread outwards as they open to liberate the pollen. The superior **ovary** consists of a large number of separate carpels, each ending in a tiny stigma (Fig. 90, C).

The Ranunculaceae. — Nearly all the plants belonging to the

FIG. 113. - Flower of the Winter Aconite (natural size), showing the deeply divided green leaves below the flower. The trumpet-shaped nectaries are visible outside the stamens.

Ranunculaceae, like the Buttercup, have numerous stamens, a superior ovary composed of separate carpels, and free floral leaves. The **foliage-leaves** are alternate and have broad sheathing bases. Most members of the family are **perennial herbs** with a sharp taste, but the Old Man's Beard or Clematis is a woody climber, which is peculiar in having opposite leaves. In the Wood Anemone and Winter Aconite (Fig. 113), the flower is protected, when in bud, by a whorl of deeply divided green leaves, which are borne high up on the peduncle.

The members of this family do not always produce a branched **inflorescence**, but sometimes bear single or **solitary** flowers, as in the Wood Anemone and Winter Aconite (Fig. 113). In the Monkshood and Larkspur, the flowers are in a raceme.

Perianth of Ranunculaceae. — A calyx and corolla are often **not distinguishable**. Thus, in the Wood Anemone all the floral leaves are white, in the Marsh Marigold they are yellow, whilst in the Hellebores they are green. Honey is often formed in special nectaries, situated between the stamens and the perianth. In the **Christmas** Rose and Winter Aconite (Fig. 113), for instance, the **nectaries** appear as little trumpet-shaped structures. In the Buttercup, a nectary, covered by a little scale-like flap, is situated at the base of each petal. The petals of the Columbine are drawn out, at their lower ends, into narrow tubes or **spurs**, within which the honey is produced.

The Fruit. — The fruit, in this family, consists either of a number of **achenes**, as in the Buttercup (Fig. 97, a), or of a number of **follicles**, as in the Marsh Marigold and Monkshood (Fig. 97, b). Each achene or follicle is formed from a single carpel of the ovary. In the follicles, there are nearly always several seeds.

The Flowers of the Monkshood. — The flowers of the Monkshood and Larkspur are **irregular**, and therefore quite different from those of other Ranunculaceae. They can only be cut lengthwise, into two **equal halves**, by sections passing through the middle of the "hood" of the Monkshood and of the "spur" of the Larkspur.

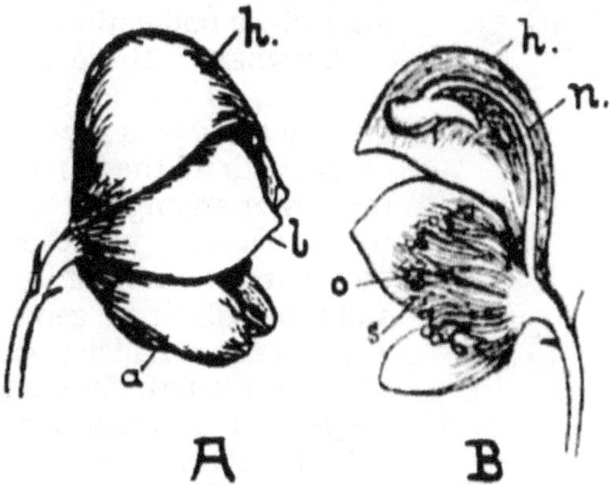

FIG. 114. Flowers of the Monkshood (natural size).
A, entire flower seen from the side; B, flower in longitudinal section a, one of the two anterior floral leaves; h., hood (posterior); l, side-member of the perianth; n., nectary O., ovary; S., stamens.

The Monkshood (Fig. 114) has a **perianth** of five purple floral leaves. The uppermost of these is shaped like a **hood** (Fig. 114, h.) and overlaps the two side-members (l), which in their turn overlap the two lowest (a). Within the hood are two curiously shaped **nectaries** (n.) borne on long stalks. There are, as usual, numerous stamens (s.) around the ovary (ot), which is composed of three carpels.

The flowers of this plant are visited by **Humble Bees**. These insects alight on the lower floral leaves and the mass of stamens, and seek the honey in the nectaries beneath the hood. Meanwhile, the **under surface** of the body becomes dusted with pollen. When the flower first opens, the stamens completely hide the stigmas from view. Later, after the pollen has been shed, the stamens bend back and wither, so that the stigmas become exposed. As a matter of fact, it is not until now that the stigmas are ready to receive the pollen. The Humble Bees, therefore, usually bring about **cross-pollination** of the flowers.

The Flowers of the Larkspur. - In the Larkspur (Fig. 115), one of the large blue leaves of the **perianth** is drawn out into a **long spur** (s) which is often at right angles to the peduncle. When slit open, this spur is seen to enclose two slender outgrowths which arise from two of the inner floral leaves. A **nectary** is situated at the tip of each out-

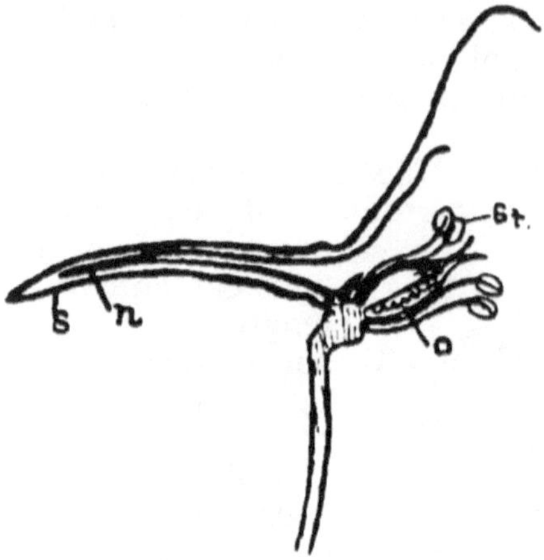

FIG. 115. Longitudinal section through the flower of the Larkspur. n., nectary; o., ovary; s., spur; st., stamens.

growth (Fig. 115, n.), and the honey formed by it collects in the spur. Bees which visit the flowers are able to reach the honey in this honey-bag, with the help of their long tongues. In so doing, they bring about pollination.

Summary. - The *Ranunculaceae*, as a whole, are distinguished by a superior ovary, with all the parts of the flower arising below it, free and usually numerous carpels, numerous stamens, and fruits which are generally achenes or follicles. The parts are usually in fives, and the perianth-leaves are often alike in colour.

PRACTICAL WORK

1. Draw floral diagrams of the following common members of the Ranunculaceae: Marsh Marigold, Columbine, Monkshood, and Lesser Celandine.

2. Sketch the entire fruits of the Buttercup, Marsh Marigold, and Old Man's Beard.

3. Draw longitudinal sections of the flowers of the plants mentioned in (2), and label those parts which remain in the fruiting condition.

4. Make a list of the insects you see visiting a Buttercup, Larkspur, Monkshood, and Lesser Celandine. Note the way in which they settle on the flowers.

QUESTIONS

1. Compare, with the help of drawings, the flower of a Buttercup or Marsh Marigold with that of some Monocotyledon.

2. Describe carefully the method of pollination of the Monkshood or Larkspur, illustrating your answer by figures.

3. What do you understand by a carpel? Describe the arrangement of the carpels and the structure of the ovary in the following: Clematis, Monkshood, Crocus.

CHAPTER XXIX

THE WALLFLOWER- AND CHICKWEED-FAMILIES

The **Cruciferae.** - The Wallflower and Shepherd's Purse belong to another family of Dicotyledons, known as the Cruciferae. All the members of this family are **herbs**, with alternate exstipulate leaves. Stems and leaves often bear branched **hairs** (Fig. 119, C), like those you noticed in the Shepherd's Purse (p. 5). The **inflorescence** is usually a raceme (Fig. 1) or a corymb (Fig. 85), but is peculiar in that it bears **no bracts**. The flowers of nearly all the members of this family have the same structure as those of the Wallflower (see Chapter IV). The four sepals usually stand upright and, with the claws of the four petals, form a **tube** (Fig. 116), although none of the floral leaves are joined. Most Cruciferae can therefore only be visited by insects having a tongue of some length.

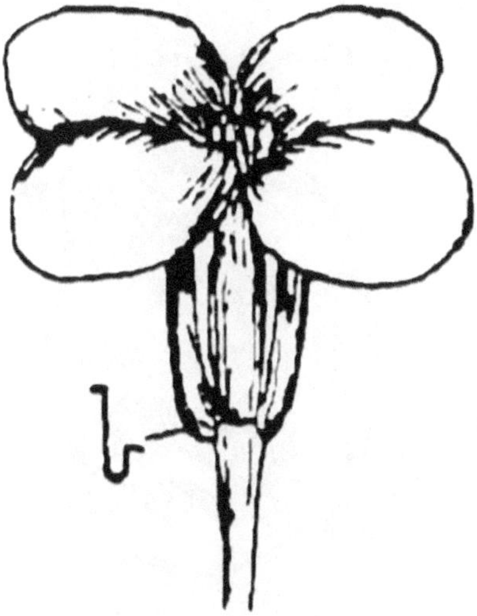

FIG. 116. - Flower of the Wallflower, showing the tube produced by the four upright sepals and the claws of the petals (natural size). b, one of the pouched sepals serving as a honey bag.

The Floral Diagram. - In making a floral diagram of the Wallflower (Fig. 117), you will notice that the four sepals are **in two whorls**. The two outer ones and the axis are in the same straight line (i.e. they are posterior and anterior), whilst the two inner ones are at right angles to them. The four clawed petals are all **in the same whorl** and alternate with the sepals (Fig. 117). Four of the six stamens are **slightly longer** than the other two, although this is not as pronounced in the Wallflower as in most members of

FIG. 117 - Floral diagram of the Wallflower.

the Cruciferae. The **short stamens** stand, one on either side of the flower, opposite the inner sepals. The **long stamens** are arranged in pairs opposite the outer sepals (carefully compare Figs. 7, 117, and 119, A). The **nectaries** have already been recognized as small swellings at the bases of the short stamens (Fig. 7, n.).

Ovary and Fruit. - The superior **ovary** consists of two carpels (i.e. is **bicarpellary**). Like the fruit (p. 126), it shows two chambers which are placed on the right- and left-hand sides of the flower (Figs. 8, D, 117). The ovules are attached **to the wall**, on either side of the partition (Fig. 118), and not to the centre of the ovary as in the Tulip and Daffodil. The **placentas** are therefore not axile, but are described as **parietal**, and this method of attachment of the ovules and seeds is distinctive of the Cruciferae.

The **fruit** of the Wallflower is, as you learned, a **siliqua** (p. 126), and many other members of the family have a perfectly similar fruit. But a certain number, like the Shepherd's Purse (Fig. 119, B), Honesty (Fig. 118), and Candytuft, have very short siliquas (often called siliculas), which otherwise show the same structure. In the Radish, the siliqua develops partitions between the individual seeds and breaks up, when ripe, into indehiscent achenes.

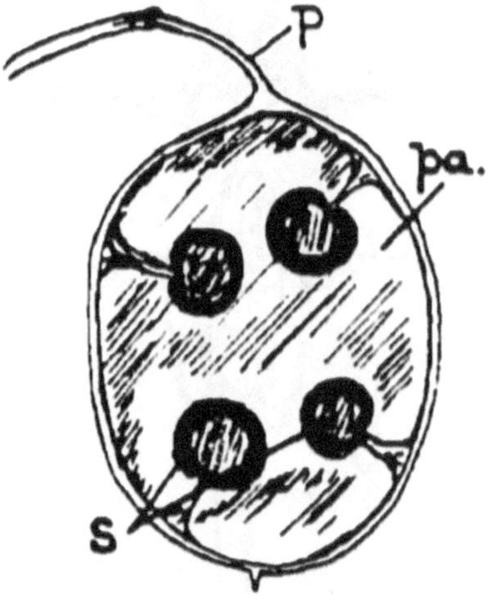

FIG. 118.-Ripe fruit of the Honesty, with one valve removed, showing the attachment of the seeds (natural size). P., peduncle; pa., partition s., seeds.

Amongst the more familiar plants belonging to the Cruciferae are Jack-by-the-Hedge, Milkmaid, Honesty, and a number of weeds, such as Charlock, and Shepherd's Purse. Several of the members of this family are useful as vegetables, for instance, the Turnip, Radish, Cabbage, Cauliflower, Mustard, Horse Radish, and Watercress.

The Caryophyllaceae. - The Chickweed-family or *Caryophyllaceae*, like the Cruciferae, includes a number of common weeds. Most of the members are again **herbs**, with simple exstipulate leaves. The latter are, however, opposite, and the nodes are often **swollen**. The **inflorescence** is the very characteristic **dichasial** cyme which was described on p. 115 (Fig. 87, B). In very many Caryophyllaceae, after the first two branches have ended in flowers, the further branches are of unequal length. Moreover, towards the tips, only one of each pair of branches may be formed.

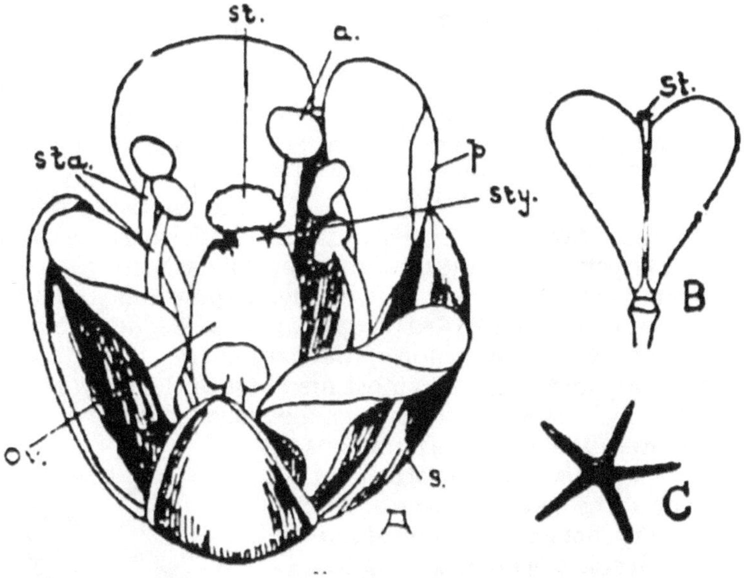

FIG. 119.
A, single flower of the Shepherd's Purse (much enlarged); S., sepal: P., petal sta., stamens: a., anther; sty., style; st., stigma: ov., ovary. B, single fruit (much enlarged) st., stigma. C, single star-shaped hair from a leaf (much enlarged).

The Flowers. - Common members of the Caryophyllaceae are the Pink, the Campions, the Stitchwort, and the Chickweed. You will easily see that the **flowers** are of two shapes, namely, **tubular and open**. Thus, in the Pink and Campion (Fig. 120, A), the sepals are joined together, and the lower part of the flower forms a tube. In the Chickweed and Stitchwort (Fig. 120, B), however, the flower is like a shallow cup, and the sepals are quite free from one another. The open flowers of the Chickweed and Stitchwort are, like those of the Buttercup, visited by quite a variety of insects for the honey, here formed at the bases of the stamens. The tubular flowers of the Campion and Pink, on the other hand, are only accessible to insects with **long tongues**.

When the sepals are joined, the **petals** have long claws (Fig. 121), which are even more pronounced than in the Wallflower. The claws

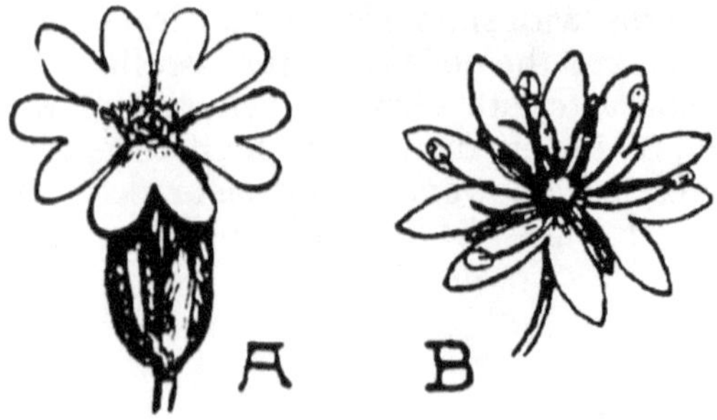

FIG. 120.
A, Flower of Campion, showing the joined calyx and the five divided petals (natural size) B, flower of Stitchwort, with free sepals and deeply cut petals (enlarged).

are completely enclosed in the calyx, whilst the blades of the petals spread out horizontally (Fig. 120, A). The free petals are frequently **deeply divided**, as in the Stitchwort (Fig. 120, B) and Ragged Robin. In the Chickweed, this goes so far that the flowers almost look as though they had ten petals.

In this family, all the whorls are **in fives**. Thus, there are five sepals (shown by the five teeth where the calyx is joined), five petals, **two whorls** of five stamens each, and a **superior ovary** composed of five, three, or two joined carpels. This is shown by the fact that there are five (Red Campion), three (Bladder Campion), or two (Pink) stigmas at the top of the ovary.

The Ovary and Fruit. - In most members of the Caryophyllaceae, you will find **no partitions** when the ripe ovary is cut across. It is, therefore, **unilocular**. The numerous ovules are attached to a central column, known as a free central placenta. The fruit is a very characteristic kind of **capsule**, which splits open at the top by a number of **teeth** (Fig. 97, f.). The latter are either as many, or twice as many, as the number of stigmas on the ovary. The calyx generally remains as a **protective covering** around the fruit. As the capsules ripen, the flower-stalks become stiff so that, after they have been bent aside by the wind, they spring back again to their original position. In this way, the ripe seeds are **shot out**.

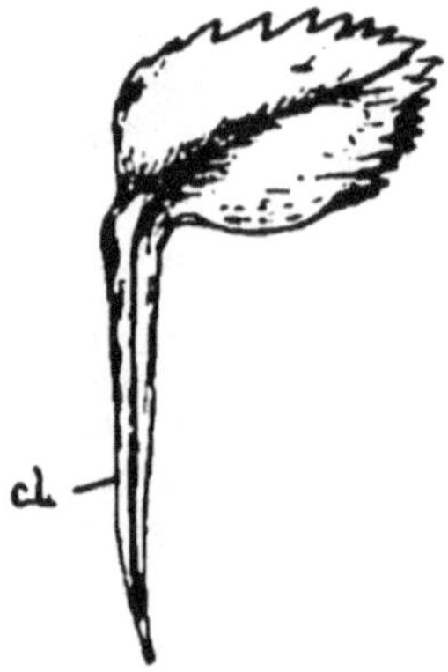

FIG. 121. Single petal of the Pink (about two-thirds natural size).
cl., claw.

Summary. - The *Cruciferae* have a raceme or corymb without bracts. The flowers have four sepals in two whorls, four petals in one whorl, four long and two short stamens, and a superior bicarpellary ovary with two parietal placentas. The fruit is either a siliqua or a silicula.

The *Caryophyllaceae* have opposite leaves and swollen nodes, and the inflorescence is a dichasial cyme. The flowers are regular, with the parts in fives. The sepals are free or joined, whilst the petals are free and often divided. The stamens are in two whorls, and the ovary is superior, unilocular, with a free central placenta. The fruit is a capsule opening by teeth.

PRACTICAL WORK

1. Draw a floral diagram and a longitudinal section of the flowers of the Stock or Jack-by-the-Hedge.

2. Draw and compare longitudinal sections of the flowers of the Pink and the Stitchwort or Gipsy Grass.

3. Draw floral diagrams of the flowers of the Pink, Campion, and Stitchwort.

4. Examine and draw the fruits of the following: Jack-by-the-Hedge, Watercress, Radish, Candytuft, Chickweed, and Campion.

QUESTIONS

1. Describe, giving one example of each, an ovary with (a) a parietal, (b) an axial (axile), (c) a free central, placentation.

2. Make a detailed comparison of the Wallflower and the Chickweed. Say how far the differences are characteristic of the families to which these plants belong.

3. Describe, with diagrams, the structure of the fruit and the method of dispersal of the seeds in any *five* of the following: Radish, Old Man's Beard, Campion, Candytuft, Stitchwort, Jack-by-the-Hedge, Lily, Marsh Marigold, Wild Hyacinth.

CHAPTER XXX

THE ROSE-FAMILY

Rosaceae. - A large and important family of Dicotyledons, including trees and shrubs as well as herbs, is that of the Rosaceae. To this, the Apple, Rose, Strawberry, and Silverweed belong. In this family, the **leaves** are alternate, generally stipulate, and often compound (Fig. 45). The kind of **inflorescence** varies greatly. Thus, in the Avens, it is a cyme (p. 115), in the Cherry, it is a simple umbel (p. 114), and in the Cherry Laurel, a typical raceme. The **flowers** are regular and usually resemble those of a Buttercup in having numerous stamens and a superior ovary composed of free carpels. If you compare longitudinal sections of the flowers of this family with that of a Buttercup, however, you will find that they differ in the **shape of the floral receptacle**.

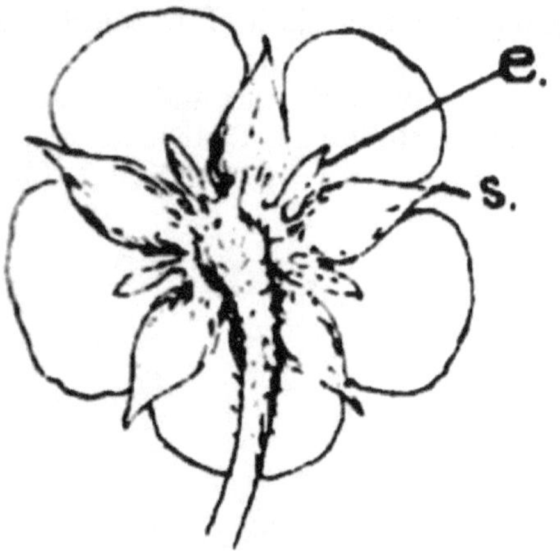

FIG. 122. - Flower of the Strawberry (slightly reduced), showing the outer (e) and inner (s) whorls of green floral leaves

The Strawberry. - In the Strawberry or Cinquefoil, the receptacle has the form of a **cup**, from the edge of which the sepals, petals, and stamens arise (Fig. 123, C). They, therefore, **stand around the ovary**, instead of arising **beneath** it. The carpels are borne on a little knob-like swelling in the center of the cup-shaped receptacle. The Cherry and Plum have a similarly shaped receptacle, but here only **one carpel** is present.

When you come to draw a **floral diagram** of the Strawberry or the Cinquefoil (Fig. 124), you will notice that there are **two sets** of green floral leaves (Fig. 122, e and s), the one alternating with the other. The inner set are the true sepals, whilst the outer are an extra whorl, found also in a few other members of the Rosaceae. The five **free pet-**

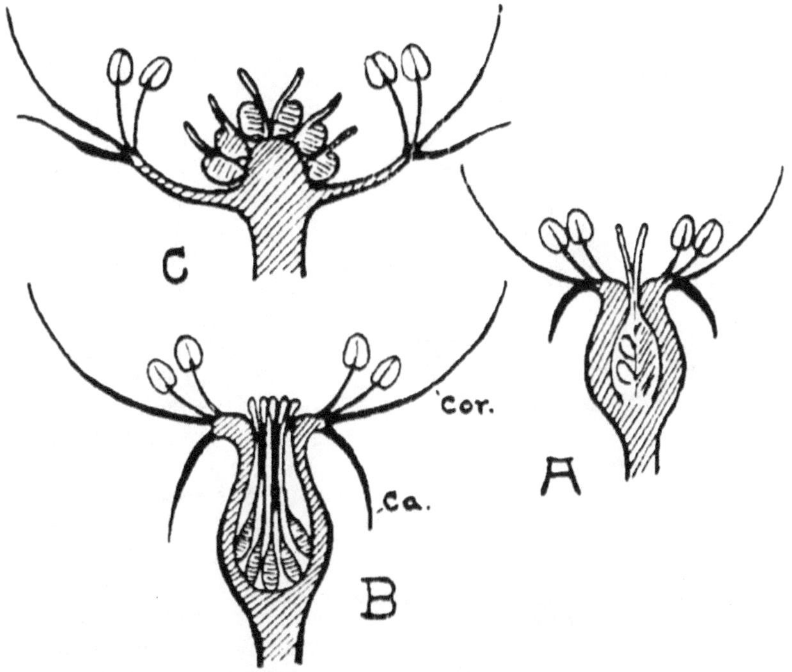

FIG. 123. - Diagrammatic longitudinal sections of flowers of the Rosaceae. A, Apple; B, Rose: C, Cinquefoil: ca., calyx; cor., corolla. In each figure the receptacle is shaded.

als alternate with the sepals. If you pull off and count all the stamens, you will probably find that their number is some **multiple of five**. You would obtain the same result with other Rosaceae having numerous stamens, whereas this is not usually the case in the Buttercup family.

The Rose. - A longitudinal section of a Rose-flower (Fig. 123, B) shows that here the receptacle is hollowed out so much that it appears like a **flask** with a narrow neck. The carpels arise from the base of the hollow, whilst sepals, petals, and stamens come off from the edge of the neck. Otherwise, the flower is very much like that of the Strawberry, but there are not two whorls of green floral leaves.

The Apple and Pear. - In the Apple and Pear, the ovary is **inferior** and completely embedded in the floral receptacle, from the top of which the other parts of the flower arise (Fig. 123, A). **Five carpels** join together to form the ovary, which consequently exhibits five compartments.

The Fruits of the Rosaceae. - The fruit, in many members of this family, is a group of one-seeded **achenes** or **drupelets**. **False fruits**, in which the receptacle becomes fleshy, are, however, quite common.

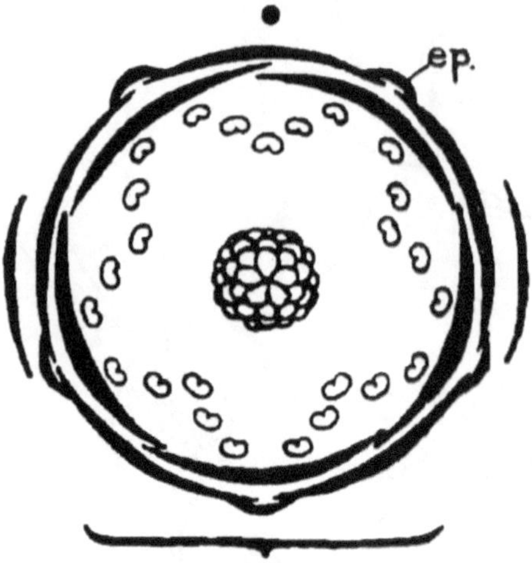

FIG. 124. - Floral diagram of the Cinquefoit.
ep., the outer whorl of green floral leaves. The two bracteoles are shown at the sides of the flower.

Thus, in the Strawberry (Fig. 100, D), the knob-like swelling, on which the carpels are borne, forms the fleshy edible part on which the true fruits (achenes) appear as dark-colored pips. In the Rose (Fig. 100, C), the whole flask-shaped receptacle containing the achenes enlarges to form the scarlet flesh of the "hip." In the Apple (Fig. 100, E) and Pear, the edible part of the fruit is produced from the receptacle, whilst the core is the ripened ovary, and the pips are the seeds.

The flowers of the common Agrimony have only one or two carpels within the cup-shaped receptacle, which is covered on the outside with numerous **hooked hairs**. The dry receptacle remains around the fruit, and the hairs upon it stiffen (Fig. 103, A), so that a **burr-fruit** which clings to animals is formed.

The Cinquefoil only differs from the Strawberry in the fact that the receptacle does not become fleshy, the whole fruit being dry and consisting of a cluster of achenes. The fruits of the Blackberry (Fig. 99, G-H) and Raspberry are similar, but here each carpel develops into a small drupe. These three fruits thus differ from those of the Strawberry, Rose, and Apple in being **true fruits**. The same is the case in the Cherry and Plum, where the **single carpel** enlarges to form a big **drupe** (Fig. 99, E-F).

In nearly all Rosaceae, the calyx remains as a **protection** for the young fruit. It can be seen at the top of the stalk in the Strawberry (Fig. 100, D, c), as a brown structure at the top of the ripe Apple (Fig. 100, E, c), and is plainly evident at the summit of the Rose-hip (Fig. 100, C).

Common members of the Rosaceae, apart from those already mentioned, are the Meadow-sweet, Hawthorn, Avens, Salad Burnet, and Sloe.

Summary. - The *Rosaceae* are trees, shrubs, or herbs, with alternate, generally stipulate leaves and a varied inflorescence. The flowers are regular and have their parts in fives. There are often many whorls of stamens, and the ovary usually consists of free carpels (except Apple,

Pear, etc.). The fruits are mostly achenes or drupelets, but the floral receptacle often takes part in the formation of the fruit. The chief **difference from Ranunculaceae** is the form of the floral receptacle.

PRACTICAL WORK

1. Draw floral diagrams of the following: Cherry or Plum, Apple or Hawthorn, and Cinquefoil.

2. Draw longitudinal sections of the flowers of the Strawberry, Apple, Cherry or Plum, Rose, and Agrimony.

3. Examine and draw longitudinal and cross-sections of the fruits of the plants mentioned in (2), and mark in each case the true fruits, the receptacle, and the calyx.

QUESTIONS

1. Explain carefully, with the help of drawings, the chief differences between the plants and flowers of the Cinquefoil *or* Blackberry and the Buttercup.

2. Describe two edible fruits belonging to the Rosaceae. Explain what parts of the flower are represented in each of the fruits.

3. What changes take place in a flower after it has been pollinated? Describe how the fruit is formed in the case of the apple or some other fleshy fruit.

CHAPTER XXXI

THE PEA- AND CARROT-FAMILIES

The Leguminosae – The members of the Pea-family or *Leguminosae* are very numerous and found in all parts of the world. Some, like the Laburnum, are trees, whilst most are shrubs or herbs (e.g. Gorse, Sweet Pea). The **leaves** are alternate, stipulate, and nearly always compound, being either pinnate (False Acacia, Fig. 18, H) or provided with only three leaflets (Clover, Fig. 125, A). The **stems** sometimes, as in the Sweet Pea, have a broad green wing on either side.

A considerable number of the Leguminosae are **climbers**, either twining round their support (Runner Bean) or fixing themselves by means of **tendrils** formed from the upper leaflets, as in the Vetch and Sweet Pea. The **roots** frequently show small swellings, inhabited by a low form of vegetable life (Bacteria). Owing to their presence, the Leguminosae are peculiar in being able to make use of the free nitrogen of the air.

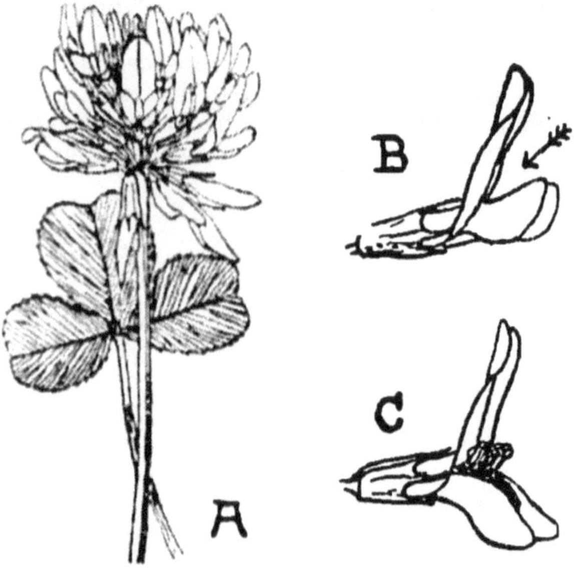

FIG. 125. – The Clover.
A, inflorescence and leaf (natural size); B, single flower enlarged, seen from the side, as it appears when no insect is upon it: the arrow indicates the direction of approach of the pollinating insect; C, the same, showing the position of the parts at the time of pollination, when wings and keel are pushed down.

Flower and Fruit – The **inflorescence** is racemose. The **flowers** are **irregular** and have their parts in fives, except for the superior ovary, which consists of a **single carpel**. The receptacle is slightly hollowed out, but much less so than in the Rosaceae. The five sepals are more or less joined together. Unlike other Dicotyledons, the odd sepal is **anterior**, that is to say, on the side of the flower away from the axis of the inflorescence (Fig. 126).

The **corolla** is very characteristic and consists of five petals with which the five sepals alternate. The uppermost or **standard** (Fig. 127,

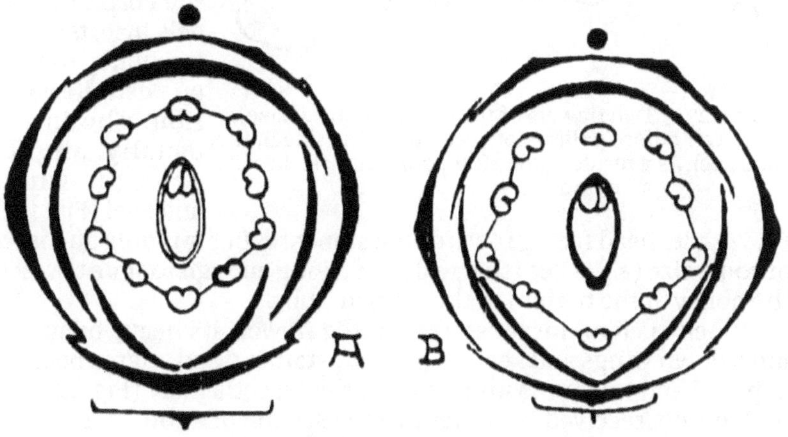

FIG. 126. - Floral diagrams of Leguminosae.
A, Needle Furze: B, Sweet Pea.

s.) is large, and overlaps the two smaller side-petals or **wings** (Fig. 127, w.). The wings in their turn overlap the two lowest petals, which are joined along their lower edge to form the boat-shaped **keel** (Fig. 127, k.). Within the keel, the stamens and ovary are concealed.

There are **ten stamens** (of which five are often longer than the other five), whose **filaments are joined** for about half their length, so as to form a tube around the ovary (Fig. 126). In the Gorse, Broom, and Needle Furze (Fig. 126, A) all ten stamens are united in this way. In the Sweet Pea (Fig. 126, B), Clover, and Bird's-foot Trefoil, on the other hand, only nine are joined, whilst the **tenth is free**. This free stamen is the posterior one (Fig. 126, B), consequently, the tube in these forms shows a slit-shaped **opening on the upper side**. The ovules are attached along the upper (posterior) edge of the single carpel, forming the ovary (Fig. 126), and the **fruit** is a legume (Fig. 97, c). At the top of the ovary, there is a long style, ending in a stigma of various shapes.

The Pollination of Leguminosae – Honey is only found in the flowers of those Leguminosae in which one stamen is free. It is pro-

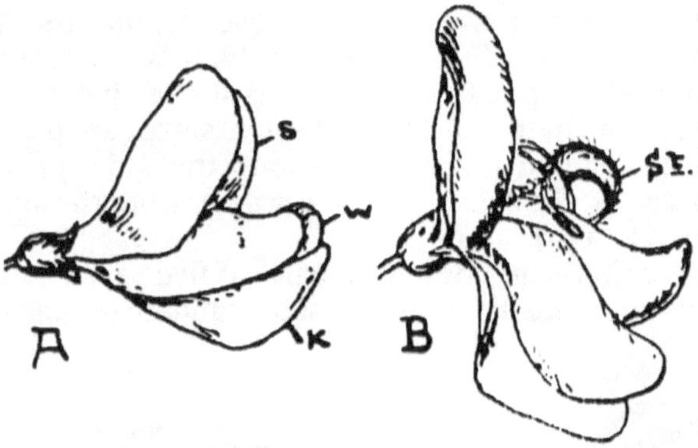

Fig. 127. - Two flowers of the Broom (natural size). A, flower before pollination, seen from the side B, the and keel. As a result, same after pollination; k., keel S., standard; st., style; w., wings.

duced at the bases of the stamens and collects **in the tube** formed by the joined filaments. As in the Larkspur and Monkshood, the irregular shape of the corolla compels insects seeking honey to take up a **definite position**. The insect usually alights upon the wings and keel (Fig. 125, B), with its head facing towards the standard. But it is only an insect of some size (e.g. a Bee) that will have a **long enough tongue** to reach the honey at the bottom of the stamen-tube.

When such an insect settles on the flower, its heavy body will **push down** wings and keel. As a result, stamens and stigma become exposed and touch the **underside** of the insect's body (Fig. 125, C). Pollen thus received is brought to the stigma of another flower as the insect goes to and fro.

The Pollination of the Broom – In many members of the Pea-family (e.g. Clover, Sweet Pea, Bird's-foot Trefoil) the wings and keel move up into their **original positions**, as soon as the insect flies away, so that stamens and ovary are again concealed. In the Broom, however, this is not the case. The flowers of this plant are also peculiar in the fact that pollen is deposited on the **insect's back**.

The stamens and style are held within the keel **under tension**, something like a bent spring. Directly a heavy insect alights and presses down wings and keel, the stamens and style **jerk out** (Fig. 127, B) and strike its body. Only the five shorter stamens, which are the first to spring out, touch the underside of the insect. The five longer ones, as well as the stigma, strike its back. A flower of the Broom, once visited, **appears broken** (Fig. 127, B), since the various parts of the flower **do not** return to their original positions. The same "explosive" method of discharging the pollen is found in the Gorse, although here stamens and stigma touch only the **lower side** of the insect's body.

Both in the Broom and the Gorse, all ten stamens are joined, and the flowers produce **no honey**. Here, as in other flowers without

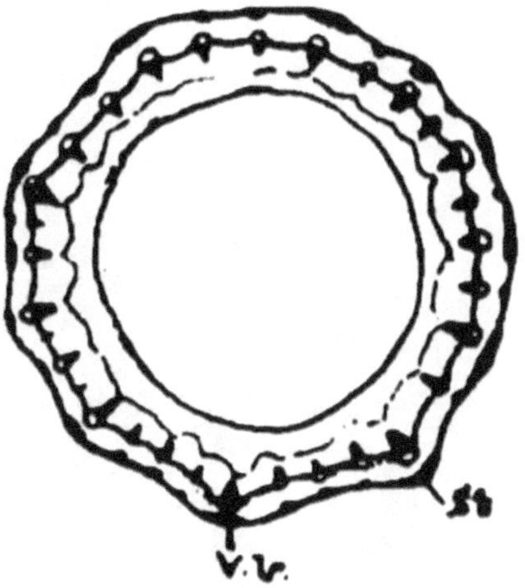

FIG. 128.-Cross-section of the stems (Fig. 128) and large, usually com-(considerably enlarged). u.b., the woody strands st.; other strands of hard tissue situated below the ribs of the stem.

honey (e.g. Poppy, Clematis), the insect feeds on part of the pollen, but while so doing, helps to transfer the rest from stamens to stigma.

The Umbelliferae – Another large family of Dicotyledons is that to which the Carrot, Hogweed, Cow's Parsley, and Parsnip belong. Owing to the form of its racemose **inflorescence** (a compound umbel, p. 114), this family is called the *Umbelliferae*. Most of its members are **perennial herbs**, having hollow ribbed stems (Fig. 128) and large, usually compound, leaves with broad **sheathing bases** (Fig. 43, C). There is often a large tap-root situated below the ribs of the stem. The root, which in the Parsnip and Carrot is fleshy, is eaten as a vegetable. Many members of this family (e.g. Fennel) have a strong odour.

Flower and Fruit – The **flowers**, which are usually white or yellow, are often very small. But the grouping of the flowers in **compound umbels**, which in the case of the Hogweed may be several inches across, renders the whole mass **conspicuous**. The flowers, except at the edge of the umbel, are always regular (Fig. 130). The five sepals appear as minute green teeth at the top of the **inferior ovary** (o.). The five petals (p.) are all alike, although in the outer flowers of the umbel some of them are often **enlarged**. Alternating with the petals are **five stamens** (Figs. 129, 130, s.). The ovary is inferior and consists of **two carpels**. Above it, is a fleshy swelling or **disc** (Fig. 130, n.), which forms the honey, the two styles projecting from its centre. When cut across, the ovary shows two chambers, each containing a single ovule (Fig. 129).

The ripe **fruit** separates into two **one-seeded portions**, which, for a time, remain attached to the split end of the flower stalk (Fig. 98, A). The halves of the fruits are scattered independently. They are either flattened and distributed by the wind (e.g., Hogweed) or bear numerous hooks and are carried away by animals (e.g., Carrot and Chervil).

Summary. - The *Leguminosae* usually have compound, stipulate leaves, a racemose inflorescence, and irregular flowers. The receptacle is slightly hollowed. The five sepals are joined. The irregular corolla consists of a standard, two wings, and a keel of two joined petals. The stamens are ten in number, either all joined or the posterior one free. The superior ovary consists of a single carpel, and the fruit is a legume.

FIG. 129 - Floral diagram of the Hogweed.

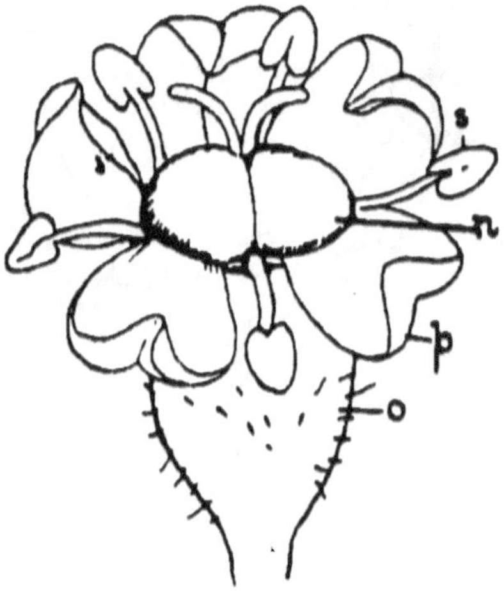

FIG. 130. - "Single flower of the Hogweed (considerably enlarged). n., disc (nectary); o., ovary; p., petal; a., stamen.

The *Umbelliferae* are herbs with ribbed, hollow stems and compound leaves with sheathing bases. The inflorescence is usually a compound umbel. The flowers are regular. Sepals, petals, and stamens are in fives. The ovary is inferior, bicarpellary, and bilocular. The fruit splits into two one-seeded portions.

PRACTICAL WORK

1. Make floral diagrams of the Sweet Pea and the Gorse. Draw the different parts of the flowers separately.

2. Draw longitudinal sections of the flowers of the Sweet Pea and the Lupine.

3. Examine the inflorescences of the Wood Sanicle, Beaked Parsley, and Fool's Parsley. Make diagrams of each, showing the distribution of the bracts and the order of opening of the flowers. Draw a floral diagram of a single flower.

4. Examine the fruits of the Hogweed, Chervil, Wood Sanicle, and Parsnip.

QUESTIONS

1. What are the chief points in which the flowers of a Buttercup (a) differ from and (b) resemble those of a Pea or Bean? What is the significance of the differences you notice?

2. Compare, by the help of drawings, the flowers of any member of the Leguminosae with those of a Monkshood or Larkspur. Enumerate the points of resemblance and the points of difference.

3. How would you recognize members of the families Caryophyllaceae and Umbelliferae when not in flower?

4. Contrast the methods of pollination found in the Broom, Clover, and Monkshood.

CHAPTER XXXII

THE PRIMROSE- AND FORGET-ME-NOT- FAMILIES

ALL the families of Dicotyledons, as yet studied, have **free petals**. There are, however, many Dicotyledons in which the petals are **joined together**. This is the case, for instance, in the Primrose, which may be taken as a first example of this kind of flower.

FIG.131.-Floral diagram of the Primrose.

The flowers of the Primrose. - The **flowers** of the Primrose are regular and have a **superior ovary** (Fig. 132). All the parts are **in fives** (Fig. 131), although this is difficult to recognize in the case of the ovary. The lower parts of the petals are joined together to form a **long tube**, while the upper parts spread out into five lobes (Fig. 132). The latter alternate with the sepals, which are likewise united into a tube.

The five stamens stand **opposite** the lobes of the corolla and are epipetalous (Fig. 131). They arise from the inside of the corolla tube, to which they are attached by very short filaments (Fig. 132). The ovary is **unilocular** and contains numerous ovules borne on a **free central placenta** (Fig. 132, middle figure), similar to that of the Caryophyllaceae. At the top of the ovary is a slender style ending in a knob-shaped stigma. The **fruit** is surrounded by the calyx and is a capsule that opens at the top by means of teeth.

The Primulaceae. - The Primrose belongs to a family known as the *Primulaceae*, most members of which have flowers of the same structure. In the Pimpernel and Yellow Loosestrife, however, the petals

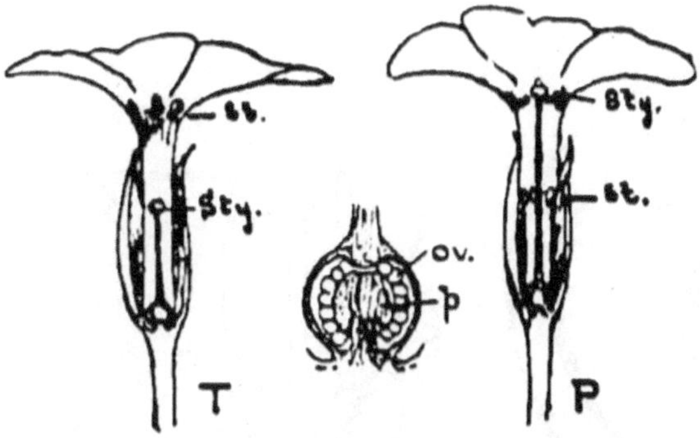

FIG. 132. - Structure of the flowers of the Primrose, showing longitudinal sections of the thrum-eyed (T) and pin-eyed (p) forms (natural size). St., stamens.; Sty., stigma. The middle figure shows the ovary in longitudinal section and considerably enlarged uv., ovule: P. free central placenta.

are only joined at their bases, so that they are **almost free** from one another. There are no petals at all in the Sea Milkwort, a succulent plant found on the seashore.

The capsules do not always open by teeth. In the Pimpernel, for instance, the whole top splits off as a little lid. Most members of the family are **perennial herbs** with exstipulate leaves.

The pollination of the Primrose. - The Primrose has **two kinds of flowers**, each produced on a different plant (Fig. 132). In one kind, the stamens are attached low down in the corolla tube, while the style is long so that the stigma lies in the mouth of the flower (**pin-eyed** Primrose, Fig. 132, P). In the other kind, the style is short, and the anthers of the stamens occupy the opening of the tube (**thrum-eyed** Primrose, Fig. 132, T).

Bees settle on the upper spreading parts of the petals and push their tongues down the tube to reach the honey formed at the base of the ovary. The pollen from the stamens of a pin-eyed flower adheres to the **insect's tongue** and, when carried to a thrum-eyed flower, is in just the right position to touch the stigma. Similarly, pollen from a thrum-eyed flower is brought to the stigma of a pin-eyed one. The two kinds of flowers of the Primrose thus help to secure **cross-pollination**.

The Boraginaceae. - The Forget-me-not family or *Boraginaceae* likewise usually have regular flowers with a joined corolla (Fig. 133) and a **superior ovary** (Fig. 134). Most of the members are herbs, having simple alternate leaves and frequently bearing stiff, bristle-like **hairs**. The **inflorescence** is cymose and often shows two main branches, which are generally coiled at their tips in a characteristic manner.

Flower and fruit. - The **flowers** (Fig. 133) have five joined sepals. In the case of the Forget-me-not, these are covered with hooked hairs, which often help in the dispersal of the fruits by animals. The corolla has a very **short tube** (Fig. 134, t.) and is commonly blue or

FIG. 133. - Floral diagram of the Forget-me-not. The bracteole is shown on the right-hand side of the flower.

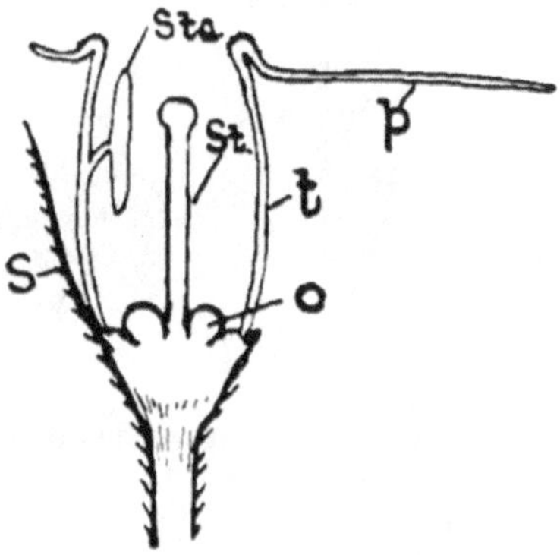

FIG. 134. - Longitudinal section through a flower of the Forget-me-not.
o., ovary; a., petal; s., sepal; St., style; Sta., stamen; c., corolla tube.

red in color. The five stamens are attached to the corolla tube (Fig. 134, Sta.), as in the Primrose, but in this family **alternate** with the petals (Fig. 133).

The ovary is composed of **two carpels** but shows four **chambers** when cut across (Fig. 133). This is due to the formation of a special partition **between** the two ovules present in each of the two original chambers. Below the ovary is a fleshy **disc** forming honey. The style often ends in a knobbed stigma. The ripe **fruit** breaks up into four **one-seeded portions** and, as in the Primulaceae, is generally protected by the calyx.

Summary. - The *Primulaceae* have regular flowers, with all the parts in fives and joined sepals and petals. The five stamens are epipetalous and opposite the petals. The ovary is superior, unilocular, and has a free central placenta. The fruit is a capsule.

The *Boraginaceae* often have stiff hairs. The inflorescence is cymose, and the flowers are generally regular. The sepals and petals are joined and five in number. There are five stamens alternating with the petals. The ovary is superior and is bicarpellary but shows four compartments, each with one ovule. The ripe fruit splits into four achenes.

PRACTICAL WORK

1. Draw a floral diagram and a longitudinal section of the flower of the Primrose and Yellow Loosestrife.

2. Draw a floral diagram and a longitudinal section of the flower of the Forget-me-not.

3. Make a list of the insects visiting the flowers of the Primrose, Pimpernel, Forget-me-not, and Viper's Bugloss.

4. Examine the ripe fruits of the Cowslip, Pimpernel, Comfrey, and Viper's Bugloss.

QUESTIONS

1. Compare, with the aid of diagrams, the structure of the flowers of the Wallflower, Campion, and Primrose. Say how the construction of these flowers affects the kinds of insects which visit them.

2. Describe three *different* ways in which flowers may be constructed to ensure cross-pollination.

3. Describe the structure of the flower and the fruit of any member of the Boraginaceae. Compare them with those of the Umbelliferae.

CHAPTER XXXIII

THE DEAD-NETTLE- AND FOXGLOVE- FAMILIES

The Labiatae. - The large family of the *Labiatae*, to which the Dead-nettle belongs, resembles the Boraginaceae in several characters. The most marked difference is that the flowers are **irregular**. All the British members of the Labiatae are **herbs**. The leaves are opposite, and the **stems** are **square** and often hollow (Fig. 135).

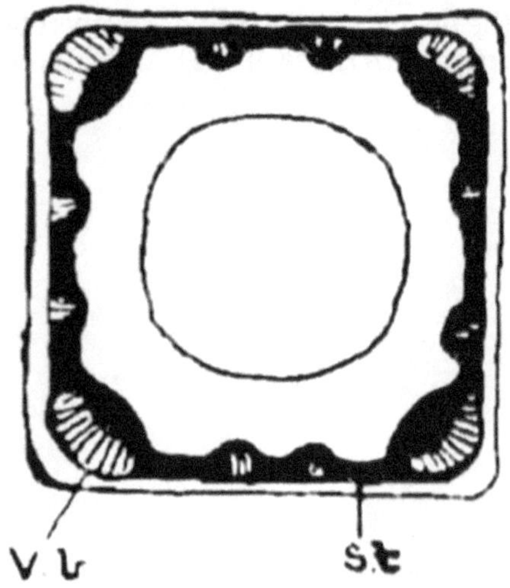

FIG. 135. - Cross-section of the stem of the Hedge Woundwort (considerably enlarged).
v.b., the woody strands: st., other hard tissue that gives support to the stem.

The inflorescence. - The inflorescence is peculiar. The flowers are borne in groups in **the axils** of the ordinary leaves, which here act as **bracts**. These groups open in order **from below upwards**, as in a racemose inflorescence. The flowers of each group, however, develop as in a dichasial cyme, the middle one being the **first to expand**, followed afterwards by the flowers on either side. Thus, the inflorescence as a whole is racemose, while each little group is a small dichasial cyme of shortly stalked flowers.

Flower and fruit. - The calyx appears as a short tube, which usually ends in five narrow and unequal teeth. The shape of the **corolla** is very characteristic, forming a short tube that ends in **two prominent lips**, an upper and a lower (Fig. 136). The upper lip is shaped like a hood (Fig. 136, h.) and is notched at its tip, where the two petals that compose it are not completely joined. **Beneath it** lie the stamens and the style.

Fig. 136. - Corolla of the Dead-nettle (natural size).
h., upper lip (hood) l., side lobes of lower lip; p. middle lobe of lower lip.

The lower lip is formed by three petals and has three lobes, of which the middle one (Fig. 136, p.) is much larger than the two side ones (l.). In the Bugle and Wood Sage, the upper lip is very small, while in the Gipsywort, the corolla is almost regular.

There are only **four stamens** since the posterior one is missing (Fig. 137). The stamens have long filaments and arise from the corolla tube. As a general rule, **two** of them are **longer** than the other two. The **ovary** is **superior** and just like that of Boraginaceae, except that here the style ends in a forked stigma. The **fruit** again splits into **four achenes** and is surrounded by the calyx.

The pollination of the Labiatae. - The **honey**, formed at the base of the ovary, can only be sucked by insects with tongues long enough to reach down the corolla tube. The flowers are generally visited by bees, which **alight on the lower lip** and almost fill out the mouth of the corolla. Their **backs** thus come in contact with the anthers under the hood. In many cases, the stamens shed their pollen before the two forks of the stigma separate, so the stigma usually receives pollen from a **younger** flower.

Among the commonest members of the Labiatae are the Dead-nettles, Woundworts, Bugle, Sage, Mint, and Ground Ivy (Fig. 15).

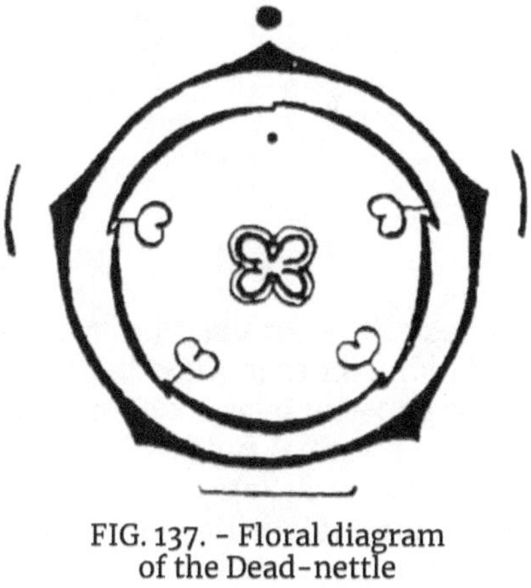

FIG. 137. - Floral diagram of the Dead-nettle

The Scrophulariaceae. - The Foxglove and Snapdragon belong to another family with **irregular** flowers and joined petals, known as the *Scrophulariaceae*. It is most easily distinguished from the Labiatae by its ovary. Most of its members are **herbaceous perennials**. The leaves are usually simple and alternate or opposite, while the stems are often square.

Flower and fruit. - The **inflorescence** is in many cases racemose

(Foxglove, Snapdragon), although in the Figwort, it is cymose. As in the Primulaceae and Labiatae, both petals and sepals are **joined**, but the **corolla** is very varied. Sometimes, as in the Mullein (Fig. 138, A), it is regular, and there are five stamens. Usually, however, it is irregular, and there are only **four stamens** (Fig. 138, C). This is again due to the absence of the posterior one. In just a few Scrophulariaceae with irregular flowers (e.g., Figwort, Fig. 138, C, Pentstemon), all five stamens are present, but the one nearest the axis produces **no pollen**. Such a structure is called a **staminode** (Fig. 95, st.).

As in the Labiatae, the stamens **alternate** with the petals and are

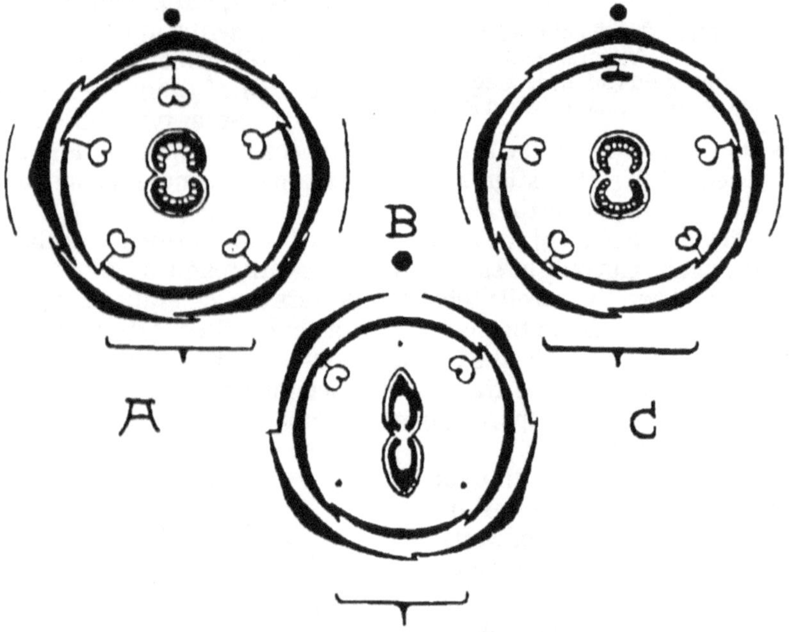

Fig. 138. -- Floral diagrams of Scrophulariaceae.
A, Mullein; B, Speedwell; C, Figwort.

attached to the corolla tube. When there are only four, two are again usually **shorter** than the other two.

The **superior ovary** consists of two joined carpels, as shown by the two-lobed stigma, and is **bilocular**. The chambers are **not divided**, like those of Labiatae, and each contains numerous ovules on a much-swollen **axile placenta** (Fig. 140, D). The two compartments are so placed that one is posterior and the other anterior (Fig. 138). The **fruit** is a capsule (Fig. 97, e) that opens in various ways.

The pollination of the Scrophulariaceae. - Insects visit the flowers for the **honey**, which is formed just below the ovary. The stigma does

FIG. 139. - Corolla of the Foxglove.

not generally receive pollen from the stamens of the same flower, since the **anthers** usually **open before** the lobes of the stigma spread apart. The methods of pollination are very varied and may be illustrated by a few examples.

In the Foxglove (Fig. 139), the hanging corolla is shaped something like a finger-stall. The stamens and stigma lie underneath the upper part of the tube, whilst the lower lip serves as the **landing stage**. As the insect sucks the honey, its back comes into contact with stamens or stigmas, according to the age of the flower.

In the Snapdragon, the lower lip of the corolla is bulged out into a **large pouch** (Fig. 140, p.), which completely closes the entrance to the corolla tube (Fig. 140, A). As a consequence, only **heavy insects**, like humble bees, are able to force open the flower (Fig. 140, B) and to suck the honey. Whilst doing this, their **backs** touch the stamens or stigmas, as in the Foxglove. In the Toadflax, the honey collects in a long **spur** formed by the corolla. Otherwise, the flowers are like those of the Snapdragon.

The flower of the Speedwell (Fig. 138, B) is almost **regular** and very unlike that of other Scrophulariaceae, except for the ovary, which is quite typical. There are only four sepals and petals and but two stamens, and the corolla tube is quite short.

Summary. The *Labiatae* are herbs with opposite leaves and square, hollow

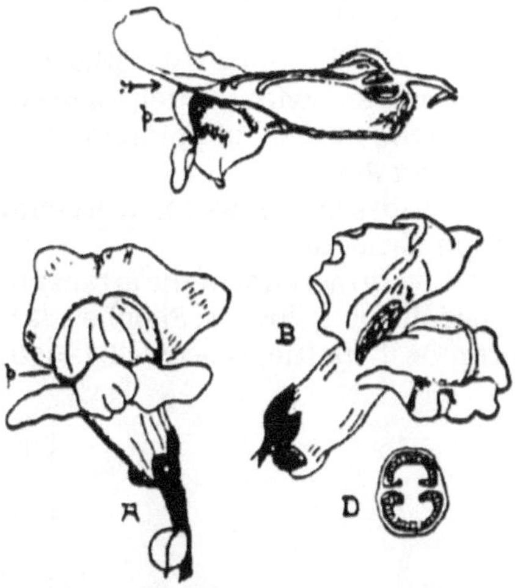

FIG. 140. - Structure of the flowers and pollination in the Snapdragon (D enlarged, other figures about two-thirds natural size). A, complete flower seen from the front; B' flower in side-view, with the corolla forced open to display stamens and stigma below the upper lip; C, flower in longitudinal section. The arrow shows the direction of approach of the insect D, cross-section of ovary showing the large axile placenta; p., pouch formed by lower lip of corolla.

stems. The irregular flowers form little dichasial cymes in the axils of the leaves. The flowers are two-lipped, and both calyx and corolla are joined. There are four stamens, two long and two short. The ovary and fruit are like those of Boraginaceae, the fruit splitting into four achenes.

The *Scrophulariaceae* are herbs with alternate or opposite leaves and a varied inflorescence. The calyx and corolla are joined. The stamens are usually like those of Labiatae, but the ovary is bilocular with numerous ovules on an axile placenta. The fruit is a capsule.

PRACTICAL WORK

1. Draw a floral diagram and longitudinal section of the Bugle and Hedge Woundwort.

2. Draw a floral diagram and a longitudinal section of the Mullein, Snapdragon, and Pentstemon.

3. Examine the fruits of the plants mentioned in (1) and (2).

4. Examine the inflorescences of the Dead-nettle, Calamint, Foxglove, and Figwort. Make diagrams to show the order of opening of the flowers, and determine the nature of the inflorescence of each.

QUESTIONS

1. Compare, with the help of drawings, the structure of the flowers and the method of pollination in the Dead-nettle, Snapdragon, and Sweet Pea.

2. Write a brief illustrated account of the characters of the family Scrophulariaceae.

3. Give an account of the arrangement and number of the stamens in the following flowers: Shepherd's Purse, Gorse, Stitchwort, Strawberry, Dead-nettle, Speedwell. Illustrate your answer with drawings.

CHAPTER XXXIV

THE DAISY-FAMILY

The Compositae. — Members of the vast family termed the *Compositae*, to which the Daisy, Dandelion, and Hawkweeds belong, are found all the world over. All the British plants of this family are **herbs**, many of them being common weeds. A large number are grown as garden plants (e.g., Dahlia, Sunflower, Michaelmas Daisy, Marigold), whilst some are cultivated as vegetables (e.g., Jerusalem Artichoke, Salsify). The lower leaves often form a **rosette** at the base of the stem. Many of the Compositae exude a **milky sap** when broken across (e.g., Dandelion).

The florets. — The **inflorescence** is always a **capitulum**. It usually bears a large number of small flowers or **florets** and is surrounded by an **involucre of bracts** (Fig. 143, A). The capitula often close up at night and open during the day, a feature well seen in the Daisy and Dandelion.

In the Daisy, Sunflower, or Ragwort (Fig. 143, A), the central or **disc-florets** are regular and tubular, each consisting of five joined petals (Fig. 143, C). The outer flowers or **ray-florets** also have a joined corolla but are **irregular**, the petals together forming a strap-shaped structure (Fig. 143, B).

In the Cornflower, where the ray-florets are tubular, the lobes of the corolla show that here also it consists of **five petals** (Fig. 141, B). However, where the ray-florets are strap-shaped, the petals are only recognizable as small notches at the end (Fig. 143, B).

Not all Compositae have two kinds of florets in their capitula. Thus, in the Coltsfoot and Thistles, **all the florets** are **regular** and tubular, whilst in the Dandelion (Fig. 141, A) and Sow-thistle, they are all **strap-shaped**.

The Disc-Floret of the Sunflower. — The disc-florets of the Sunflower, owing to their large size, show the structure of the flower very clearly. Each floret arises in the axil of a scaly **bract**. The **ovary**, as in all members of the Compositae, is **inferior**. The calyx is represented by two scaly teeth. The corolla is tubular, and the **five stamens** arise from its inner side and alternate with its five lobes (Fig. 142). The **anthers** are joined along their sides to form a **tube** surrounding the hairy upper

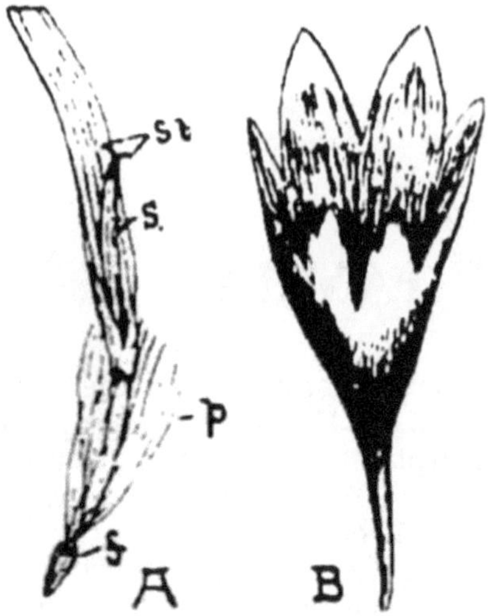

FIG. 141.
A, Strap-shaped floret from the capitulum of a Dandelion (enlarged) f., ovary P., pappus S., anther-tube: st., stigmas; B, neuter floret of a Cornflower (enlarged).

part of the style (Fig. 143, D). The latter ends in two lobes, the stigmas, which, in the young floret, are closely **pressed together**.

The Ray-Florets. — The ray-florets of the Sunflower have neither stamens nor anther-tube; i.e., they are **neuter**. This is also true of the ray-florets of the Cornflower (Fig. 141, B), but in many Compositae (e.g., Ragwort, Fig. 143, B) they have ovary, style, and stigma, although there are **no stamens**. In the Dandelion, Sow-thistle, and others, all the florets have both stamens and stigma (Fig. 141, A). Where the ray-florets are neuter or contain only an ovary, they serve chiefly to **attract insects** to the more inconspicuous disc-florets.

Fruit and Pappus. — The **calyx** in the Compositae is **always small**. In most members, the place of the sepals is taken by a number of fine hairs, the pappus, arising from the top of the inferior ovary (Fig. 143, B, C; Fig. 141, A, p.). The latter has only a **single compartment**, which contains one ovule. The fruit is an **achene**, in which the fruit wall and seed coat are indistinguishable from one another (p. 130); this is easily seen in the Sunflower.

If there is a pappus, it remains at the top of the ripe fruit and **helps in dispersal** by the wind (p. 133, and Fig. 101, E).

The calyx of the Burr Marigold appears as two or three stiff spines at the top of the ovary. In the ripe fruit, each of these spines bears a number of **backwardly directed teeth**, like the barbs of an arrow (Fig. 103, C). The fruits cling to animals by means of these spines and are thus dispersed.

FIG. 142. - Floral diagram of a disc-floret of one of the Compositae.

The Pollination of the Compositae. — If you examine a young capitulum of the Sunflower or Ragwort, you will find that the wide-spread stigmas are clearly visible in the outer disc-florets (Fig. 143, A and C). Those further towards the centre, however, show nothing of the stigmas, but in some of them, a little **heap of pollen** will be seen on the top of the stamens.

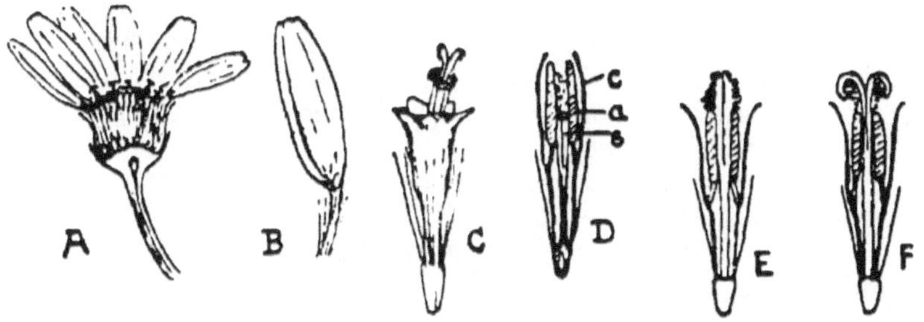

FIG. 143. - Structure of the flowers and pollination in the Marsh Ragwort (.4 natural size, other figures somewhat enlarged).
A, Capitulum cut through lengthwise B. Ray-floret; C, Disc-floret, with the stigmas just separating and showing the heap of pollen at the top of the stamens; D, the same in longitudinal section, before the style has grown up the anther-tube; E, the same with the style just emerging from the anther-tube F. the same, showing how the two stigmas finally curve back.

In the young disc-florets, the style is **short**. The stamens shed their pollen **into the** little **tube** formed by the anthers, and after that, the style begins to grow (Fig. 143, D). Its hairy tip thus gradually **sweeps the pollen out** of the anther-tube (Fig. 143, E), so as to form the little heaps just noticed. The two lobes of the stigma remain closely pressed together until they come **above the tube**, by which time all the pollen has been swept out (Fig. 143, C). Then, however, they bend apart and are ready to receive pollen from a **younger** flower.

Insects, such as Flies and Bees, are often seen crawling over the capitula of Compositae, seeking the **honey** formed at the base of the style. They thus usually carry pollen **from the inner to the outer** florets of the disc. The two lobes of the stigma **continue to curl back**, so that they finally touch some of the pollen still clinging to the anthers of the same flower (Fig. 143, F). Thus, **self-pollination** is brought about in case cross-pollination has not already taken place.

Summary. — The *Compositae* have capitula consisting of (a) all tubular florets (Tansy), (b) all strap-shaped florets (Dandelion), or (c) tubular disc-florets and strap-shaped ray-florets (Daisy). The calyx is often represented by a pappus, which aids in the distribution of the fruit. The petals are joined. The stamens are five, alternating with the petals, and have their anthers joined to form a tube. The ovary is inferior, bearing a style ending in two stigmas. The fruit is an achene, in which both the fruit wall and seed coat are joined.

PRACTICAL WORK

1. Examine longitudinal sections of young and old capitula of the Daisy, and note the order of opening of the flowers and the growth of the receptacle.

2. Examine capitula of the following: Cornflower, Sunflower, Cat's-ear, and Thistle. In each case, draw the different forms of florets, notice the distribution of the bracts, and whether the flowers contain stamens or ovaries or both.

3. Draw disc-florets from the Sunflower to show the different stages in pollination.

4. Examine the fruits of the Salsify, Burr Marigold, Nipplewort, Dandelion, and Thistle.

QUESTIONS

1. Give a short description of a Daisy plant or a Dandelion plant.

2. Describe the structure and functions of the calyx in the following plants: Dead-nettle, Campion, Primrose, Dandelion, Burr Marigold.

3. Describe, with the aid of diagrams, the inflorescences of the following plants: Chickweed, Dead-nettle, Daisy, Foxglove, Buttercup.

4. Describe the method of pollination in the Compositae.

CHAPTER XXXV

A WALK IN SPRING

Spring Plants. – If you take a walk in spring, you will notice that many of the earliest flowers to bloom are those growing in the **woods** and **hedgerows**. Most of these plants are of **low growth** and, owing to their surroundings, are well **sheltered**. At the same time, it is necessary for them to bloom before the trees and shrubs overhead cast too deep a **shade** for the proper production of flowers.

FIG. 144. - Photograph of a clump of Snowdrops in bloom. (Photo, E. J.S.)

If you dig up a number of early-flowering herbs, nearly all of them will be found to have underground **storage organs**. Thus, there are swollen roots in the Lesser Celandine (Fig. 24, B), a corm in the Cuckoo Pint, a rhizome in the Wood Anemone, and a bulb in the Snowdrop and Daffodil. This store of food enables them to produce their flowers **early** in the year.

The Flowers of the Hazel. – The very earliest plants to flower are generally trees and shrubs, like the Elm (Fig. 149), the Poplar, and the Hazel. In these, the flowers open some time before the **leaves** appear.

If you examine the long, dangling yellow **catkins** of the Hazel (Fig. 145, 3), you will see that only stamens are present. Each Hazel catkin contains a large number of flowers, but these have **no petals or sepals**. Each flower consists of a little bunch of stamens, which arises in the axil of a large bract. These are the **male flowers**. Those which contain the ovaries (i.e., the **female flowers**) look just like the ordinary winter buds, except that a tuft of crimson **stigmas** projects from the top (Fig. 145, O).

At the time when plants like the Hazel and Elm come into flower, **few insects** are about. The pollen, in fact, is not carried to the stigmas by insects but **by the wind**. Owing to the large number of stamens that each Hazel catkin contains, a great quantity of pollen is formed. The light catkins are swung to and fro by every breeze, and thus the pollen is shaken out of them. **Much** of this **is wasted**, but since so much is produced, some is almost certain to reach the stigmas of the female flowers.

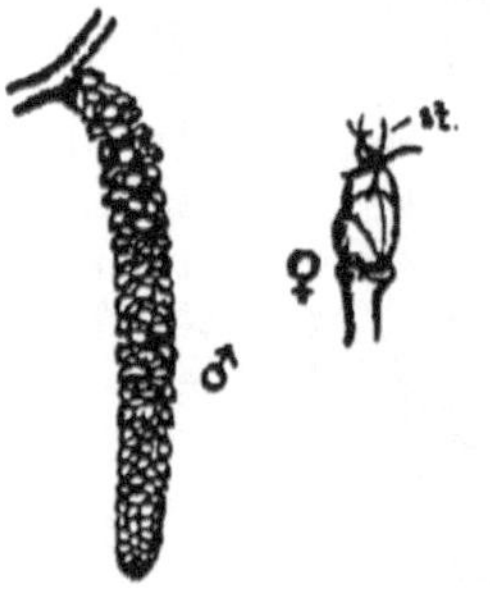

FIG. 145. - Male (♂) and female (♀) catkins of the Hazel (natural size). st., stigmas.

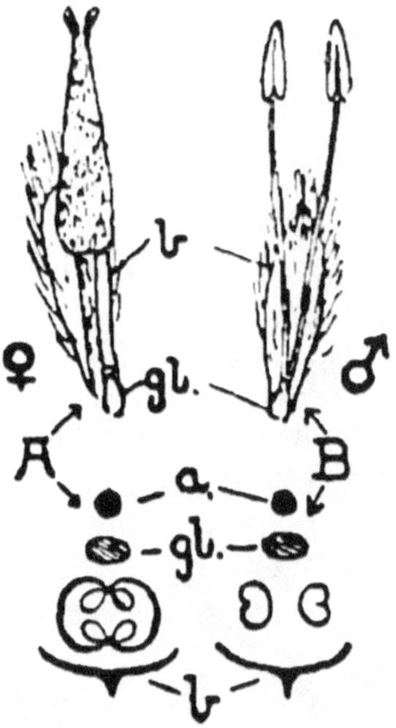

FIG. 146. - Structure of the flowers of the Goat Willow (enlarged). Single male (B) and female (A) flowers are shown above, and the corresponding floral diagrams below. a., axis of the catkin; b., bracts; n., nectary.

The Flowers of the Willow. – In the Goat Willow, both male and female flowers are grouped in **catkins** which, unlike those of the Hazel, are borne on **different trees**. Each flower arises in the axil of a large, hairy bract (Fig. 146, b.). In the male flower, there are **two stamens** (Fig. 146, B). In the female flower, there is a **one-chambered ovary** bearing two stigmas and containing numerous ovules on two parietal placentas (Fig. 146, A). Both kinds of flowers contain a small **nectary** at their base (Fig. 146, gl.). The Willow blooms later than the Hazel and is visited by **insects**, which are attracted by the honey and the sweet scent.

The Flowers of the Dog's Mercury. – Amongst early-flowering herbs, the Dog's Mercury is one of the very first and is often pollinated by the wind. This also has **male and female flowers** on different plants. Both kinds are **inconspicuous** and have a perianth of three green leaves (Fig. 147). The male flowers possess several stamens (Fig. 147, 3), which have long filaments and large anthers. The female flowers contain a single ovary bearing two large stigmas (Fig. 147, O).

The Cuckoo Pint. – A very peculiar flowering plant of the early spring is the Cuckoo Pint (Fig. 148). The inflorescence is a **spike**, the axis of which is fleshy. The whole is protected by a **huge** green sheathing **bract**, so that only the purple-colored end of the spike is visible (Fig. 148, A). The flowers themselves are situated at the base of the spike and form two groups.

The lower group consists of **female flowers**, each composed of nothing but an ovary. The upper group consists of **male flowers**, each with a few stamens. Still higher, where the enveloping bract is narrowed to a kind of waist, there are numerous **stiff hairs** that curve downwards (Fig. 148, B, h.).

Small flies, attracted by the evil smell and the purple tip of the spike, crawl down into the swollen base of the sheathing bract. They are unable to escape because the way out is blocked by the hairs, which will only bend downwards. Until these wither, the insects **remain imprisoned**. The female flowers ripen some time **before the male**, so that if the insect bears pollen from another Cuckoo Pint, it will, in its wanderings, bring about **cross-pollination**. Before the hairs wither and allow the insects to escape, the anthers of

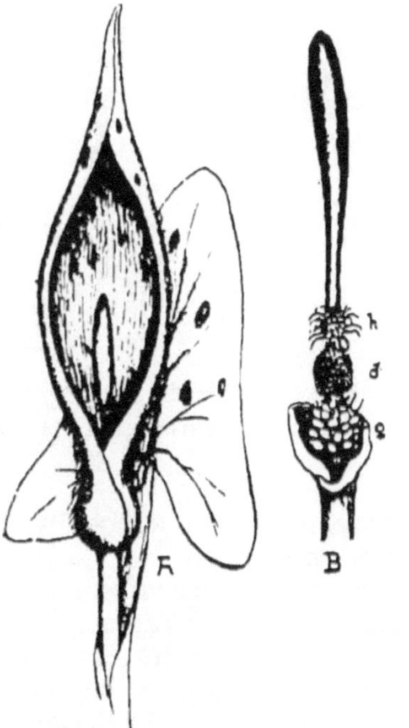

FIG. 148. - Inflorescence of the Cuckoo Pint (slightly reduced): A, leaf with complete inflorescence showing the large sheathing bract; B, spike after removal of the bract; H, hairs; ♂, male flowers; ♀, female flowers.

FIG. 147. - Flowers of the Dog's Mercury, the male on the left, the female on the right (somewhat enlarged).

FIG. 149. - Two twigs of the Elm. showing flowers, but no leaves.

the stamens open. As the flies crawl out, therefore, they become **coated with pollen**.

Other Spring Flowers. – Not all the spring-flowering trees have stamens and ovaries in separate flowers. For instance, **both** are present in those of the Elm (Fig. 149). This is also true of most herbs that bloom in the spring, e.g., the Barren Strawberry, the Lesser Celandine, and the Dog Violet. The flowers of the last-named are **irregular** and visited by insects for honey. The nectaries are at the ends of projections from two of the stamens, which reach down into the **spur**.

Summary. – All the early-flowering plants have stores of food, either in their underground organs or in their twigs and branches. Several are pollinated by the wind and have the stamens and ovary in different flowers. Wind-pollinated flowers differ from insect-pollinated flowers in producing a large amount of powdery pollen, easily shaken out of the flowers, and in not having a conspicuous perianth.

PRACTICAL WORK

1. Make lists of the flowers you find in bloom each week, and note where the plants grow that first come into flower.

2. Place a shoot of the Hazel bearing young catkins in water over a sheet of white paper. Notice the large quantity of yellow pollen that is shed.

QUESTIONS

1. Give the names of three plants with wind-pollinated flowers. Describe, with sketches, the stamens and stigma of one of them.

2. Describe the changes which two of the following undergo in the course of a year, saying clearly what each is like in the winter and in the summer: Bluebell (sometimes called Wild Hyacinth), Lesser Celandine, Crocus, Oak, Dahlia, Daffodil.

3. Mention *two* flowers, one with bright-coloured petals and one which has no petals, and suggest a reason for the differences between the two.

CHAPTER XXXVI

A WALK IN SUMMER

Weeds. - The summer is the time when most plants are seen at their best. As you wander through the cornfields, you can find numbers of **weeds** amongst the green-stemmed Wheat and Barley. Sometimes the fields are red with the flowers of Poppies or golden with Marigolds and Charlock. Here, too, are to be found the Groundsel, the Thistles, the Fumitory, and the scarlet blooms of the Pimpernel.

Nearly all of these weeds are **quick-growing annuals** which produce **abundant seeds.** The seeds or fruits are easily scattered and very soon grow into new plants. Weeds of a similar kind are found on every waste piece of ground. The weeds of **Grass-lawns**, on the other hand, are often **perennials**, like the Plantain and Dandelion. The leaves of the Plantain and Daisy (Fig. 44) form a rosette and rapidly kill off the Grass which they cover.

Woodlands. - In passing through the woods you notice that most of the **flowers** are **over**. This is because the shade in summer is **too deep** for the production of flowers. After part of a wood has been cut down or **coppiced**, the **increased light** allows for a much more vigorous growth of herbs.

Scarcely any plants can thrive in the deep shade of a **Beech-wood**, so **very few** herbs or shrubs are found on the ground beneath the trees. Beech-woods, however, when coppiced, are, apart from the pastures on the chalk-downs, the chief home of the British Orchids (e.g., Butterfly Orchis, Fly Orchis, and Twayblade). In the **more open parts** of Beech-woods, herbs like the Dog's Mercury, Wood Sanicle, and Wild Strawberry often flourish in springtime before the trees overhead come into leaf.

Beech-woods are found more particularly where the soil is chalky, whilst Oak-woods thrive on clayey or sandy soils. In an **Oak-wood,** the shade is **not nearly so deep**, and there are usually numerous shrubs, such as the Maple, Hazel, and Hawthorn. On the ground, there is a **luxuriant growth** of herbs (Fig. 150), even in the height of summer. Characteristic herbs of Oak-woods are the Wild Hyacinth (Fig. 150), Yellow Dead-nettle, Wood Anemone, Primrose, and Lesser Celandine.

Nearly all the herbs growing in woods are **perennials**. They usu-

FIG. 150. - Ground-flora of a damp Oak-wood in early spring, Harpenden, Herts., showing Wild Hyacinths and Dog's Mercury. (Photo, F. J.S.)

ally have leaves separated by **long internodes**, with **large**, thin, fresh green **blades**. The chief difficulty woodland plants have to battle with is the shade. This not only prevents the production of flowers but also **interferes with assimilation** by the leaves. This is why so few plants can grow in a Beech-wood in the height of summer.

The effect of shade. - All the herbs, and even the lower branches of the trees and shrubs, place their leaves to get the **greatest amount of light**. This is well seen in the photograph of a seedling Sycamore (Fig. 151). Here the blades are arranged so that those near the top of the stem **do not shade** others lower down.

On the horizontal branches of the Hornbeam and Beech, the leaves are often placed in a sort of **mosaic**, in which smaller leaves fill in the spaces between the larger ones. In this way, all the leaves on a branch form a **single layer** without overlapping. You can see the same kind of thing in a plant of the Dog's Mercury or Enchanter's Nightshade if you look down on it from above (compare p. 65).

Fields and meadows. - Quite a **different growth** of plants is met with in the fields and meadows. In such situations, there is plenty of light and plenty of water. **Mowing and the grazing of animals** prevent the growth of any tall herbs, and the dense carpet of Grasses makes it difficult for any but **perennials** to exist. The plants are very varied,

FIG. 151. - Photograph of a seedling Sycamore, taken from above, to show the leaf-mosaic. (Photo, E. J. S.)

including, apart from the Grasses, many of our commonest flowers. Here it is that Buttercups, Daisies, Dandelions, and Clovers are found in greatest abundance (Fig. 152).

Heaths. - Should your wanderings take you onto a heath, you will find that the dense vegetation consists mainly of a few shrubby **evergreens**. These grow to a very **uniform level** (Fig. 153). In the meadow and the woodland, the broad, thin blades of the leaves allow transpiration to go on freely. On the wind-swept heath, the leaves of many plants are **very small**, as in the abundant Heath and Heather (Fig. 74, A). In other cases, they are replaced by **spines**, as in the Gorse (Fig. 77, B). The plants consequently **transpire very slowly**. This is necessary not only because the plants are evergreen but also owing

FIG. 152. - Vegetation of a meadow. The chief plants seen are the Dutch Clover, Buttercups, Daisies, Yellow Rattle, and numerous Grasses. (Photo, E. J. S.)

to the **exposed situations** in which heaths occur and the **dry nature of the soil**. This is often sandy, and the top layers contain much dark brown, partially decayed, humus or **peat**, which interferes with the absorption of water by the roots.

Summary. - Your walk then will have taught you that different situations have each their own particular kind of vegetation. In any given spot, whether it is a wood, a meadow, or a heath, the plants that grow there are more or less suited to the conditions under which they live. You have already become acquainted with other illustrations of this fact in studying the plants of dry and wet places (Chapters XX. and XXI.).

FIG. 153. - Photograph of Heath, Hindhead, Surrey. (Photo, E.J.S.)
Note the uniform level of the vegetation.

PRACTICAL WORK

1. Make a list of the plants growing in a Beech-wood, an Oak-wood, and a Pine-wood. In each case, notice whether the plants are in flower or in fruit, and whether they are annuals or perennials.

2. In any wood or plantation, make a list of the plants (a) in the shade, and (b) near the edge or by the paths.

3. Study the plants on a heath, in a meadow, a cornfield, or a pond, in the same way as described under (1).

QUESTIONS

1. Give as full an account as you can of the plants which grow in any hedge you know.

2. Name three plants that commonly occur as weeds on waste ground or on garden beds. Why do they spread quickly over a wide area?

3. When do the following plants come into flower and into leaf respectively: Elm, Dog's Mercury, Ivy, Beech, Lesser Celandine, Meadow Saffron, Honeysuckle, Hazel, Hawkweed, Groundsel?

4. What is the chief difficulty against which plants in woods have to struggle? Say how this difficulty is overcome by the way in which the plants grow.

www.ingramcontent.com/pod-product-compliance
Lightning Source LLC
Chambersburg PA
CBHW032008180726
48283CB00008B/2589
* 9 7 8 1 7 6 1 5 3 9 0 0 8 *